Worse Things Happen at Sea

Worse Things Happen at Sea

David O'Connell

The Pentland Press Limited
Edinburgh • Cambridge • Durham

First published in 1994 by
The Pentland Press Ltd.
1 Hutton Close
South Church
Bishop Auckland
Durham

ISBN 1 85821 157 3

Typeset by CBS, Felixstowe, Suffolk
Printed and bound by Antony Rowe Ltd., Chippenham

Dedicated to the passengers and crews
with whom I have shared a happy and exhilarating life.

My thanks to my family and friends
who have provided moral support during the writing of this book.
Special thanks to Cathy for her hard work and inspiration.

CHAPTER 1

New York is a fascinating place, I'd been told, and I could well have found it so, had I been in the right frame of mind, which I most definitely was not. Sitting on the edge of a cab seat, heart pounding, hands sweating, willing the driver to develop some sense of urgency was not, I felt, the best way to appreciate the flavour of this amazing city.

To make matters worse, I was beginning to doubt my reasons for being here at all. Why, I asked myself, had I given up my secure job in England to embark on a job at sea? I'd been well established in a desirable country practice; good income, pleasant surroundings, smart sports car, fashionable country cottage; all the trimmings. Life had indeed been a 'bed of roses' and might well have remained so, had I not killed my wife.

Even so, I could have stayed in my job because nobody else suspected that I'd been responsible. The death certificate stated: 'Death due to cerebrovascular accident, secondary to brain tumour'.

It did not add; 'Contributory factor - neglect by her husband, her doctor'. That was my secret, and one I'd have to learn to live with, but I could not live with it in the same job and in the same area, surrounded by memories. I'd tried for three months, but in the end had resorted to browsing through the medical journals looking at advertisements.

The advertisement that had led to my present predicament had caught my eye late one evening. Sitting alone in the cottage, in silence apart from the sonorous ticking of the hall clock, and well into my third scotch and water, my thoughts had been mainly centred on Alice, or more precisely, her absence; listening to the sounds she wasn't making any more and looking at the shape that wasn't filling the chair on the other side of the fireplace. I'd almost given up on the medical journal and was idly considering what other occupations I could take

1

up. Apart from medicine the only skills I had were interior decorating and stone-wall building, learnt over years of renovating our cottage and garden. That had been a labour of love and Alice and I had spent as much time drinking coffee and admiring our handiwork as we had in physical work; hardly a good basis for earning a living. Having discarded that idea, I flicked over one more page and the advert hit me like a breath of fresh air:

WANTED
SHIP'S DOCTOR
LARGE PASSENGER LINER

This, I thought, could be the answer; a way of taking the job away from the memories. It could also be considered as running away from my problem; but then running away might be the sanest course of action. They wanted a doctor between thirty and forty years of age, so at thirty-five, I was in with as good a chance as any. I decided to apply for the post.

Three weeks later I'd attended an interview which had gone quite well, but I was still not mentally prepared for the shock of receiving the formal letter offering me the post.

Up to that point it had been only a possibility, something to play with in my mind, much like climbing to the top diving board at a swimming pool, idly wondering whether to make the dive.

Now I was standing at the end of the board, toes curled over the edge, looking at the water far below and thinking of the safety of the platform behind me. It was not too late to turn back. I remembered my father teaching me, as a young boy, to dive; 'Don't look at the water Mike, look straight ahead. You've made your decision – do it!'

I agonized for a whole week, afraid to take the decision, toes curled over the edge, thinking of the security behind me. I'd dealt with patients in the same dilemma, afraid to make a change in their lives, preferring to settle for the familiarity of their painful existence, rather than jump into the unknown.

I don't know how long I would have stood there, paralysed, if it hadn't been for a push from behind. My partner invited me to make up a foursome. I knew it would happen eventually of course. I could imagine him discussing it with his wife; 'Can't let Mike stay in on his own like that every evening; we must get him out to meet people, help him get over it.'

I appreciated his well-intentioned motives, but it was the beginning of a mating-up process that I didn't want - not yet.

I made the decision: resigned from the practice, bought the uniforms, and made the dive.

Now here I was, three months later, in a taxi heading for the ship, but seriously wondering if I was going to make it in time.

There wouldn't have been a problem, had I not decided that I needed more shirts and interrupted my journey from the airport to call into Macey's. I didn't think it would be difficult; a similar shopping trip into Marks and Spencer's, even as a lone male, would have taken a few minutes. Macey's turned out to be an entirely different project:

'What type of shirt are you looking for, Sir; work shirt, sport shirt, open neck, cut-away collar, body fit, loose fit, regular fit, button cuff, link cuff...'

'Just an evening shirt, please.'

At this point the shop assistant looked at me, her pretty but plastic face barely concealing her wonderment at my ignorance on the subject of shirts: 'I'm afraid you're in the wrong department,' she said. 'You require the "Evening Wear" Department. That's level four; turn right at lingerie, and left at nightwear, you'll find the department right opposite ski-wear.' Then, with a plastic afterthought, she added; 'Have a nice day.'

Twenty minutes later, after getting lost in perfumery, I found the right department, bought three semi-suitable shirts and emerged, senses reeling, into the stifling heat of New York's streets.

I'd been confidently advised that Macey's was only minutes away from the dock-side by cab. Add to that the half an hour to get a cab to stop, and another ten minutes to explain to a Latin American driver where to go, and time is running out.

I gave him the name of the liner, but it meant nothing to him. I explained that it was a ship.

'Ah, si, el barco - boat, compriendo! What kinda boat?'

'Passenger ship - going to England.'

'Si, England. Lovely place. I gotta brother live in England. He marry a plump nurse there. Is verra happy.'

At this point I resorted to the New York street map I found tucked in the glove compartment and pointed out the docks to him:

'Why you no say before, 49 Street, is easy, but we miss the turning already.'

He found another turning, down a street of high, grimy tenement buildings with people of all races leaning against railings and sitting on steps: the sort of place where you invariably get shot or stabbed, in American cop movies.

My hands were now as clammy as the cab seat, my trousers were sticking to my legs and I was developing that prickling sensation of panic. I searched the cab driver's face for the least hint of urgency, but he was otherwise preoccupied; flicking cigar ash away from between his thighs. He was certainly a competent man, managing to drive, balance a cigar in the corner of his mouth, regularly smooth his large moustaches into line, and keep up a voluble conversation, simultaneously. He was not so good at urgency.

I interrupted the life story of his brother.

'My ship leaves at 3.30!'

'Is no problema.'

Is a bloody big problema, I thought, looking at my watch - 3.29 already!

We did arrive, five minutes later. I thrust him a handful of dollars and lugged my cases through the dock building onto the quay.

Hell she's big, was my first thought, looking up at the mountainous black ship, *and I'm going to be doctor on that!*

Bloody Hell, she's moving, was my second thought as I noticed the slowly increasing gap between it and the quayside.

In my experience no form of transport left on time. I'd met the exception.

In fantasy I contemplated leaping from the quayside, through the port-side shell-door entrance which was still open and still only four feet away, but while I contemplated my past indifferent competence at the long jump, and my present load of luggage, the opportunity was vanishing as, slowly, the mountain moved away. I managed to fling the Macey's bag of shirts into the ship, as partial compensation for my absence, but the ship's security officer, standing at the entrance, looked wryly at me and muttered into his walkie talkie - 'Looks like the new

4

Doc's staying in New York, Sir!'

At this point self-pity overcame me. It seemed nothing could be worse than standing alone in a strange place, watching your new job moving slowly but inexorably away.

Instead of standing on this noisy foreign quayside with its smell of oil and sounds of New York stevedores shouting at each other, I could have been lying back in my garden chair, enjoying the scent of the honeysuckle Alice and I had planted, listening to the chirping of thrushes and blackbirds, and admiring the plants we had nurtured and the natural-stone wall I'd carefully rebuilt.

The rose climbing the wall would now be in full bloom, its blushing pink petals blending with the dainty blue of the clematis threading its way through the brambles.

Of course, the chair beside me would now be empty and Alice would not be making us a jug of lemonade, but I'd still have the job, and my only concern would be getting to evening surgery in time – evening surgery never floated away!

I would have been secure until retirement, provided I'd avoided gross malpractice and sexual abuse of patients.

Why had I been daft enough to miss the ship, just to buy some shirts that I could probably have managed without anyway? Perhaps pure miscalculation; or perhaps my subconscious was pulling me back, trying to make me miss the ship so that I could return home, to safety.

The ship's agent came to my rescue. He grasped my hand as if I were a long lost friend; 'You must be the missing doctor! It looks like you're a celebrity. Everyone's been hunting for you for the past hour. They decided to sail without you eventually.' He didn't look as worried as I felt, but then it wasn't his job at stake.

'I was afraid that would happen. Looks like I've lost my job before I even started it.'

He shrugged his shoulders, as if this were an everyday occurrence. 'No sweat, Doc, worse things happen at sea.'

If he meant that as a consolation, it didn't work. I replied, rather caustically, 'I don't think I'm going to get a chance to test that theory.'

'There 's no problem, Doc, the pilot's launch is leaving soon; you can hitch a lift on that. It'll be a choppy ride, but you'll get there.'

True to his word, within minutes he'd bundled me and my luggage into the launch and I set off on the choppy ride down the Hudson River.

To say that I felt relieved would be a massive understatement. Just a few minutes before I'd all but written off my new job. It had been made quite clear to me that a permanent post was subject to me avoiding any big mistakes on my first voyage, and I reasoned that missing the ship was just about as big a mistake as could be made. I'd resigned from my practice on the confident assumption that I could cope with most problems that would be thrown my way, but I hadn't reckoned on this one. Now I knew that I would at least reach the ship and, although I guessed that I'd be in some form of trouble, I could afford to relax a little.

Relaxing, however, was not exactly easy as the launch seemed to be doing a lot of bouncing, so that to keep my balance I needed to grip the rail very firmly. I suspected that the launch had hung around waiting for me, and was now making up for lost time. We were leaving the towering New York skyline behind and were rapidly catching up on the Liner. The two tugboats which had guided her into the main river were veering off and each gave a cocky farewell blast on its whistle; but it was the responding boom from the huge ship that almost blasted out my eardrums. Perhaps the skyscrapers didn't rock as the sound bounced off them, but I imagined they did. I felt myself surrounded by enormity; the huge buildings, the overpowering noise and the ship, now looming up. I was entering a new and huge experience in my life and my surroundings seemed to confirm this impression.

We hit the wake left by the tugboats at speed, and the resultant salty spray provided an ample baptism for my new life. Luckily I would not be needing my drenched sports jacket for much longer; very little longer in fact, as we were now pulling alongside, and ropes were being lowered from the shell door. Soon we were made fast and a set of steps were lowered to the launch. Before climbing them I looked upwards to gauge the size of the vessel, but the curve on the towering bulkhead obstructed my line of vision so that only some of the row of faces peering over the ship's rail were visible.

I handed up my luggage, then followed it. As I stepped through the shell-door, I was greeted by the security officer who had witnessed the earlier arrival of my shirts. There was more than a hint of sarcasm in his voice as he handed me the Macey's bag; 'Welcome aboard, Sir. I expect you'll be needing these.'

CHAPTER 2

My relief at arriving on board was so great that the security officer's sarcasm had little effect on me. I had arrived; and for the time being my job was secure. I had very little idea of where exactly I was, except that it was at the back end, and about ten feet up from the water. I'd not given much thought as to where on the ship I'd head for now that I was on board, but the security officer gave me a clue; 'I think you're expected in the hospital, Doc; Sister's waiting for you. One of the medical attendants is on his way to help you with your luggage. Best of luck!'

The sarcasm which had earlier been evident in his voice had been replaced by a hint of sympathy. It did not surprise me that I was expected in the hospital, nor that I should be meeting the senior nurse, nor that she should have the title of 'sister'; but I was puzzled by the sympathy in his tone and wondered what he knew that I didn't.

I pulled my cases away from the shell-door to await the promised assistance. The alleyway that I now stood in seemed to stretch on forever, confirming that the impression of size that had struck me from outside the ship was no illusion. In the distance, approaching from the front end, I could just make out a swaggering uniformed figure.

It eventually materialized into a short rotund man in his early fifties.

'You must be the doctor we've been waiting for,' he said as he took my hand. 'I'm Patrick, Patrick O'Brien; pleased to meet you.' There was a soft Irish lilt to his voice which I found very welcoming.

'You must be the medical attendant?'

'You're right enough there, Doctor,' he replied, then added as if to establish his correct credentials. 'Mind you, there's two of us, but I'm the senior.'

'Well, I'm very pleased to meet you Patrick. Thanks for coming to my assistance with the cases.'

'Think nothing of it, Doctor. You see it's a kind heart I have, and I don't mind interrupting my tea to help a gentleman such as yourself. Besides, Sister asked me to meet you: and I'd not be inclined to say no to Sister Sally!'

Behind his large spectacles his eyes had a distinctly impish twinkle that suggested that life was a continuous joke to him. His thinning hair was strategically groomed, to present as youthful an appearance as possible. Even carrying two of my cases he walked with a cocky swagger.

'How far is it to the hospital, Patrick?'

'A couple of hundred yards yet, Doctor. I hope you're fit, there'll be plenty of walking for you on this ship; the beauty's almost a quarter of a mile long.'

By the time we reached the hospital he'd discovered that I was half Irish myself and we'd explored the possibility of our common ancestry. I'd also learned a lot about who was who on board.

'You'd be wise to be wary of Sister Sally; she's as pretty as an angel, but the Good Lord was none too generous with her temper.'

Entering the hospital he introduced me; 'Doctor Vaughan, this is Sister Sally Scott.'

Then, appearing to sense danger, he vanished.

There was, I was sure, a pretty face behind the countenance that met me, but it was not about to be revealed. I could have sworn that frost was forming around her sharp little features. She could be described as petite; a man with a large pair of lungs could have blown her over if he were foolish enough; but what she lacked in height was more than made up by her look of determination.

'Well, Doctor Vaughan, better late than never, I suppose. There are several things we need to talk about.'

I'd expected a bit of small talk first, but she pressed straight on with her authoritative briefing:

'First there's the duty rota. You'll alternate as first on call with Doctor Crawley. He's on tonight. The emergency drugs are kept in the treatment room and your emergency bag is refilled every day with the essentials, if you remember to tell me what you've used, of course.'

'That sounds clear enough, Sister. I'm sure I'll soon get the hang of it.'

'I certainly hope so. You haven't made a very good start.'

I hadn't expected to be hugged and kissed, but this was turning out to be an extremely frosty reception. Perhaps an apology would turn away her wrath:

'Oh, you mean my almost missing the ship. Look, I am sorry about the trouble it's caused, I misjudged the time it took to get here from the airport.'

'Well that's a misjudgment you can't afford to make too often, Doctor Vaughan. You have broken the first commandment, "Thou shalt not miss the ship". It is illegal for a passenger ship to sail without a doctor on board. Luckily there are two on this ship so we could have just managed without you. Our smaller ships have only one doctor.'

I wondered how many other commandments there were. Was she always like this or was she just putting me through a baptism of fire?

'Well I suppose the ship could wait a few minutes.'

'Have you any idea how much it costs in extra port charges for every minute's delay in casting off?'

'Can't say that I have, Sister.'

'A lot more than your salary, Doctor.'

Well, that had put me in my place. Doctor or not, I was a very small cog in this ship's operation, and there was no doubt about who ran the medical department.

'I get the point; I promise to be a good boy in future, Ma'am.'

'You'd better! Anyway, it's time for you to get into uniform. The Captain wants to meet you before dinner. You know where your cabin is do you?'

'Yes, Patrick filled me in. I think he's taken my cases there.'

'Right, see you in the morning then. We all meet here at 0830 hours ... sharp.'

As I made my way to the cabin I felt like a chastised schoolboy and wondered how I was going to get on with this miniature martinet.

By this time we were well clear of land and into the Atlantic proper, so the ship was moving around a bit, not much, but enough to cause a slight giddy feeling and for my feet to land in not quite the expected place when walking upstairs; enough to make me aware of the sensation of being at sea.

I was pleased to get into my cabin and sit down for a minute. It looked very comfortable, with a separate sleeping area, plenty of surfaces, my own bathroom and a porthole to look out of. It provided a good view of a vast expanse of ocean which was not at all blue, but the typical grey of the Atlantic. The waves looked big to me, with foaming white crests, and I wondered if this could be classed as a rough sea.

My experience of seafaring up to now had been limited to cross-channel ferries and playing around in dinghies, and that none too successfully.

I recalled the last holiday I'd spent with Alice learning to sail in the Lake District. 'Thank God you're not a sailor!' she'd commented, quite acidly for her, after I'd capsized us for the third time in as many hours.

We'd become very wet and cold and, although we'd laughed it off, I couldn't persuade her to venture into the dinghy again for the rest of the holiday.

Her headaches had started that week; nothing too bad, nothing that a couple of aspirin wouldn't clear up, but they took the edge off her appetite for food, and other things. It had briefly crossed my mind that she'd been trying to avoid my attentions, but Alice wasn't like that; she was direct and honest, brutally honest on occasion; she wouldn't have used a headache as an excuse.

Still thinking of her, I unpacked my cases and, finding the framed picture of her, placed it in pride of place on the desk, next to the head of my bunk. She seemed to be looking straight at me; a twinge of guilt made me shudder briefly. It was time for a shower.

Refreshed and ready to start my new life, I donned my uniform, wondering why the black jacket and trousers were called 'blues' – something I'd have to find out. The bright brass buttons and the gold and red insignia on the lower sleeve brightened the overall appearance, and gave it a sense of importance. For the first time I began to feel that importance; now, officially, I was an officer on board one of the greatest liners in the world.

'Well, what do you think of me now?' I asked Alice, while I preened myself in front of the mirror. 'Now I'm a real sailor!'

But the face in the picture did not seem impressed. It didn't surprise me; she never had been one for instant praise.

A further look in the mirror confirmed that my white collar and black tie were straight. I'd best look smart to meet the Captain.

As I left the cabin I felt strangely unprotected; *God,* I thought, *I hope no passenger asks me any questions I'd be expected to answer, wearing such a uniform; I wouldn't even be able to direct them to the nearest lavatory.*

Now find the Captain. I hadn't asked Sally where I had to meet him and I didn't fancy ringing her to find out. I presumed he'd have to be somewhere at the front end and pretty high up, to see where we were going. I headed forward and then up 'A' stairway to find the bridge. After climbing 80 feet or more, I realized that I would need to get fit to do this regularly.

Arriving, breathless, I announced myself through a security intercom on the locked bridge door; 'It's Doctor Vaughan, I'm looking for the Captain.'

'Hang about, Doc, I'll press the buzzer; push the door when you hear it.'

Sure enough the door opened as I pushed it in time with the buzzer and the light above it.

'Come in, Doc, be with you in a minute.'

The invitation came from a figure hunched over a set of charts, evidently joining points together with a ruler and pencil. From the back I judged him to be stocky and of medium height; his voice suggested that he was near my own age. He wore the same uniform as me, but the insignia on his lower sleeves were black on gold.

Eventually, satisfied with his artistry, he turned to me; 'Hi, Doc, I'm Pete Hardy, Chief Navigating Officer; welcome aboard.' As he took my hand I noticed that my observation about his height wasn't far out, in that he was slightly taller than me, but his broad, mildly pock-marked face looked so well lived-in that my estimate of his age could have been ten years too low. His canny, but friendly eyes were clearly making as rapid an appraisal of me.

'Thanks for the welcome, Pete; I've been in the dog-house up till now.'

He shrugged; 'Don't worry about it, it'll soon blow over.'

'So, you know all about my late arrival?'

'Of course, nothing escapes my notice. What's your first name, by the way?'

'Mike.'

'Right, Mike, I'd better show you around, as you're new to ships.'

He seemed to take great pride in showing me around his domain, explaining the details of the satellite navigating instruments, the back-up magnetic compass and the radar equipment; I watched the beam sweeping across the dark screen, now and then outlining a small vessel. He demonstrated how to work out the distance and direction of any ship in the vicinity.

His enthusiasm was building up as he explained the other instruments lining the bench, but I was by then finding it difficult to take it all in, so impressed was I by the view from this lofty position, looking out over the fore-deck far below, and further below that again, the sea. The waves that had seemed large from my cabin now looked small, but the roll of the ship that I'd felt mildly in my cabin was now much more evident, presumably magnified by the greater height, much like being at the top of a metronome. I began to feel dizzy and then suddenly remembered the Captain.

'I'm enjoying the tour, Pete, but I think it's time to meet the Captain.'

'OK, I'll show you the rest another time. You'll find the "old man" down the stairs, first cabin on the right. See you around.'

The stairway to the Captain's cabin consisted of only a dozen steps, but it was long enough for my apprehension to build up, wondering what sort of man I was about to meet and how serious an opinion he'd have about doctors missing his ship.

The door was open, with just a curtain over the entrance. I knocked on the bulkhead.

'Come in.'

I entered and walked across to meet a towering man.

'Nice to meet you...at last, Doctor.' Every word was spoken with slow courtesy. A very well-disciplined, immaculate man this. It didn't help that his 6' 3" height dwarfed me so that his words had the added force of gravity, as they dropped from his granite features onto my head. I began to wonder if keel-hauling and flogging were still part of naval custom.

'You had a comfortable journey?'

'Not exactly, Captain.'

'Pity.'

Clearly he was not prepared to waste too many words on sympathy.

'You've probably heard of my late arrival?'

13

'Yes.'

I felt that this was not going to be an easy interview. The sparseness of his words was disturbing, and his great height put me at a disadvantage. He looked every bit the master of this great vessel. I judged him to be old enough to be showing signs of greying; but these were absent from his jet-black hair which was smoothed flat with Brylcreem away from his long, strong features.

'Care for a drink, Doctor?'

'Scotch and water, please.'

The offer of a drink was a welcome sign of humanity in an otherwise robotic demeanour. Standing rigidly, with arms hanging from his shoulders, hands in line with his trouser creases, he presented an unnervingly symmetrical appearance. His composure was so profound that he had no need to place a hand in a pocket, or smoke a cigarette. Neither his long, slim body, nor matching face, betrayed any sign of emotion. I guessed that he had been taught as a small boy to stand straight, and that he was still obedient to that long departed teacher: except for the slight bowing of his head, due no doubt, to a lifetime of talking to people shorter than himself, which would include most.

I accepted my drink, pleased to note how stingy he was with the water - I was in need of a little anaesthetic.

'Please take a seat.' He indicated the chair I was to occupy.

Settling himself into his preferred armchair opposite me he crossed his legs, lowered his half-rim spectacles and, looking over them and above his poised glass, he directed his full attention to me. I felt the real purpose for the meeting had arrived. His pose was very deliberate as if remembered from serious interviews in his youth. I could imagine his father interrogating him in a similar manner. His eyelids had not blinked for what must have been a full fifteen seconds.

'Now tell me, Doctor, about your reasons for coming to sea?'

'Well, Captain, I was finding general practice very tedious and lacking excitement. I needed a change.'

I really did not need that question; I was trying to forget what was behind me, and keeping the truth from the imposing man was going to be difficult.

'I understand that there is more to it than that. I was very sorry to hear of your bereavement.'

How did he know about that? He must have been briefed. I had deliberately asked the medical director who had appointed me to keep my details a secret. I'd wanted to make a fresh start without any reminders of Alice's death. He had agreed; but now it seemed that my confidence had been betrayed.

'I'm surprised that you know about it, Captain. The medical director in Southampton agreed to keep the information to himself; not to let anyone on board know, so that I could make a fresh start.'

'Yes, but I'm not "anyone", Doctor. I have total responsibility for this ship at sea and important details about senior officers are part of my responsibility.'

I could see why my medical background should be important to him, but not my private life.

'I don't understand why anyone should know about my personal life. I am not a criminal, and my medical record is clean.'

'I don't doubt that, Doctor, but your recent bereavement is also an important detail. Someone on board has to know, in case it affects your behaviour. That someone is me - understood?'

This was a new concept to me. The man opposite me was in complete command of a large community; afloat and isolated from the world except by radio. I had to concede; his point was valid.

'Understood, Captain, but no one else needs to know?'

'The information is safe with me, but you can't keep it a secret for ever, you know.'

He was right, the facts would become widely known eventually. Someone would meet somebody who knew me, perhaps a passenger. That didn't bother me. I just needed a few weeks to begin my new life without reminders and without sympathetic gestures; just to be accepted for myself.

'I realize that, Captain, I just need a few weeks to settle in first. I don't want people making allowances for me out of sympathy. You know the sort of thing I mean?'

'I certainly do. You need to find your feet. Now, tell me about the rest of your life. What medical experience have you had before coming to sea?'

'Very mixed, Captain. I spent five years in the Army before doing general practice in England.'

'Ah, you're a military man then?'

'That's putting it a bit strong, Captain. I was a doctor in the Army; not much soldiering involved in that.'

'Perhaps not. My father was a brigadier, you know. Most of my family have been involved in some form of military service.'

Somehow that didn't surprise me, his mannerisms suggested that he'd had a disciplined childhood and his accent implied an upper-class background.

'Is that how you came to sea then, Captain, from the Royal Navy, perhaps?'

'Good heavens, no. I was the black sheep of the family; ran away to the Merchant Navy when I was sixteen to get away from all that regimental stuff. I started my career stoking boilers!'

That would explain how his accent had lost any of the condescending, cutting edge, so often found in the upper classes.

The whisky was starting to have its effect and I felt a warm glow developing. The movement of the ship didn't seem so bad, and the Captain was looking more human. Given a long time, I felt that I could get to like the man.

'What I wanted to know, Doctor, was whether you have any particular specialities? They must have taught you something in the Army.'

Oh God, I thought, *he must be expecting me to do major operations.* 'You weren't thinking of any serious specialities, like major surgery, were you, Captain? I understood that that sort of problem could be evacuated ashore by helicopter, if necessary. I've dealt with most things, from delivering babies to stitching up drunken soldiers, but I'm not master of any particular speciality.'

'But I expect you could put your hand to most things, if need be, Doctor? I was thinking more of the little, everyday things that crop up; the crew don't get much time ashore to get their problems sorted out, you know.'

He shifted a little uneasily in his chair, his supreme equanimity disturbed for a moment.

'Well, Captain, I would certainly do my best to cope with any problems, large or small, on any part of the anatomy.'

'That is all that can be expected of you, Doctor. If I can help with any problem, please feel free to ask me. You might be able to help me with a little problem that I have?'

'Of course, any time.'

'I'll let you settle in for a day or two first, then I may come down to see you. Well, must be getting on; time for dinner shortly; must dress you know.'

I was dismissed.

As I made my way to the door I felt my chest relax, breathing more easily now that the interview was over and the expected blasting hadn't happened. He seemed to have overlooked my earlier difficulties. Almost through the door now ...

'Oh, and by the way, Doctor ... miss the ship again and you're fired.'

* * * * * * *

After my meeting with the Captain the after-effects of the harrowing day's experiences were beginning to take their toll; I decided to give dinner a pass.

The ship was definitely moving about now. Trying to walk a straight line down the long alleyway to my cabin felt like being on a fairground board-walk, bouncing from bulkhead to bulkhead. At first I thought it was the whisky, but I knew I could take more than the Captain had served me. By the time I'd got used to the ship's rolling from side to side, it started rocking from end to end as well. One second I was climbing uphill, the next running downhill, trying to keep up with my legs. I overshot my cabin and had to retrace a few yards. On the next pass I grabbed the cabin door handle and swung into the cabin. The next roll of the ship hurled me, luckily, in the direction of my bunk and I gratefully collapsed on it.

Lying down was an immense relief for a short while; until the bunk decided to try to throw me out. Ships bunks can be very determined, but by spread-eagling my limbs the damage was limited to a mere churning of the head and stomach. Then the flying started - not me, but the items which I had left lying on the desk top next to the head of the bed. First the picture of Alice slid from end to end of the desk gathering momentum until it hit the raised lip of the desk, giving it vertical lift off with a trajectory aimed at my head. This was closely followed by a writing pad and other sundries which I collected around

17

me and tried to ignore. Too late, I remembered the full water jug, now rumbling with increasing speed toward me. The cascade of water made further rest impossible so I struggled out of bed to assess the damage and try to trap down any further missiles. By this time everything movable in the cabin had moved; glasses, bottles, ice container, table lamp, standard lamp all lying on the deck, some glasses and bottles smashed, some still rolling. In half an hour the Atlantic had turned an immaculate cabin into a state of chaos.

I struggled out of bed to clear up the mess but it was a losing battle. No sooner had I replaced one thing than something behind me fell over. To make matters worse, my need to tidy the cabin was losing the battle against my need to vomit.

I telephoned the bridge and explained my predicament to Pete.

'No problem, Mike. I'll send Gwilym to help you out.'

'Who's Gwilym?'

'You'll find out.'

Ten minutes, and the entire contents of my stomach, had passed before I found out;

'Allo, Doc. I'm your bedroom steward. In trouble, is it?'

The deep, melodious Welsh voice of Gwilym was slightly soothing. His tone conveyed a mixture of pity and long-suffering patience. His 5'10" frame was slightly bent with his shoulders drooping in sad weariness. The expression on his dark Welsh features reminded me of a sheep-dog, well used to service, but never quite reconciled to it. In his late fifties a large part of his brain appeared to be engaged in contemplating his retirement; at least it didn't seem to be concentrating on the problem at hand.

'Trouble is, Doc, when you're new to the sea you don't know how to put things to stop them rolling about?'

'Yes, but what the hell do we do about it?'

'Oh, don't know exactly, Doc. It's a bit of a mess!'

Between vomiting bouts I explained to him how sorry I was for being new to the sea and eventually managed to get some action. Glasses were stowed in cupboards and wet towels put under the rows of bottles to stop them moving.

Once under way he seemed to be very efficient. I felt that he'd had to make a decision about whether he liked me or not before getting into action. He must have seen a lot of doctors come and go, and probably enjoyed being in a temporarily superior position with the newcomers.

'Getting a bit rough now, Doc; not feeling too well is it?'

The sounds of my retching made the question seem a bit superfluous, but it was probably the best I'd get in the way of sympathy.

'Perhaps a glass of port and brandy, Doc?'

I retched again. 'Just help me sort out the bed, I can't stay in it with this rolling, Gwilym.'

'Always said bunks should be athwart the ship, not like this; less throwing about the other way.'

'That's not much use now, Gwilym, the bugger's screwed in place!'

'Suppose you're right, Doc. Dieu, it's getting rougher now; better get your lifejacket.'

'Bloody Hell, Gwilym, it's not as bad as that is it?'

'Oh no, Doc, you haven't seen a proper rough sea yet. Just need the lifejacket to put under your mattress.'

With that he lifted the outer edge of the mattress and laid the stretched-out lifejacket under it. It was as if he'd extracted enough sport from the occasion, at my expense, and was now prepared to be sympathetic and helpful.

'Now get into bed, Doc.'

It sort of worked; I was wedged in a valley between the propped-up outer edge of the mattress and the bulkhead.

'Not much rolling about like that, Doc. Might be a bit of up and down, mind you! Nos Da.'

'Good night, Gwilym.'

He departed, no doubt pleased that he'd demonstrated some of his nautical experience. Probably he was heading for a night-cap with his buddies; I could imagine the conversation:

Dieu, you should have seen the mess the new Doc was in! Green as a cabbage and his cabin a real tip. His face was a real picture when I offered him a port and brandy. Don't know if he'll last: he thinks we're in a hurricane!'

Well, I thought, *I'll show him - I'll last! I've made a bad start, but I'll make up for it, if I can just get over this nausea and headache.*

Headaches were a new thing to me and I wondered if Alice's had been the same, or worse. She hadn't complained about them too much after we'd returned from our Lake District holiday. When she did I sometimes took her for a drive with the car hood down; the fresh air seemed to help. Sometimes we'd resorted to aspirin.

'Get me a gin and tonic, and some aspirin, would you, Mike?' she asked me one afternoon.

'You shouldn't take alcohol with aspirin,' I'd reminded her.

'If I'd wanted your medical opinion, I'd bloody well have asked for it,' she'd snapped.

We never drank alcohol in the afternoon and she didn't usually swear. I think that was when I began to get concerned, especially when I noticed that the usual small bottle of aspirin in the medicine cabinet had become a large one. I'd thought that perhaps that was an economy measure and that her more frequent headaches were because of her mother's recent illness.

I did try to take some action.

'Why don't you let me get a specialist opinion on your headaches, Alice?' I'd enquired.

'Don't be silly, Darling; why see somebody else, when I've got a clever doctor like you for a husband?' she'd replied.

Well, I'd been clever all right! I had missed what was right under my nose. If she had been a patient I'd have taken action weeks earlier. Perhaps it is true that the cobbler's children are the worst shod?

I felt something sticking in my ribs. It was Alice's picture, still lying on the bed where the storm had tossed it. I tucked it under my pillow.

CHAPTER 3

The following morning the sea felt less rough, not much, but enough to enable me to wash, shave and dress without falling. I'd slept most of the night, eventually managing to ignore the 'up and down' that Gwilym had promised. I felt green and a look in the mirror confirmed it, but it was time to get to work.

As instructed, I reported to the hospital at 0830 hours, prompt, for the morning hospital report and meeting. I met the rest of the team: John Crawley, the senior doctor; Mary and Janet the junior sisters, and of course Sally, who appeared to have forgotten our previous encounter. She led the meeting with the previous night's report.

'Pretty busy night, so had to call on Mary for extra help. Thirty-two seasick, one passenger with a fractured ankle from falling off a bar-stool – waiting in Ward 1; one crew punch-up – both waiting for X-rays; one mechanic with a 'Dear John' letter crying into the small hours and wanting to be excused duties; one hysterical female passenger who has decided she doesn't like it at sea and wants the Captain to turn the ship back; and two elderly couples with luggage gone missing with all their tablets. The bridge forecasts increasing rough seas, maybe storm force 9-10; and there is a queue of seasick passengers lining up the stairs. Any questions?

There were quite a few questions I'd have liked to have asked, but Sally's tone was not encouraging any. She'd had a busy night. Her report was brief but concise. Clearly she didn't think any questions would be necessary. It was now time for action. I was comforted to find her as brief with the rest of the team as she'd been with me the previous day.

John Crawley took over; 'No questions? OK then, meeting over. Mike, you start the crew surgery, the nurses can start on the seasicks, and I'll check the fractured ankle. See you later.'

That was the briefest meeting I'd ever attended. Within seconds everybody was in action. Syringes and needles were appearing from cupboards and drawers and an assembly line had formed with a medical attendant at one end fixing the needles to the syringes, one nurse next, drawing up the drug into the syringe, and the other nurse pulling in passengers from the queue outside. There was no room for anyone else in the small treatment room so I departed to find the crew surgery.

In the tiny alleyway outside the crew consulting room were gathered what seemed like a large proportion of the ship's 1000 crew-members. Some were leaning against the bulkheads, some sitting on the bench, one crumpled in the corner, crying his eyes out.

I was wondering where to get started when help arrived; 'There's a large crowd for you this morning, Sir, not a very good start I'm afraid. By the way, I'm Terry, pleased to meet you.'

He was a thin man with a face to match. His expression was half glum and half smile, and his voice was very matter of fact, with a broad Geordie accent. He was dressed in a uniform of black trousers and white open-necked shirt, bearing the shoulder insignia of a Medical Petty Officer. He gave me the impression of a seasoned campaigner, probably ex-Royal Navy. I thought he'd probably be a good source of information about the running of the hospital.

'Nice to meet you Terry. I'd like to have a chat with you later and perhaps you could show me around your domain, but I suppose we'd better get started on the sick and lame first.'

'More lame than sick this morning, Sir. I've laid out the notes on your desk. I'll X-ray the bruisers from last night's Charity Boxing match.'

'Charity Boxing Match?'

'Aye, Sir, fighting over the new blond hairdresser, Charity Box.'

'That's a damn funny name!'

'Real name's Barbara Box, Sir, but she's given so many "donations", she's known as Charity.'

'Regular occurrence is it, Terry?'

'Aye, one per voyage on average.'

'Did you say that you were doing the X-ray?'

'Aye, Sir, Jack of all trades, that's me; dispensing, X-rays, plastering, pathology. Better be getting on now.'

I started on the crew surgery which reminded me of my Army days doing sick parade.

First there were the easy, minor coughs and colds needing a drop of linctus. Next came a batch of bruises and cracked ribs. It appeared that the Charity Boxing match had been extended into a free-for-all. Nothing serious with that lot, though several waiters would be off duty because of black eyes which wouldn't go down well with the passengers. They'd end up serving the officers for a week which wouldn't please them – no tips!

The next two were engineers, one with a deeply embedded splinter in his finger and the other a metal foreign body in his eye. They would have to wait until a quiet time, so I took them to one of the wards to rest and wait.

Returning to my little consulting room I found an embarrassed-looking waiter standing waiting for me. I looked at his notes headed Julian James, Waiter First-Class Passenger Restaurant.

'Well, Julian, what's the problem?'

He shifted from foot to foot. 'I don't know if I've got a problem, Sir, so I wanted you to look at it for me.'

'What do you want me to look at, Julian?

'Well, it's probably nothing really. I think I've got a discharge.'

His fresh, young face was pinking up.

'Have you been doing something unwise?'

'Only once, Sir, about three weeks ago.'

'When did you notice the discharge?'

'Only yesterday, Sir, but I've been looking for one for weeks.'

'Then we had better have a look. Let's go round to Terry's laboratory.'

The hospital laboratory was very tiny, more like a cupboard really, but there was room to sit at a microscope and do some simple tests. If I'd deduced correctly that Terry was ex-Royal Navy, he'd probably know more about this sort of problem than I did.

I dug Terry out of the X-ray developing room and presented the problem.

He nodded knowingly, as if this were an everyday occurrence to him. 'Aye, Sir, I'll deal with him.'

He carefully put on surgical rubber gloves and proceeded to examine the organ in question, then started massaging it to find the discharge. I was still feeling nauseous, so decided to leave.

'I'll get on with the rest of the surgery, Terry, and leave you to it.'

'No problem, I'll make a slide and let you know the result.'

The remaining patients were a mixture of sprains, backaches, and rashes that were quickly sorted out and I was about to leave to sort out the two engineers with splinters when I remembered the crumpled heap in the corner of the alleyway.

He was still there, sobbing into his boiler suit.

'You'd better come into the office, Lad.' I persuaded him to his feet and accompanied him along the alleyway, his head still low and his walk no more than a shuffle. Sitting him in front of my desk I started to prise his story out of him.

'It's nae use, Doc. Ye cannae do nothin' fer me. Ma life's in tattered shreds; there's a black, gloomy cloud over ma head, wi' nae silver lining; and there's nae light at the end of ma tunnel.'

If I hadn't already observed him showing obvious signs of distress I'd have thought he was pulling my leg using such graphic phrases, but he seemed to be sincere.

'I take it you're feeling depressed, Jock!'

'Och, that I am, Doctor. An' me name's not Jock, it's Angus ... Angus Colquhoun.'

'Sorry, Angus. The nursing sister told me that you had a problem with your girlfriend. Is that what's depressing you?'

'Aye, the wicked harlot. Here's me sweating me heart out in the ship's boiler room, and risking me life in storm and tempest to earn a penny to buy us a home, and she, the hussy, indulging in lust and depravity.'

Whatever had happened at home, he'd certainly taken it to heart. He must have been nursing his bitter thoughts all night, to express them so clearly.

'Weren't you expecting anything like this?'

'No, I thought everything was all right, then out of the blue I get this letter, telling me the whole sordid story. Mind you, she ends it pretty enough, saying "it grieves me to hurt you so, but I have to follow the yearnings of me heart." Some heart!'

24

He wiped the tears from his face with the sleeve of his greasy boiler suit, leaving further oil streaks down his already grimy cheeks, and thrust the crumpled, stained, damp letter at me.

'I'd rather not read your letter, Angus, but it sounds to me as if you're better off without her. A good-looking young chap like yourself will soon find a good woman to replace her.'

'Ya dinna ken, Doc. How can you understand the depth of agony that this is causing me?'

'What don't I ken ... er ... understand, Angus?'

'It's ma brother that the harlot's sleeping with, me own flesh and blood conspiring against me, treating me like a piece of dirty flotsam, washed up and discarded on the shore.'

'Ah, I see, I'm beginning to "ken" your problem now. Tell me, are you very close to your brother?'

'Aye, Doc, nigh on raised him since my father died. He's a bit younger than me, you see, an' he's no much use at anything practical, but he's a good lad, or was till this happened.'

'And is she your first girlfriend?'

'Aye, well, first "proper" girlfriend; we planned to marry when I'd enough saved. I should have spent it all on me'sen, an had a good time, like the other lads on board.'

'Look, Angus, you can't do anything about it until we get to Southampton. Why don't you get back to work, to help keep your mind occupied, and we can talk some more tomorrow. Perhaps it would help to decide what upsets you most; losing your girlfriend, or your brother's friendship?'

'Aye, well, I'll try, Doctor. I don't want me mates thinking I cannae pull ma weight. They're beginning to think me a cry-baby, even the nursing sister tore me off a strip; threatened to report me to the Captain if I didn'a pull me'sen together and get back to work. I'm no shirker, Doctor, I just cannae see the point of going on.'

'Angus, just hang on to yourself. You're going through the worst bit now, it'll get better later. I'll talk to your boss and explain your problem. Come and see me tomorrow.'

'Aye well, thanks, Doctor, I'll do my best.'

As I watched his short, stocky figure shuffle off to report for duty I thought how nearly I'd dismissed him as a histrionic cry-baby myself.

Why had Sally torn him off a strip? Why can't people tolerate a man crying? Why should he have to keep his anguish inside? He had looked a pathetic little figure, crying over his Dear John letter, but he was hurting deeply and the world around him was alien. I could feel an echo of his pain in me, but I didn't want to know – 'Push it back, it's not good for you, Mike.'

I telephoned the Chief Engineer to explain the situation, and asked him to keep an eye on him in case he decided to drown his sorrows literally, by jumping into the Atlantic.

I felt that I should have spent more time with the poor lad but my stomach was beginning to churn with the increasing roll of the ship and I'd nowhere near finished work. Besides, I wanted to talk to Sister Sally.

I found her in the Treatment Room and managed to attract her attention between injections.

'Sister, I know you're busy, but could I have a word with you about young Angus, you know, the mechanic with the "Dear John" letter.'

'Yes, I know him, I could hardly forget him, he spent most of the night pestering me for sleeping tablets.'

'Well, I'm concerned that he's going to go off the rails, he seems deeply depressed.'

'Look, Doctor Vaughan, this sort of thing happens all the time. They seem to expect their girlfriends to hang around for them at home, while they're living it up in every foreign port.'

Hell, I thought, *what's the matter with her! She's got a real down on him. Something's upset her. Perhaps it's not just me.*

'I don't think that he's like that. He's really in love with his girlfriend.'

'Well, he'll get over it. He's best at work; he can't expect to shirk duty every time there's a problem at home.'

Perhaps I'd caught her at a bad time. She'd been working all night and looked dog-tired. Still, she'd no right to question my medical opinion, even if she was tired.

'I was asking for your help in looking after him; not your opinion on his moral fibre! I've decided on that.'

'Well, you'd better use your moral fibre to sort him out. Ask Janet to keep an eye on him, she's on duty now. I should have been off duty hours ago, I'm dog-tired and ready to flake out as soon as we've sorted out most of this seasickness.'

It was no good. I didn't think that I'd ever get on with the little martinet. Better drop the subject.

'All right, Sister, I'll talk to Janet later.'

The subject was closed. She turned on her heel and within seconds was busy filling syringes again. I decided I could talk to Janet about Angus later in the day. Time now to get back to the remaining problems.

I remembered the waiter with his embarrassing problem and so searched out Terry, still huddled in his small laboratory.

'What's up with the waiter, Terry?'

'Ah, no great problem there, Sir, there are no evil beasties on the smear – look for yourself.'

After many years of not using a microscope, it took me some time to focus it properly, but eventually a clear view of the beautifully prepared slide revealed none of the gonococcal bacteria that show up as pairs of evil looking little red dots in cases of gonorrhoea.

'You reckon that there's nothing wrong with him then, Terry?'

'Aye well, that's for you to decide, Doctor, but in my opinion he's been playing with himself too much, trying to find a discharge. Often happens when they feel guilty and worried about a casual pick-up in a foreign port. Can't leave their peckers alone, until one day they irritate it so much they produce a discharge. Quite harmless, of course, but it scares the daylights out of them.'

'Hope you're right, Terry.'

'That's for you to decide, Sir. I'm just the Medical Petty Officer.'

'Well, thanks for your opinion, Terry. Could you send him in to see me?'

Julian appeared, still red-faced and ill at ease. 'What have I got, Doctor? Is it something serious?'

'No, nothing serious, Julian. I think that it's a case of digital urethritis.'

'Oh my God! What does that mean, Sir?'

'Well, I think that you've been examining it too often, making it weep a bit.'

'Will it recover?'

27

'Yes, I'll give you a course of tablets, but keep your hands busy elsewhere for a week or two.'

'What about work?'

'Well, there's a rule that waiters suffering from a discharge have to be kept off duty.'

'I know that, Sir, but I'm saving up hard to buy my sister a word processor 'cause she's got polio and can't get about much. If you put me off duty I'll lose all my tips.'

I began to feel sorry for him. As I was sure that there was very little likelihood of there being an infection present, I decided that I could afford to help him out by letting him go back to work.

'Well, as there's no sign of serious problem, I'll stretch the rule for once. You'd better get back to the restaurant now.'

'Thank you, Doctor.'

There were still the two minor injuries to deal with. What I really wanted to do was lie down on the examination couch and die, but I reckoned I could last another half-hour.

Making my way back to the main hospital felt like being a pinball bouncing off the bulkheads of the narrow alleyway. In the distance I could hear trolleys rolling about, and the sea was now crashing against the sides of the ship with determination, each lurch being accompanied by a loud bang.

The queue of seasick passengers seemed to be no less, some vomiting onto the deck, some into the large plastic bags provided.

I looked into the Treatment Room to find a nurse. Most of the narrow space was occupied by a large pair of buttocks belonging to a voluminous American lady heaving over the sink, groaning and retching. With lightening speed a needle entered the large volume of flesh and two millilitres of clear fluid were plunged home by Sister Janet.

'That's number 69,' she said, grinning at me, 'How are you doing? You're still looking green.'

'Don't mention it, I'm fighting it back. What's that you've just planted in her bum?'

'Phenergan; marvellous stuff, stops the seasick within minutes and puts them to sleep for an hour or two.'

'Sounds great. I'm about to operate on the two splinter cases in the ward, any chance of help?'

'I've dealt with the finger already. You'll have to do the eye. Everything is set up in the theatre, you'll have to help yourself I'm afraid.'

I was not looking forward to dealing with the metal fragment in the centre of the engineer's eye. I remembered the first time I'd been shown how to do it, by a specialist;

'If you haven't got a steady hand, forget it Lad, give the job to someone else. That delicate, transparent skin over the front of the eye is precious, if you dig around it with your clumsy hands you'll ruin the man's vision for life.'

Watching him perform the operation had made me feel sick, but I'd had to do it myself later, as an Army doctor. That had been on dry-land, dry, stable land. How the Hell could I do it bouncing around the Atlantic like this, and feeling sick as a dog before I'd even started?

I laid the poor man on the operating table and by setting the angle-poise magnifying glass over his face I could clearly see the tiny, offending, sharp fragment. The concentration of focusing on the object was making my nausea worse, especially as both patient and doctor were rocking in time with the ship. I think he had noticed the colour of my face and the beads of sweat on my forehead, as he was looking rather alarmed.

'What are you planning to do, Doc?'

'Oh, just lift the fragment of metal out of your eye,' hoping I sounded a lot more confident than I felt.

He glanced at the array of sharp instruments on the trolley, then back at me. He said nothing, but a hint of disbelief blended with the alarm already showing on his face.

'Don't worry, I'll deaden the eye first with drops.'

'Thanks, Doc,' he said with semi-conviction, or could it have been sarcasm?

I put the anaesthetic drops into his eye and sought out Sister Sally, to discuss the problem.

'I'm a bit worried about operating on his eye in these rough conditions. What are the chances of the weather improving?' I asked.

'There's no reason why the weather should improve! Could well be worse later. Of course, if you don't think you can cope, I'll get Doctor Crawley. He managed to do an appendicectomy in a Force 9 gale last year, but he's busy setting the fractured ankle right now.'

My God, I thought, *you don't miss a chance to put me down; but I won't give you the satisfaction of seeing me give up!*

'No, thank you, Sister, I'll manage.'

There's no point in putting it off, I thought, *leave it much longer and the metal will start off a rust mark in his eye.*

On my way back to the operating theatre, Terry stopped me; 'Is the ship's rolling complicatin' yer operation, Sir?'

'It certainly is, Terry, I've never done anything this delicate in these sort of conditions before.'

'Best to fix your hand firm against his face then, so's you both move together, in harmony, so to speak.'

'You reckon that would work?'

'Seen it work before, Sir, but you're the doctor.'

'Thanks, Terry.'

Returning to the theatre I began to feel respect for the alarmed patient. Ship's Engineers are a stoical breed and he wasn't going to admit to being afraid; alarmed maybe, but not afraid. I wouldn't have swapped places with him.

I made everything as stable as possible; battening down the instrument trolley and tying it to the operating table to prevent them from parting company. Now ready to go, I selected the best instrument, reassured him that there was nothing to it, provided he kept his eye still, and pressed the heel of my hand firmly against his face. As an added precaution I took a firm grip of his right ear to prevent us parting company.

I examined my hand – steady as a rock, until viewed through the magnifying glass which showed the instrument making violent swings. I held it nearer to the sharp end to reduce the movement and waited for the next lurch of the ship. I had estimated that there were ten seconds between the lurches so I'd try to catch the lull. The ship lurched, we both rocked together – now the steady bit – in with the instrument, under the edge of the tiny metal fragment, slightly breaking the surrounding transparent skin. I worked the fragment loose then flicked it out quickly, before the next lurch. The tiny piece of metal flew off somewhere, I didn't care where. It was out of the eye.

I put an antibiotic ointment into his eye and padded it over. 'There you are, I told you it was nothing.'

'Thanks, Doc, the eye feels much better, but can you do something for my ear?'

I examined his right ear and noticed the bright red fingermarks where I'd gripped him, to hold his head still.

'Sorry about that, but that should get better by itself. I'll see you this evening to check your eye.'

I would have liked to wallow in a bit of pride in my handiwork, but there wasn't time. The concentration and tension of the operation was the last straw. I needed a sink, quickly. The treatment room was still full of naked buttocks, but I was desperate. Another lady passenger was already occupying the sink. With an 'Excuse me, madam' I eased my head alongside hers and together we heaved in mutual misery.

A hand clasped my shoulder. 'You'd better come with me, Doctor.' Sally guided me into the examination room. 'Just drop your trousers.'

'I didn't think you cared, Sister.'

'I don't! Turn round and lean over the couch.'

I looked over my shoulder to see Sally advancing with a syringe. I didn't like the glint in her eye.

God, she's making me pay for breaking the first commandment, I thought.

The needle entered my buttock, surprisingly smoothly, the two millilitres of Phenergan stung its way into my flesh.

'That's it, pull 'em up. You'd better go to bed now. I didn't think you'd last as long as this. I'll have you woken up in two hours. Sleep well.'

Those were the kindest words she'd spoken to me, they felt almost as good as a blessing from the Pope, and in my weakened state they brought traces of tears to my eyes.

As I stumbled to my cabin I thought about the last 24 hours. My practice and home in England now seemed a lifetime away. If I was looking for change I'd certainly found it. If I was escaping boredom and safety, I'd achieved that too. Could I cope with these changes?

With relief I crumpled onto my bunk, cocooned myself within the blankets and let myself roll with the ship. It then occurred to me that part of seasickness was due to trying to fight the movement of the sea. Best to accept it and learn to live with it, like I'd have to learn to live with the strangeness of this new environment with its myriad of personalities all working together in close confinement; having somehow to resolve their conflicts within the discipline of the ship. I was beginning to understand the tension that had caused the fight over Charity Box.

My nausea was vanishing now and I spread myself out. The double bunk felt very spacious, until I realized that it was the first time I'd been alone in a double bed. After Alice had died I'd moved into the spare single bed, because I couldn't bear the smell of her perfume still lingering on the sheets; neither did I want to wash away that intimate connection, so I'd left them untouched, unlaundered.

I'd considered getting rid of everything that reminded me of her, sheets, pillowslips, perfumes, clothes, pictures; but for every moveable memory in the cottage there were hundreds of immovable memories in my head. If I couldn't scrub my mind, why bother with the rest? Besides, she would be very hurt if her possessions were missing if she came back, and there were times when she did come back.

One evening, out of habit I'd poured two drinks and taken them into the sitting room. I'd placed hers next to her chair and sat opposite with mine. I'd chastised myself for being stupid and absent-minded, but left her drink there anyway. Then she had started talking to me: 'You've poured me a double, Darling. How did you know I had a headache?'

'You've always got a headache lately, Alice. You know that.'

'I'm sorry, Darling. Have I been irritable? I've been trying to keep it from you.'

'You can't hide much from a doctor.'

'But you didn't know I had a brain tumour, did you?'

It had been an uncanny experience. She was sitting there, as real as life. I even recognized the dress she wore - it was one I had picked out for her birthday; the emerald green colour matched her eyes. One minute we were talking about the present, the next about her death. Afterwards I thought I must be going mad, but at the time it seemed quite natural.

'No, Alice, I didn't know you had a tumour, and I can't forgive myself for not spotting the signs earlier. I might have saved you.'

'But maybe you wouldn't have, Darling. Maybe it was too late when the headaches started, then we'd have had months of anguish and perhaps there would have been a horrible operation that didn't work. We were happy right up to the end, weren't we?'

'Oh yes we were, Alice. But now you're just trying to comfort me. You always did that; trying to find the bright side of all my problems. Death hasn't changed you.'

'Don't be silly, Michael, you were my husband, not my doctor. Stop feeling guilty! Kiss me.'

Her lips were so real and so inviting. She looked as pretty as ever. I'd almost reached her chair when the telephone rang. It was a patient, with a headache of all things. We'd talked about how bad it was and how long she'd had it, and I'd arranged to see her the next day. Of course, when I returned to the sitting room Alice had gone. I'd been so angry at the interruption.

Perhaps it was an effect of the Phenergan injection, allowing me to think about this more freely. Even sexual memories were beginning to stir, lying in this strange bed. Memories of her long, brown hair falling over my face as we tumbled happily together. Suffocating in her breasts for as long as I could before coming up, gasping for air; sometimes pretending to be dead, holding my breath until she'd get worried and slap my face. In retrospect, that had been a macabre thing to do, but she had laughed. It was all fun. Even coming too soon when I was drunk had been fun. She'd never let me be serious for long. There was so much I missed about her.

I wondered if I'd ever feel aroused again. I wasn't looking for any new romance, just to feel whole.

The only woman I'd so far developed any relationship with was Sister Sally, and that certainly wasn't likely to become a loving one. Any warmth in her soul was well camouflaged. She didn't seem to like me and I don't think it was just because I had broken the first commandment.

These thoughts floated away as the Phenergan injection took its effect and a wonderful drowsy feeling enveloped me.

Drifting into sleep the words of a doctor friend came back to me. When I had told him that I was becoming a ship's doctor he'd commented: 'Lovely life, Mike, piece of cake. An hour's work in the morning, sleep on the sun deck all afternoon, boozing, eating and dancing all evening.'

'Where's the sun deck?' I wondered.

CHAPTER 4

I awoke of my own accord. The violent lurching of the ship had settled into a gentle roll and for minutes I lay still, indulging in the pleasant sensation of being rocked, like a baby in a cradle. The cabin around me was alternately lightening and darkening in rhythm with the ship's roll as the shafts of steely grey afternoon light reflecting from the sea entered the porthole. Far below, the rhythmical rushing noise from the bow wave added harmony to the overall lulling sensation, and I began to appreciate some of the attractions of a seafaring life.

'Looking at my watch I realized that I had slept solidly for four hours, so Sally had either failed to wake me, or decided to leave me in peace. A call to the hospital confirmed the latter. Evidently the storm was abating and the pressure of work had eased off. Hunger was beginning to awaken, so I dressed and went to the hospital to scrounge a sandwich from the tiny hospital galley.

Dr Crawley was there finishing of the treatment of his last passenger case. 'You look better, Mike. When you've finished your sandwich let's go for a drink. I've just about finished here.'

Apart from our brief introduction this morning this was the first contact I had had with John. He seemed very much in command of himself and at ease in his environment. His tall, slightly fleshy body could afford the slight stoop of his shoulders and his long, rangy limbs could encompass as large a territory as he wished to control. His handsome, aquiline features were marred only by an unnecessary handlebar moustache which was tinged slightly more with grey than his long dark, loosely swept-back hair, which collapsed over the right side of his face into a forelock that regularly encroached over his eye. Perhaps because of the slipping forelock his head resided slightly to the right of centre, giving his gaze an impression of earnest inquisitiveness, but his eyes added a hint of arrogance, forced, as they were, to look down his fine long nose. Nobody, least of all himself, I felt, would have denied his good looks.

I reckoned him to be much the same age as myself and I was curious to learn his background. I'd wager he was ex-Royal Air Force with that moustache - that could be the only excuse.

'Tell you what, let's go to my favourite bar, on upper deck aft. It's quiet at this time of day, and the view's good.'

He was right, the view was good, with its absorbing panorama of the sea and the wake of the ship pluming out behind us into the distance. John ordered a Vodka Gimlet and I thought a Bloody Mary might help put me on my feet.

This felt very civilized. Refreshed by the sleep and beef sandwich, headache and nausea gone, I realized how wonderful it is just to feel normal.

'Well, how was your first morning, Mike?'

'Pretty damn hectic. I didn't expect life at sea to be a doddle, but I felt like a scrambled egg by the time I'd finished surgery.'

'You'll get used to it; you managed to cope, that's the main thing.'

'Yes, only just managed though, and I'm bothered over a tussle I had with Sally, over that mechanic with the "Dear John" letter; she's pretty damn obstinate in her opinions. I think I've got on the wrong side of her.'

I was hoping to get some insight into Sally's behaviour from John. Perhaps find out if he had the same problem.

'Well, tact and diplomacy aren't her strong points, but she's a bloody good sister, and runs the department as well as any nurse I've ever met. Better than most. You'll have to respect her opinion, she's been at sea a damn sight longer than you.'

Naturally he would have to defend her, particularly to a newcomer: I'd not have respected him for doing otherwise. However, a bit more explanation wouldn't have come amiss, and it wasn't necessary to put me down so hard.

'That's as maybe, but it's only seafaring that I'm a novice at. I've been a doctor for ten years and that should count for something.'

He hesitated before replying, as if considering whether to change tack, but his eyes hardened again and his air of superiority returned.

'Look, Mike, you've a lot to learn about medicine at sea, it's different. Life is not all beer and skittles; it can be damn hard work and we have to pull together, as a team.'

Perhaps he was trying to warn me of something, or perhaps deferring some explanation until he knew me better.

Approaching John, on his port side, was a vision. Tallish, blond, mid-twenties with legs all the way up to her swaying hips. He couldn't see her from his position, and didn't even notice her leaning over the back of his chair. Her musky perfume had reached my nostrils; his must have been blocked!

'Really, John, what's all this stuff about hard work? Are you trying to frighten the new doctor back ashore? You didn't seem too intent on hard work in the nightclub last night.'

It was obvious that he knew her voice well because his response was instantaneous. 'Bloody hell, Susie, don't you miss anything? As you're here you'd better join us for a drink and meet our new junior doctor, Mike Vaughan.'

'I'd be delighted to, Doctor Crawley. Pleased to meet you Doctor Michael. As I can see that John isn't going to introduce me, I'll do it myself – I'm Susie, the social hostess on board.'

She shook my hand, maintaining the grip for slightly longer than was necessary. It is possible that John noticed this because his eyes hadn't left her.

'I'll have a glass of champagne, John. I think you can afford it with the profit you're making from your private practice.'

I didn't know much yet about the private practice, except that passengers were charged a standard fee for medical services. Susie seemed to be clued up on it.

'That's none of your business, Susie! Mike, could you go and get Susie a glass of champagne from the bar?' He said this with the air of someone well used to being obeyed.

Well, being the junior doctor was one thing, being Doctor Crawley's 'go-for' was quite another. I was about to express this opinion when Susie saved me the trouble; 'No, do it yourself, John. I want to talk to Michael.'

With ill-grace John left to fetch her drink.

There was something about Susie's deep blue eyes that grabbed me, and drew my gaze directly into them, or more accurately into one of them as she appeared to have a slight squint. This resulted in her left eye having a greater intensity about it – she made no effort to look away.

'I do hope that John isn't boring you with his old sea-dog tales, Michael. He can go on a bit if you let him.'

'No, Susie, we were just discussing some medical problems. I take it you know John well?'

She glanced across at John, standing at the bar, as if trying to decide how to reply. 'Not as well as he'd like, but that's another story. Anyway, we should be talking about you, you're the new boy.'

I was surprised by this honest revelation, but by quickly changing the subject she'd warned me to avoid persuing any further.

'Hardly a boy, Susie.'

'That's just a matter of definition. Scratch any man and you'll find a boy beneath the veneer, and your veneer isn't very thick.'

This conversation was reaching the personal level very rapidly, and I began to feel uneasy. There was an aggressiveness about her manner that was disturbing. I wondered if social hostesses were taught a form of conversational Karate. I felt my defences were being penetrated.

'Oh, I've always prided myself on having a strong professional veneer, for protection mainly.'

Not much of a counter-attack, but it was the best I could manage.

'Yes, I can see that, but it's only in your forehead and mouth, it's your eyes that give you away.'

So she'd been observing mine too. Perhaps the eyes are the windows of the soul, but I'd rather keep my soul hidden for the time being. 'I don't think I'm flattered, Susie.'

'You should be.'

I wasn't sure I wanted this conversation to continue. She was making me feel naked, so when John returned with the champagne I was both disappointed and relieved.

'Had to crack a new bottle just for you, Susie, but I suppose you're worth it.'

'You know I am, John. So was the girl in the nightclub last night, I noticed.'

I couldn't understand what was going on between these two. She was definitely teasing him, but seemed to be flirting with me.

'That's none of your business either. Anyway, it could have been you, if you weren't such an obstinate cat.'

'Obstinacy has nothing to do with it, John. We tried all that, remember?'

'Yes, I remember! Anyway, what have you been chatting to Mike about?'

'That's none of your business, Doctor Crawley!'

I broke in, to try to ease the mounting tension; 'Actually we were just talking about some of the problems I've been having getting used to the ship.'

'Yes, well, Mike's learning to feel the ropes, Susie. It's all a bit strange for him to start with. There's no substitute for experience.'

'And you have plenty of that, John!'

'Plenty where it matters, Susie.' His meaning was obvious. Hands behind his head, trunk and limbs at full stretch, his body language was obvious. The arrogance, showing clearly in his eyes, was intentional.

'Vulgar Pig. Drink the bloody champagne yourself!'

He'd have had difficulty drinking that glassful. She'd poured it, with deliberate care, over his crotch.

John's embarrassment was scarcely noticed by the other occupants of the bar. Susie had carried all their eyes with her, as she swayed, head held high, out of the room.

The champagne had the desired effect. His arrogant pose quickly disappeared as he scrabbled for serviettes to mop his trousers. 'Bitch!'

I wanted to laugh, but I finished my drink instead. There weren't many comments appropriate to the occasion but it couldn't be ignored.

'Well, she's quite a bombshell!' maintaining as neutral a voice as possible.

'She's a bloody menace. Thinks she can poke her nose in anywhere.'

'Pretty nose though, John.'

'I can see you've been taken in by her charms. Well, I'd be careful if I were you: there's a lot you don't know about her, yet.' He'd regained his poise. A short sniff as he swept his forelock away from his eye, the only sign that he'd been in any way disturbed by the incident.

He rose to take command. 'I think it's time I showed you round the public rooms, show you the layout of the ship. Can't have you getting lost.'

It suited his mood to be the tour guide, and I welcomed the opportunity to discover more of the glamorous side of the ship.

First we briefly visited two more of the bars; it was interesting to see how different in atmosphere they were; one clearly ideal for after-dinner brandy and cigars, the other for more romantic late-night occasions, with private little areas partly partitioned off, each with its own small table light. I wondered how much time I'd get to spend in either of them.

Our next port of call was the Princess Room. He paused, to let me take it in.

This is elegance! I thought. It was large enough to take several hundred people comfortably. Pale, subtly lit walls and arches edged a large polished parquet dance floor. This was surrounded by groups of pale, low-backed leather seats, each group nesting its own circular glass drinks table. 'What's this room used for?'

'It's the first-class entertainment room. You'll be coming here for the Captain's cocktail party, later in the voyage. That'll involve looking smart and chatting to the passengers.'

'Sounds glamorous.'

'Just part of the job, Mike. Something else you'll get used to.'

The mood was suddenly shattered by a piercing Tannoy announcement; 'STARLIGHT, STARLIGHT. BOILER ROOM, BOILER ROOM.'

'What the hell is that?'

'That's us, we're Starlight - let's go, quick.'

Forget the lifts - too slow. Down stairway after stairway, taking the steps three at a time. Down into the bowels of the ship. Enter the working alleyway; from elegance to industrial thoroughfare, crew members everywhere, some in waiter's uniforms, some in boiler suits, running.

'This way, run.'

We ran aft, past Printers Shop, food storage areas, crew administration offices, security office, on to the boiler room entrance.

A frightened mechanic was waiting for us; 'This way, Sir, quick.'

'What's happened?'

'Steam pipe's burst, Sir. Couple of mechanics caught in the blast. Sister's there already.'

Opening the door, the heat and noise were overwhelming. Now down the metal runged ladder, across the metal platforms to a group of huddled figures. Engineers everywhere working on the broken pipe.

'Where are the patients?'

'Can't hear a bloody word above this noise,' John shouted at me. 'Look for the Sister.'

Sure enough Janet's white uniform was easily spotted against the blackened deck. She was leaning over a mechanic who seemed to be unconscious. John joined her. She turned to me, pointing just beyond where I stood; 'Another one, down there.' she shouted.

After pushing my way through a gathering group of engineers I could see him, hanging, his arm caught between a rail and the edge of an engine block. One side of his face was reddened and peeling where the steam had hit him and knocked him off balance. The other side was white with shock.

'Jesus, he's swinging by his arm. For God's sake get down there and support him.' I directed two of the strongest-looking engineers, who quickly climbed down to the deck below, where they grabbed him and eased him up a fraction.

The immediate panic over, I assessed the situation. *Looks like his shoulder is dislocated and his arm is wedged above the elbow,* I thought.

One of the senior engineers pushed his way forward; 'What do you think, Doc? Lift him, or cut the railing and lower him?'

'Cut the railing,' I shouted.

Within seconds a large pair of cutters appeared and the railing was removed.

'Now take him down, slowly. Support his arm.'

By this time the rest of the medical team had arrived; Terry, Patrick, Mary and Sally, carrying between them stretcher, oxygen cylinder, resuscitation equipment, emergency bag – the lot.

'Let's give him a whiff of Entinox to ease the pain, before we move him.'

Climbing down to the relative quiet of the deck beneath the platform, I placed the mask over the man's face and as he breathed in the mixture of oxygen and nitrous oxide, I recognized him; 'Angus! I thought you had enough problems, without this.'

He pushed the mask away. 'Sorry, Doc. It was mae own fault, got careless. I unbolted the wrong flange. Am ah hurt bad?'

'No, nothing too bad, Angus. I'll have to patch your face up for a wee while and put your arm back in place. Otherwise you're fine. Now breathe this gas in; it'll take your pain away.'

'Och, the pain's none too bad, Doctor.'

'Yes, but it may be worse when we move you.'

Now that was a problem; with his arm stuck out like that we'd not be able to get him into the wrap-around cane stretcher to lift him out. I daren't let him walk. He looked shocked; besides which, he might have injured something else too, perhaps his back. I was pleased to see Terry had joined me.

'Could you keep the anaesthetic going, Terry. I want a word with John.'

'Sure, no problem, Sir.'

I left Angus in his capable hands while I climbed back up to the platform, where John was still examining the other mechanic. 'How are you getting on?' I asked.

'OK, this lad was unconscious but we've brought him around. He's not too bad.'

'I'll need your help with mine. His arm's dislocated, and we can't get him in the stretcher. I think we'll have to treat the dislocation here.'

'Right, let's have a look at him.'

We climbed down to join Terry who was still administering the light anaesthetic.

'You're right,' John said quickly, 'dislocated all right. We'd better reduce it here. Which method do you fancy, Kocher's method or Hippocrates? He's your patient.'

As textbooks play a small part in a doctor's life after qualification, I had to dragnet my memory to recall which of these names referred to which method, and I wondered if he was testing me, perhaps digging for a flaw in my knowledge.

I recalled that Kocher's method involved twisting the arm outwards, a manoeuvre that needed more room than was available in the cramped conditions, and was usually done with the patient sitting.

'I'd prefer Hippocrates.'

It seemed odd referring to an ancient Greek physician in this noisy mechanical environment.

41

'OK, I'll hold his shoulder, you can do the donkey work.'

I took off my right shoe. *If he was on an operating table this would be straightforward,* I thought. *In this situation I'll have to lie on my back.*

There wasn't much space but I managed to position myself alongside Angus, sardine fashion, allowing me to feel for the ball of his humerus with my toes. Now, by pressing with my foot, and pulling his arm with both hands, I had good control. This had worked before on a hulking soldier; the stronger the patient's arm muscles, the harder the pull needed on the arm. 'OK, ready,' I said.

John held the top end firm and I started the donkey work, pulling to overcome the muscle tension. Press the ball towards its socket with my toes; nothing happened. Pull harder; slow, steady pull. Sweat was now pouring down my face from the heat and exertion. Pull; press harder with the toes.

Clunk.

'Ouch!'

The two sounds simultaneous; the satisfying clunk meant that his shoulder joint was back in place; the 'Ouch', that he'd felt it, even with the anaesthetic.

'OK now, Angus?'

'Och, yes, Doctor, didn'a hardly feel a thing.'

'You're a bit of a liar, Angus, but you're a good patient.'

All I had to do now was tether him into the stretcher and get him hoisted back through the boiler room, up into the working alleyway, and into the hospital via the back entrance.

We then took him into the treatment room where I could examine him more fully. John joined me. 'Well, you're not just a pretty face. That was a nice bit of work you did.'

'Thanks, first time I've done a dislocation for years, and never like that before!'

'Yes, it was a bit unconventional. What do you make of his condition now?'

I felt sure the question was intended to assess my knowledge; after all, he was responsible for ensuring that I was capable. He'd probably carry the can if I fouled up. 'Well, I want to check him for other injuries first. We don't know what he might have damaged when he fell over the rail; but it looks like the burn is not too bad, probably only first degree.'

'Right, I'll leave you to it. Better check the other chap.'

He seemed satisfied that I could cope, and in spite of his overbearing manner, I felt pleased by his compliment on my performance in the engine room.

By now Sister Janet had anticipated my requirements by laying up a trolley with dressings and instruments. After making sure that he hadn't injured any other part of his body, I set about examining his face. Under close inspection, in a good light, I was relieved to find that the burn wasn't too serious; so Janet and I set about cleaning it up. First cutting away the loose, peeling, dead skin, then removing the grease from the pink flesh underneath. I could see from Angus's face that it was hurting him a bit, which was a good sign; it showed that the flesh was still living. He remained stoical throughout the procedure, but he looked worried.

I felt it was time to cheer him up, so, more for his benefit than for Janet's, I remarked; 'Well, Sister Janet, we've made a good job of that and I think he's probably got away with first degree burns only. If we cover it with antibiotic gauze, a week or two should see him back to his handsome self. How does that suit you, Angus?'

'Could ye no make me more handsome, Doctor? Mebbe ah'd get ma girl back then.'

'I think you'd do better as you are, Angus. "Handsome is as handsome does" remember.'

'Ah'd no thought of it like that before, Doctor. Thanks anyway.'

'You're welcome. Now get some sleep.'

I met John in the alleyway.

'How did you manage with young Angus's face? Was it much of a problem?'

'Not really, just needed tidying up and cleaning. I reckon he'll be fine in a few weeks.'

'You've had your first taste of action then, Doctor Vaughan. See what I mean about medicine at sea being different?'

I could see what he meant all right. He meant, 'You ain't seen nothing yet, and you're still a novice'. He was probably right though and I'd no doubt learn a lot from him in the coming weeks. I just wished I could like him.

'Well, it's different in some respects, but the basics are the same.'

'But there are a lot more basics to know about. Remember there are no specialists to back you up on board ship.'

That thought had already been niggling in my mind. Most doctors have a few blind spots. I just hoped that his weren't the same as mine.

'Between us we should manage,' I commented.

'Always have done. The nurses are well clued up as well.'

'Yes, I've noticed. Sally seems to be well informed; I just wish she wasn't so prickly. I could have done with her backing me up over Angus this morning. She didn't have much sympathy for the lad!'

'Look, go easy on her will you. There's reason for her being prickly about that sort of problem at the moment. She's just been let down herself; her fiancé, at home. He's gone off and married a nurse from the local hospital. She's not got much sympathy just now for men in a similar position. Anyway, she's a damn good Sister; don't upset her.'

That explained a lot. Perhaps it wasn't just me she didn't like; probably men in general after an experience like that. 'OK, I get the point; but we still need to pull together as a team. Can't let our personal problems interfere with the job.'

'That's easier said than done, Mike. You'll find out. By the way, you're doing evening passenger surgery. It started ten minutes ago. Patrick will show you the way, he's in the galley.'

With that, and a flick of his forelock, he departed, leaving no chance for a reply to his comment. I felt he'd fired a warning shot across my bows. I admired his loyalty to Sally, but didn't think he was doing her any favours by ignoring her attitude. It wasn't right to let your own problems affect your work - but wasn't that exactly what had happened to me? Wasn't that the main reason I came to sea? Coping with Alice's death had severely affected my attitude to patients. I could easily have become bitter and twisted. *People in glass houses shouldn't throw stones,* I thought.

With relief, I realized that I was beginning to feel more enthusiasm for work, probably because the challenge of the new environment was all-absorbing. I hoped it would last. Now I'd better find Patrick and get to passenger surgery.

Sure enough I found him in the tiny hospital galley, sitting on a small stool, surrounded by a cloud of smoke; can of beer in one hand, the other holding a cigarette cupped within his palm. He looked like a mischievous Irish leprechaun.

'You're not busy are you, Patrick?'

'Oh, not at all, just finished the washing-up. Thought I'd better be steadying my nerves, after all that excitement in the boiler room. If you know my meaning, Doctor?'

This came out with practised ease. He'd probably been using the same sort of excuse for years.

'Yes, I understand, Patrick. I can see you must have been very shocked.'

By now he had disposed of both cigarette and beer can into the waste bin, and was making a futile gesture with his hand to wave away the smoke. 'This grill's been making a terrible lot of smoke lately, Doctor. Perhaps we'd better be getting the engineers to have a look at it?'

He was trying to make me an ally to his surreptitious habit, realizing, of course, that I was too new to discipline him about smoking in the hospital.

'You could be right. Now, if your nerves are quite steady, perhaps you could show me to the passenger surgery?'

'Sure, that would be my pleasure, Doctor. Shall I be carrying your bag for you?'

You scratch my back, I'll scratch yours, I suppose. You overlook my habits and I'll look after you is what he meant. 'That sounds like a good idea. I've got some files to take.'

We climbed the stairways then made our way aft, in the direction of my cabin. This didn't seem quite right. 'Are you sure we're going the right way, Patrick? We're heading towards my cabin.'

'I was thinking that you'd maybe want to go there first, Doctor.'

'Why?'

'Well, your back is covered in grease from that operation you did in the boiler room. I've never seen it done that way before. It was a comical sight, you on your back with your foot in the poor lad's armpit.'

I'd completely forgotten the mess I'd been lying in, and opportunities for inspecting your back are few and far between.

'Well, it worked.'

'It did that, right enough, Doctor.'

We arrived at my cabin door. 'You'd better come in and wait while I change, Patrick.'

He settled himself into a chair while I dug out a fresh shirt and pair of trousers.

'I was thinking you handled yourself pretty well today, Doctor.'

'Which bit of today?'

'In the Boiler Room of course. I wouldn't be knowing about the rest now, would I, Doctor?' Which was as good as saying that he did know about the rest. He'd probably witnessed my altercation with Sister Sally and everything else that had happened.

'I don't know, you seem to know a bit about most things.'

'Well, you can't be blaming me for my natural powers of observation, now can you? For instance, I could tell you something about Angus you didn't know.'

'Such as?'

'Well, he almost got himself killed in the bar at lunchtime, taking on one of the deck-hands over Charity Box.'

'Oh God, she's not causing trouble again, is she?'

'Well, only in a manner of speaking; she wasn't there herself, you see, but this deck-hand started talking about her, calling her a whore. Well, the next thing, young Angus is taking great exception to his manner of speech, saying he has a strong objection to the word "whore", and is up and at him for all the world like a bull terrier; and this deck-hand, being built like a side of beef, is about to knock Angus into next week. If we'd not all jumped on the pair of them, young Angus would not have been around to have the accident in the Boiler Room.'

I somehow couldn't imagine Patrick getting involved in fisticuffs. He was too wily for that. 'It's a wonder you didn't get injured yourself then Patrick.'

'Well, I was acting more in the role of referee, if you understand, Doctor?'

That was more like it. 'Yes I do, Patrick. Now let's get to the surgery, I'm late enough as it is.'

He left me at the surgery.

It was tiny, with its ten-foot by six-foot area filled with desk, sink unit, small drugs cupboard, examination couch and, of course, Janet; 'You made it then, Doctor. I've got a fair number of patients lined up

46

for you. Have you dealt with Americans before?'

'No, I haven't, Janet.'

'Then you'll find it interesting, Doctor. Watch out for the language, it's not exactly the same as English.'

Sister Janet had already taken the details of the patients in the waiting area and presented me with a sheaf of cards. 'The first two are an elderly husband and wife from Texas. Their luggage was lost in transit and they're both on a long list of medications. He's had a triple artery bypass and is taking everything from blood thinners to vitamin pills. She's a chronic bronchitic on two inhalers and a host of pills. They both packed their pills and potions in their main luggage cases so we're starting from scratch.'

We sat them down in the small consulting room and asked them to describe their tablets.

The wife took up the lead: 'Ma husband's had a very serious operation you know, Doctor, and we are none too happy about losing our luggage and medication. Isn't that right, Howard?'

'Sure is Mary Lou.'

'Now you tell these people all about your tablets, Howard.'

'Well now, let me see; there's them there blood thinners that Doctor said is reel important, kinda stops ma arteries clogging up. Them's kinda off white, so to speak, with a little bitty line right 'cross the middle.'

'Do you know what the name is, Sir?' I tried.

'Well ... kinda pretty little name; coulda had a "c" in it someplace ...'

I could see we were getting nowhere fast. There were another five tablets of his to sort out, before we started on hers! I looked at Janet; 'Where do we go from here, Sister?'

'Let's try that big American formulary, Doctor.'

Luckily, apart from the listing of drugs, this book had dozens of pages of pictures of tablets. Perhaps they'd be able to recognize their tablets from this.

'Right, Sir, let's see if you can find them amongst this lot.'

'Give me ma spectacles, Honey,' - to his wife.

'Howard, you old fool, you know darn well you packed 'em in your suitcase, along with mine!'

'Well, you said to put them someplace safe!'

'You shoulda had more sense, Howard. You shoulda packed 'em in the hand luggage, jus' like I said!'

They were flowing into battle with an ease evidently born out of many years of practice.

'If you're so goddam clever, why didn't you do the packing yerself, 'sted a sittin' on yer butt all day reading them brochures?'

'Howard Sinclair, if yer gonna bad-mouth me like that in front of these people, you can sort it out yerself. I'm gonna leave you to yer own devices!'

'Now, Mary Lou, do'n you go flashin' off like that, let's be peaceable fer a little while. You'll only go an set off yer asthma agin.'

This was getting off to a good start! My first American patients, and I'd started off a family feud.

I took Janet to one side; 'We can't go on like this, Sister. Try to find a magnifying glass and sit them outside, under a good light, to study the pictures themselves. Get them to tick off the possibilities, then we can get on with the rest of the surgery.'

A magnifying glass was found in the hospital and we sat them, still feuding, under a standard lamp in the corner of the waiting area.

Janet brought the next patient in. One of those large American ladies who'd expanded over the years in every dimension God had given her. She managed to fill most of the 10 x 6 room, refusing to take a seat, which was just as well as she'd have amply overflowed the small chair available.

'I cain't sit down and it's the shipping Line's fault! First they make me sick as a dog by throwing this goddammed boat around, then they try to burn my fanny off!'

I glanced at Janet for help. She whispered in my ear: 'It's not what you think - by "fanny" she means her backside.'

'Oh, that's a relief!'

'I can see you're not very happy, Mrs Myers, but it would help if you could explain how your fa..., er, rear end was injured.'

'Stoopid, imbecile waiter threw a flaming crêpe Suzette over my ass!'

I'd have to make some enquiries into this! I could imagine that she had the ability to annoy - but I couldn't imagine even the most unstable, emotional waiter taking aim at her rear end with a dessert that took a lot of time and skill to prepare.

48

'Perhaps we'd better take a look at the injury?'

'Too darn right you will!'

With remarkable lack of ceremony she pulled her dress up to her waist, dropped her panties and turned to present her amazingly large behind for my examination.

Sure enough, there was an inflamed streak of flesh down the one cheek. Luckily most of the heat had been taken by her clothes, so the flesh was unbroken.

'First degree burns only, I think, Sister. Could you put something on it?'

'Delighted, Doctor – something slightly acid do you think?'

Janet had a flippant side to her nature. I prayed that Mrs Myers hadn't heard her whisper.

'Better take this seriously, Janet,' I hissed, 'or we'll be sued as well!' In a calmer voice; 'Some vaseline gauze and an antibiotic ointment might be better.'

We heaved her onto the couch and Janet set to work. In the distance I could hear the family feud continuing. Mary Lou appeared to be winning; asthma or no asthma.

After completing the dressing we sent the fat lady outside to fill in an accident form and Janet collected the next patient.

'Please God, send me a nice American next; there must be millions of them!' I thought.

My prayers were answered. One of the daintiest little old ladies walked sprightly into the room.

'It sure is nice to meet you, Doctor. All my friends say how charming and polite you British doctors are.'

'I'm flattered, I hope I can live up to the reputation.'

'Ah'm sure you will, Doctor, smart-looking feller like you.'

'Well thank you! Perhaps you'd better tell me what the problem is?'

'Not too much of a problem really, Doctor; I'm not sure I should really be wasting your time! You see, every morning I do my aerobics, so this morning I joined the "golden door" keep-fit class run by that lovely young lady, just below your hospital. I realize that I'm not so fit as all those other young people there, but I usually manage to keep up with the class. Today I felt quite dizzy half way through. Silly really. I'm all right now, but thought I should get a check-up, just to be safe.'

49

'Better get you on the couch and have a look then.'

Looking at her 5' 1" stature I decided she would need the step to reach the couch. 'I'll just pull the step-stool out for you,' I offered, and leant over to get it.

I felt a light hand on my back and heard a faint swish. Looking up, to my amazement, I found her lying, prim and proper, on the couch. Noticing my look of amazement she smiled primly at me. 'Never done a fence vault, Doctor? Not bad for 76, eh!'

You certainly aren't, I thought.

I didn't expect to find much wrong with somebody who could perform like an Olympic gymnast, but listening to her heart, the tell-tale signs were there. Instead of a nice regular 'lub-dup... lub-dup' the heart sounds were jumping around all over the place.

I returned to my desk to make some notes and spoke quietly to Janet; 'Fibrillating I think, Sister. Rate's about 130 per minute. We'd better arrange an ECG.'

But Millie had overheard and was not to be kept in the dark. 'What have you found, Doctor? You can tell me, I'm a big girl now you know!'

'I was about to explain to you, Mrs Montrose. Your heart is beating a bit fast, and not in regular rhythm.'

'A bit like jazz you mean! I love jazz, don't you?'

'Come to mention it, I do, but I'd prefer a bit of slow classical music in your chest!'

'Not in a minor key, I hope.'

'Why not?'

'Bit sad are minor keys, and I don't want to be sad. Anyway, how're you going to get Glenn Miller out of my chest? By the way, call me Millie. I think we can be friends; in fact I think we should be now you've had your head so close to my chest!'

There was a small twinkle in her eyes and just a hint of flirtation in her smile, with her head cocked slightly to one side.

'Right Millie, first we do a heart tracing – ECG.'

'EKG in American, Doc.' There was a bravado in her spirit, which would not allow her to be cowed by doctors. I could see that she would not let me get away with anything.

'OK, EKG. If I'm right in my diagnosis I will start you on some tablets. Can't get rid of Glen Miller I'm afraid, but we can certainly slow him down a bit.'

She sat bolt upright and started to swing off the couch. 'Right, let's go for it!'

It seemed like this was just one more adventure for Millie, another little hurdle to jump.

'Steady on, Millie, no more fence vaults for the moment. In fact I want to arrange a wheelchair to take you to the hospital.'

'Oh, please, Doctor, don't make me look pathetic. I can walk it; I'll behave, I promise.' She seemed used to getting her own way, with her demure smile.

'We'll compromise. Sister Janet here will walk you down so that you can lean on her arm - if you feel it necessary, that is.'

I watched them walk along the long alleyway, towards the hospital. It looked like Janet was doing the struggling to keep up.

'Can't be too serious,' I thought. 'Still, you can't be sure with people like Millie.'

Thankfully the remaining patients were straightforward and easily satisfied; when the last one had left I went over to the elderly Texan couple, still sparring verbally in the corner of the waiting area.

'Well, how many of those pills have you recognized?'

'Silly old fool, can't tell green from blue: but I reckon we've picked out most of them,' said Mary Lou.

Miraculously they appeared to have chosen a collection of pills that were approximately suitable for their respective conditions. At least they were happy with the colours. Now all we had to do was find the British equivalents in our pharmacy and try to get the dosage correct. This was easier said than done as the strength of tablets don't always exactly match up on both sides of the Atlantic. The only safe thing to do was choose the lower dose pills and work up until the clinical condition was satisfactory.

First I examined them both to note the condition of their hearts and lungs, and record pulses and blood pressures. I then arranged to check them every day to make sure they stayed well. It occurred to me that I could radio-telephone their doctor in Texas to help me sort it out, so I took his details from them and booked a call through the radio-room for the next morning at a time he would be in his office.

They left, clutching a handful of carefully labelled bottles. Arm in

51

arm they proceeded along the alleyway, still deep in conversation. 'Ah shure hope that English Doctor knows what he's about; he talks kinda funny! How long d'ya reckon they train 'em in England?'

'Now don't you be silly, Howard. Man's bound to know what he's doing - cain't read his writin', always the same with these educated fellers!'

By now Janet should have done the ECG on Millie, and a visit to the hospital proved me right. I studied it carefully.

'Looks like she's fibrillating all right, but no signs of any underlying heart attack. How's she feeling at present, Janet?'

'Perky as anything - can't stop her talking!'

'I'll start her on Digoxin, but I'd really like to admit her, at least overnight, just to keep an eye on her. Do you think we can persuade her?'

'It'll take all your charm, and a following wind! She was planning on doing the "light fantastic" in the Princess Room tonight.'

'Hell, can't have that. I'll try my charm. Back me up if she looks like hesitating.'

She was standing looking through the ward's porthole. As the hospital is almost at sea level, the view of the bow-wave rushing by at almost 30 miles per hour is fascinating.

She turned around on our arrival. 'Sure is one helluva view through this window. I s'pose it's watertight?'

'It hasn't leaked since I've been on board, Millie. How would you like to enjoy that view for a day? I'd like you to stay with us until we've got your heart rate controlled.'

'Oh now Doctor, don't you think that's taking it a bit far. That lovely Joe Loss is playing in the Princess Room tonight and I've had an ambition to dance to his music for years.'

I was developing the impression that treating this little firecracker was not going to be easy. Up until now my experience had been almost exclusively with British patients who were mostly compliant, often too compliant, accepting my word as gospel. There was no such religious faith in Millie. Perhaps all Americans were like this.

'Well he's there again tomorrow night, Millie. I'd feel happier if you left it till then.'

Janet came to my aid. 'Doctor's right you know. Better lose a day of

52

your voyage now, than make yourself worse and spoil the rest of the trip.'

'Oh damn it, s'pose you're right. I'll stay on one condition, Doctor; you give me a dance tomorrow night?'

She'd got me cornered. How could a gentleman refuse? Besides, from the evidence to date, she'd probably be good fun to dance with.

'I can't guarantee tomorrow night, Millie. It'll take two days to get your heart rate down, but I'll do my very best the night after; provided I'm happy about your heart. Will you accept that bargain?'

'Best I can beat out of you I s'pose. Shake on it, Doc!'

We shook hands.

'Now get into bed and start your tablets. A nurse will be checking your pulse and blood pressure from time to time. I'll see you tomorrow morning.'

She obeyed.

CHAPTER 5

It was time to shower and get ready for dinner. Once in my cabin I changed my mind and drew a deep bath, using some bath salts that had been left by the previous occupant. I wallowed in the warm, frothy water, watching it slop around me, imitating the movement of the sea outside. I reflected on how full of contrasts my day had been; from the luxurious ballroom to the grimy, hot and noisy boiler room. From hulking pugilist sailors, to a dainty little old lady. From feeling sick as a parrot, to wallowing in a warm bath.

As the bath bubbles caressed my chest, the worries of the day began to fade and a sense of relaxation developed. It was a moment for gentle philosophical thought, such as contemplating the nature of the universe, but it was the nature of my body that grabbed my attention. Something was arousing me in a way that hadn't happened for months, and it was some moments before I realized that it was fleeting thoughts of Susie that were responsible for the change.

Don't be stupid, Mike, you've only just met the girl!

Still, there was something about her eyes, perhaps it was her slight squint that, perversely, made them so attractive; *That's daft, you don't get excited over eyes, you must have noticed the other bits!*

But I couldn't remember the other bits, acceptable as I am sure they were: just the eyes, and her flaunting mannerisms, her open, almost aggressive flirtation. *That's it, she's just a flirt! Forget it, she's obviously already led John a merry dance, she's just a tease. Get your mind above your belt!*

But that was easier said than done. I'd been sexually aroused and dismissing her as 'just a tease' wasn't good enough. Maybe it had been that musky perfume that had bypassed John's nostrils, but excited mine. *Oh God,* I thought, *it was Alice's perfume!*

Alice had found out very quickly that that particular musky fragrance had turned me on.

There is nothing quite like guilt for killing the libido. I had never considered cheating on Alice and, even though she was dead, thinking sexually about someone else felt like betrayal. She was still very much alive in my head and being attracted to someone wearing her perfume seemed doubly disloyal. I knew this to be illogical, but logic has little to do with feelings. Thankfully my thoughts were interrupted: 'Not still in the bath, is it, Doc? I've laid your evening suit out for you: bit creased it was, but it'll soon drop out.'

'Won't be a minute, Gwilym.'

'Better stop playing with your "submarine", Doc; you'll be late for dinner.' His casual overfamiliarity was evidently well established. He probably considered it a perk of the job, but I wasn't feeling ready for it at that moment.

'Less of the cheek, Gwilym. If you want to be useful, fix me a Scotch and water. I need it!'

If his remarks hadn't clashed with my mood over Alice I might have found them funny. He, however, did not appear to be put out. 'I'll just leave it on the side for you. Will you be needing anything else for later; bottle of champagne perhaps?'

The man must have a degree in innuendo, I thought. *He's wasted as a bedroom steward; should be a politician. No point in fighting him.*

'Not tonight, thanks.'

'OK then, I'll bring your tea in the morning - eight o'clock suit you?'

'Yes, that's fine, Gwilym.'

'Right. I' ll knock before I bring it in for you; just in case.' He'd won, and he departed quietly with his triumph.

As I got out of the bath the telephone rang; it was John.

'Did you know that you were dining with the passengers tonight?'

'Yes, I was just about to ring you to find out which restaurant, first or second class?'

'You can have first class; give you a treat for your first night.'

I didn't care which restaurant I dined in. First class probably had a fancier menu, but I was starving; eggs, chips and beans in a corner café would have made me happy tonight. Anyway, I didn't understand why

John was being so generous. He'd not so far overwhelmed me with consideration.

'Thanks, that's kind of you!'

'Think nothing of it, Mike, *bon appetit.*'

As I dressed for dinner I tried to fathom out the reasoning behind his 'generosity', but it eluded me. I couldn't yet figure him out. It wouldn't have mattered if we didn't have to work so closely together. No doubt his good points would be revealed in time.

My bow tie was taking a lot of fixing. The mirror image was confusing my fingers. Alice had always done it for me, after watching me struggle for ten minutes. Well, she wasn't here, so I dug out a ready-tied one from the drawer. It didn't look as professional, but it passed muster. Eventually, satisfied that I looked smart enough in the black trousers, dress-shirt and white monkey jacket, I set off for the first-class restaurant.

Entering the Atlanta restaurant felt a bit like walking on stage. The raised entrance gave a good view of the hundreds of passengers already seated, but gave them an equally good view of me as I stood wondering which was my table.

However, it did give me an opportunity to take in the details of the luxurious dining room which stretched the full width of the ship, so that there was a sea view on each side through the almost full-length windows. On the starboard side the sun was setting and its reddish light reflecting off the mirrored pillars gave a flattering glow to many of the faces. The elegance of the room was well matched by the expensive dinner-dress of its occupants and I doubted if much of the jewellery glittering in the evening light was anything other than the real McCoy.

Directly in front of me, and framed by a pair of silver classical statuettes, was the Captain's table. His equally classical figure was clearly the centre of attention for the passengers dining with him.

The hum of pre-dinner chatter blended surprisingly well with the quiet music being played by a harpist in the far corner of the room.

The mixture of perfumes floating around made it difficult to detect any aroma of cooking, but what little I could smell was stimulating my appetite. I was therefore pleased when the Maître D' arrived. He guided me down the short set of stairs and into the dining room proper.

As we weaved between the tables he briefly described my table guests to me; 'They're a nice group of people, Doctor. I hope you have a pleasant meal. By the way, the gentleman on your right is rather deaf.' With that he introduced me to my six guests who were already seated, eased my chair out for me to sit down, and departed.

As I introduced myself to each guest individually I formed the impression that they were pleased to meet me, except for the teenage girl travelling with her parents who had, I felt, expected something a little taller. However, a kick from her father prompted a little smile and a 'Nice to meet you, Doctor'.

The son was more enthusiastic. He stood up and almost took my arm off with a bone-crushing hand-shake. 'Been looking forward to meeting you, Doctor. I'm going to Medical School next year and want to find out all there is to know. I'll bet you can tell some interesting stories?'

The elderly couple to my left were a little difficult. She nudged her husband and shouted in his ear; 'HENRY! THE DOCTOR SAYS HE'S PLEASED TO MEET YOU!'

He looked up from his menu; 'Eh? Oh, yes. Nice to meet you too, Son.'

He returned to his menu.

His buxom wife looked apologetically at me; 'He's going a bit deaf you know, Doctor, but he can be a very entertaining man. CAIN'T YOU, HENRY?'

'Oh, yes, yes - if you say so Dear.'

I ordered the wine and we chose from the menu while the budding young doctor alternately plied me with questions and gave his opinions on all the major health problems of the world. I thought that he would probably end up either as a world-renowned professor, or a first-year drop-out, when his ideals had been punctured by reality. Whatever, he was a pleasant, well-meaning young man.

I was feeling distinctly peckish by now and, looking forward to Cream of Mushroom soup, Beef Wellington and, to follow, Flaming Baked Alaska, I hoped that I wouldn't be expected to expound too much to the young man whilst trying to get outside it!

The buxom wife on my left prodded my arm to draw my attention: 'The waiter wants to serve you, Doctor.'

I looked up; *I know that face*, I thought.

The waiter smiled; 'You know me, Doctor. You treated me this morning. You were so kind to me that I asked to be put on your table.'

'Yes, of course... Julian!'

I remembered his blushing young face and his tricky problem. I glanced at his hands - remembering my advice to him,and noticed, to my horror, that his right thumb was well submerged in my soup! I prayed that Terry's diagnosis had been right:

'How nice of you, Julian!'

CHAPTER 6

I didn't expect to feel hungry after the large meal I'd eaten the night before, but on waking my first thought was of bacon and eggs and I'd been told that breakfast in the officers' wardroom was good. As it was already eight o'clock I washed and dressed at speed. Gwilym's promised pot of tea had arrived, but one swig was enough! From its temperature I guessed it had been delivered at least an hour before. Gwilym was an enigma. At least the tea in the wardroom would be hot.

As it was situated just below the bridge, the wardroom was easy to find. It was already half-full with fifty or so officers grouped around three long tables. I stood for a moment, unsure where to sit, as I knew hardly any of the faces present. Someone waved to me and I recognized him as Pete, the Chief Navigation Officer.

'Sit down, Sailor, you're looking lost.'

I sat opposite him, pleased to see a friendly face, and poured myself a coffee. 'I don't think "sailor" is a very good description, Pete. I've spent half my time on board being sick as a parrot!'

'Doesn't surprise me. You were a fine shade of green when I met you on the bridge! Not ex-army are you by chance?'

I couldn't see the relevance of this question. He must be telepathic.

'You're right. Spent five years in the Medical Corps. How'd you guess?'

'Easy, all the same you ex-army chaps: walk straight, stand straight, sit straight. Sea gets them every time. You need to relax a bit, take the movement in your knees. Walk smart, but don't march!'

'Don't listen to him, Mike; thinks he knows everything, lording it from the bridge all day. What he needs is a day in the engine room - that'd teach him about hard work. Get his hands dirty for a change.'

I turned to discover the source of this comment and recognized the engineer who'd organized the cutting free of Angus in the boiler room.

Before we could acknowledge each other, Pete had joined battle. 'Ignore him, Mike; always the same these engineers - grumble about working in muck all day, then claim it as a bloody virtue!'

'Well, Mike's not afraid of muck; are you?' he said turning to me. 'You got stuck into it all right, fixing up young Angus.'

I was beginning to feel like a shuttlecock in their game.

'By the way, we've not been introduced - name's Andrew. You remember me from yesterday?'

'Of course, but you look different without the grease on your face.'

'There you are, another bloody snob!' He added a wink to indicate the insult was meant for Pete, rather than me.

The battle was terminated by the arrival of our bacon and eggs which took first priority. Pete topped up my coffee.

'It's always a bit like this, Mike. Old rivalry between Navigators and Engineers. We used to have separate wardrooms. When we first combined, there was a hell of a lot of friction: now it's only banter - most of the time. Andrew's always stirring it, but he's OK; for an engineer, that is.'

I sensed that this was probably quite a compliment. 'I notice you still sit at separate tables.'

'Well, old habits die hard. Anyway, how're you settling in? Captain asked me to keep an eye on you. He thought you looked a bit green too!'

I sensed that this was more than a casual enquiry, even though most of his attention was on the extra sausage he'd acquired from a passing waiter. The Captain would not have told him anything confidential, but he probably had told him to keep an eye on me, for some trumped-up reason.

'That's not surprising. I wasn't exactly looking forward to meeting him after missing the ship!'

'Wouldn't worry about that - water under the bridge.'

I suspected that 'not worrying' was a major part of Pete's philosophy. He'd probably survived many a scrape himself; he had a well-seasoned, contented sort of face, although it looked slightly battered, probably from an earlier, rougher life as a junior seaman, toughing it out around the dock-sides of the world. He was slightly taller than short, and his stocky frame carried the moderate amount of fat you'd expect from his healthy appetite.

'It wasn't water under the bridge at the time. I felt like I'd committed a capital offence.'

'Yes, suppose you would, but how'd you get on with the old man?'

'It was unnerving to start with. He's an imposing sort of chap, but he got more human before I left.'

'Yes, he does when he relaxes, which isn't often. He thinks that you're all right though, for a quack, that is.'

'What makes you think that?'

I was keen to know what the Captain thought of me. In spite of his stiff mannerisms I felt he'd be a good man to have as an ally.

'Well, he must do, as he's planning to come down to see you. He usually hates visiting doctors. He's been off-colour for weeks now and I've been dropping hints that he should see the quack.'

I suddenly recalled the Captain's transitory fidgeting and his mentioning that he had a small problem.

'Yes, he did mention that I might be able to help him. But why hasn't he been to see John?'

This could be a useful opportunity to discover more about my colleague; a bit sly, but I was curious.

'He's spent a lot of time socializing with John over the years. Now he feels too embarrassed to consult him. I think he's daft: what's the use of having a tame quack if you don't use him?'

I could understand that. I thought I'd rather consult a stranger than have my veneer disturbed by a friend.

'I don't think that's strange; I think I'd be too embarrassed to consult a doctor I knew well socially.'

'Well, I'd rather he got sorted out, weeks ago; he's getting to be an cantankerous blighter of late. John would have fixed him up; he's a bloody good doctor – he's patched me up a few times.'

'You must know him pretty well then?'

'God, yes, sailed with him for years. Not much I don't know about John! Not my cup of tea exactly, but he can be good company, when he's not trying to impress. Had a few runs ashore with him and the old man, to the odd night-club. Had to carry him back once. Thinks he's back in the Air Force when he's drunk! How are you getting on with

61

him, by the way?'

So, I was right. John was ex-RAF; that was the excuse for the moustache.

'Haven't seen much of him yet. We've both been busy. He seems competent.'

I was not going to reveal my friction with John at this early stage. It was easier to remain neutral.

'Typical quack reply! Never commit themselves. Anyway, I didn't mean medically. I meant how d'you get on socially?'

'We haven't had a chance to meet socially.'

'Come off it, Mike. I saw you talking with him and Susie in the bar yesterday.'

'I thought you worked on the bridge.'

'Not all the time; have to get out and about; keep my eyes on things. Lot of responsibility in my job. Not much escapes me.'

I could tell that. His eyes had been scanning the room, almost subconsciously whilst we were talking. I wondered how much this skill had helped him achieve his senior position.

'That wasn't a social conversation. We were just discussing some medical problems over a drink.'

'Not with the lovely Susie around you weren't. She's not one for shop talk. She seemed to be taking a lot of interest in you.'

I wondered how he'd managed to observe all this. I hadn't noticed him in the bar.

'How do you know? I didn't see you around.'

'Ah well, you wouldn't, your eyes were too busy occupied elsewhere!'

He was right. I had been very absorbed at that moment. I felt pleased that someone else had noticed her interest in me, but annoyed that my interest in her had been so obvious.

'I think you were imagining it.'

'Not me. I'm a keen observer; have to be, it's part of my job. Helps me to anticipate problems.'

'Well, there are unlikely to be problems in that direction with me.'

I wasn't convinced of this, nor was I sure that I wanted to be convinced; part of me wanted to get to know her better, but the other part felt too guilty and rejected the idea. I wanted to play it down.

'Don't you believe it; I can spot a storm brewing from miles away.'

'Especially if you started it yourself! You're making too much out of it, Pete; it was a casual meeting. She's a friend of John's.'

'You obviously don't know the whole story. John and Susie had a fling a year back. Seemed to be getting quite lovey-dovey: then, don't know what went wrong, but it suddenly broke up, quick as it started. The air was blue for weeks after in the hospital. The nurses almost put a contract out on him.'

I couldn't tell whether Pete was plain nosey, or if he had a genuine interest in what was going on. Perhaps he had an interest in Susie.

'Well, I did notice some tension between the two of them.'

'There would be, especially if she takes a fancy to you. Just a warning, Mike.'

Then, with a glance at his watch; 'Twenty to eight; time for work. See you around.'

He got up from the table and strolled out of the room.

Oh damn! I thought, *ten minutes late for the hospital meeting! I hope Sally's in a better mood.*

It was quicker to use the stairs than wait for the lifts, but descending the nine stairways to the hospital with both speed and dignity was impossible. I sacrificed the dignity.

The meeting was already underway when I arrived and Sister Sally was well into her report, but she broke off to greet me.

'Good morning, Doctor Vaughan, nice of you to join us - we're only half way through the report.'

'Sorry, Sister. I think I'm still suffering from jet lag.'

'Not the bottled variety, I hope. Now, if I may resume?'

It was obviously too early in the day for bonhomie. 'Please go ahead, Sister.'

I found myself a perch on the examination couch with the others, who'd shifted up to make room for me.

Sally continued: 'You'll be pleased to hear that the seasickness has petered out, and I've had a fairly quiet night's duty.'

She directed this at me, with only the slightest of sarcastic smiles.

'As the others have already heard, Doctor Vaughan, there was only one case of note; a British passenger admitted by Doctor Crawley - suspected gangrene of the foot. He's in ward one and is on intravenous antibiotics.'

63

She barely paused for breath before proceeding. Even after a night's duty her uniform looked smarter than the other nurses. But the tiredness was showing in her petite face and she clearly wanted to be finished and in bed.

'The other two in-patients, Mrs Millie Montrose and Angus Colquhoun, are stable. Angus is quite comfortable; he had some pain in his shoulder but that settled with Paracetamol. Mrs Montrose is being rather difficult – refusing to stay in bed. She's wandering around, wanting to chat. She keeps asking when Doctor Vaughan is coming to visit her. I told her that Doctor Vaughan is very busy, but that he will call on her as soon as possible. I trust that that will be before you start crew surgery, Doctor.'

She had a charming way of making requests. How could a man refuse?

'Yes, of course; I'm looking forward to it. It's a pleasure talking to her.'

'Quite. Well, I've finished my report, so if there are no questions I'm off to bed.'

You'd have had to be pretty damn fast off the mark to have inserted a question within the two seconds it took her to disappear. Her sudden departure galvanized the rest of us into action. The thought of visiting Millie cheered me up, so I set off for the ward.

I found her lying in bed, eyes closed, arms folded across her chest; 'Good morning, Mrs Montrose.'

She sat up in bed, suddenly wide awake: 'Millie, please Doctor.'

'Sorry. Good morning, Millie.'

'Good morning, Doctor. And before you ask, Ah'm feeling quite well. How much are you going to charge me for that consultation?'

'I don't work only for money, Millie!'

'I know that, Doctor. I'm only teasing you. I've been so looking forward to your visit; it can be a long, boring night in hospital, you know.'

'I thought you'd be sleeping, Millie, letting your heart recover?'

'Well, I've been doing some of that as well.'

She didn't look ill, sitting up so sprightly in bed. Inactivity clearly didn't suit her, but she wanted me to know that she had fitted in some of my instructions to rest; in between her other activities.

64

'As well as what, Millie?'

'Oh, this and that. A little bit of socializing.'

This must have been the 'being rather difficult' that Sally had referred to.

'Yes, Sister told me that you'd been doing a bit of chatting.'

'Well now, I wouldn't be calling that chatting, Doctor, not with your Sister Sally. She's not a happy gal, you know, she told me straight out – "You get back to your bed, Mrs Montrose; you are disturbing the other patients".'

She pulled a long, sad face to show me that she had been hurt by Sally's rebuke.

'Well, perhaps she was right, Millie?'

The hurt could not have gone deep as her sad face had suddenly changed into one of childlike innocence, her eyes looking out from under raised eyebrows. She should have been an actress; perhaps she was for all I knew.

'Oh Doctor, you know I wouldn't disturb any patients. I only wanted to talk to her, quiet like.'

'So, did you get back to bed, as she told you?'

'Eventually, I did just that, Doctor; but not before I'd made her talk to me.'

Sally had omitted from her report that she'd lost the battle with Millie. I was developing respect for this determined little lady on the bed in front of me.

'You got Sally talking, Millie?'

'Why yes. It wasn't easy, mind – that gal's got an outside like an armadillo; inside though, she's as soft as Mississippi Mud Pie.'

'What mischief have you been up to, Millie?'

'Now, Doctor, would I get up to mischief?'

There was an unmistakable twinkle in her eyes. I'd met few people who'd looked as capable of mischief as her. It could well have been her middle name.

'Probably, Millie. I'm beginning to see through you – you're not as sweet and innocent as you look!'

'I only talked to her about her heartbreak.'

How she'd discovered about this was beyond me. I'd only learnt of Sally's problem briefly, from John, the day before. I was sure it wouldn't be common knowledge. I was not going to add to her information.

'Doctor Crawley did mention something like that to me.'

'Ah yes, but did you know that she'd been supporting that fella who jilted her? giving him money for his night-classes, to become a lawyer. Damn lawyers, all the same! Bet you he was spending her money on that other gal all the time, buying her nice dresses I don't doubt. I'll bet your Sister Sally ain't got too many nice dresses.'

Sally must have cracked under her interrogation. She hadn't struck me as someone who'd give up her secrets easily. Millie probably now knew more than any of us about the problem that was making Sally so bitter. She'd given me an insight into her. I tried to imagine the little martinet in a silk cocktail dress, with a smile on her face. Yes, she probably would be very pretty, but the only smile I'd so far seen was the very brief, sarcastic one she'd thrown me.

'I wouldn't know about that, Millie. Sally doesn't talk to me like she has to you.'

'Well, it's about time somebody talked to her, before she thickens up that armadillo hide too much.'

I didn't feel able to continue this conversation. In a way Millie had shown me up with her insight. As a doctor I should have learnt by now that aggressiveness is almost always a sign of underlying hurt.

'Millie, you are supposed to be in this hospital as a patient, not a social worker. I'm sure Sally is capable of sorting out her own affairs.'

'Now you're getting stuffy on me, Doctor. Too much "stiff upper lip" about you British. Sometimes you cain't see the wood for the trees.'

She was clearly beginning to win this discussion, so I thought it best to change the subject;

'I think we'd better leave this battle, Millie, and let me check your heart out.'

I placed the stethoscope bell onto the little square of chest that she demurely offered to me.

Her heart was still jumping around, but it had slowed from 130 beats per minute to 96.

'Looks like you're progressing a bit, Millie. Your heart's slowed down a bit already. Digoxin usually takes a bit longer than this to work.'

'Haven't got time for your fancy medicine to work, Doctor. I just lie here imagining myself as an orchestra conductor. "Easy does it" I say to ma heart, "Andante, andante", time and time again I say the same thing, and I reckon it's working; not that it would work without the help of your tablets though, Doctor, I'm sure they're helping too.'

I thought that she'd added this last remark more to avoid offending me than out of conviction.

'Well, they've worked for hundreds of years now, Millie. Ever since somebody crushed the leaf of a foxglove and found it strengthened up old people's hearts.'

'Well now, who on earth thought of doing that. And to such a pretty flower. How did they think of such a thing?'

Trust her to think of that angle, I thought.

Medicine to Millie seemed more like a game than the serious scientific discipline I believed it to be.

'Well, that's a mystery I've never been able to work out, Millie. If you can solve it, tell me. Anyway, I must get on now. I have my other patient to see in the next ward.'

'Oh, you mean Angus. He looks like a real nice boy, but I cain't hardly understand him; he does talk in a funny kinda way. Even more funny than you, Doctor.'

I shouldn't have been surprised that she knew about Angus. I guessed that 'cracking' Sally, hadn't taken up the whole night.

'Haven't you met a Scotsman before Millie?'

'Ah, is that what he is; cain't say I have; but don't you worry, I'll learn to understand him.'

I was sure she would. I little thing like a language barrier would be a minor hurdle for her talents.

'I'd rather you spent more time conducting your heart, than running around the hospital, Millie.'

'Oh, Doctor, I cain't help taking an interest in people. I'd be so bored if I couldn't socialize a little. Besides, the young lady who came in to see him last night came into my ward by mistake. Naturally I had to be civil and show her the right way.'

She was becoming a mine of information. I thought I'd have to be very careful what I said in front of her, although she could probably read my thoughts. However, I was curious about this late-night visit to

Angus.

'What young lady was that, Millie?'

'Now how would I be knowing that, Doctor. I'm only a passenger.'

'Sorry, I forgot!'

This was only part jest. I had almost forgotten that she was a passenger. I'd begun to think of her as a social worker.

'Anyway, she looked real cute to me. Dress was a bit short for my taste, but she had a real pretty face; too much make-up mind you but, underneath, a really pretty face.'

This was very encouraging. I'd taken a real liking to Angus so the possibility of a new romance developing for him was very welcome. It would help lift him out of his depression.

'Did you catch her name by any chance, Millie?'

'Well we weren't introduced, but he did call her Barbara.'

By now I was pretty sure that Millie was playing games with me. She had me on the hook with her titbits of information, and she knew it.

'Barbara, ... wait a minute ... not Barbara BOX, was it?'

'Well, how would I know that? They weren't exactly talking formal, Doctor! Anyway, now that I've told you all I know, you can tell me when I can leave this hospital and return to my cabin.'

'I've been considering that already Millie. I'll ask Sister to do another ECG, sorry, EKG on you. If that's all right you can carry on with your cruise. But no aerobics for the present.'

'What about our dance, Doctor?'

'Don't worry, Millie. I won't break my promise, but not tonight. I want to be sure that your heart is stable first.'

Her manner suddenly became coquettish. She was such a master of poses I became convinced that she had been an actress. In true Hollywood style she fluttered her eyelashes at me.

'You sure are a cautious man, Doctor, but so *masterful!*'

'Is that a compliment, Millie?'

'Now, Doctor, if you cain't work that one out, Ah'm sure not goin' to tell you.'

There was only the slightest hint of mockery in her eyes as she lay back, in obedient posture, on the bed. The perfect patient; accepting my advice, taking my tablets, trusting my word. Without doubt though, her eyes said 'I'm one step ahead of you, Doctor, in spite of your degrees.'

I wonder what you've been up to all these years, I thought, *and I wonder what you're going to get up to once my back is turned?*

'I'm going to visit Angus now, Millie. I'll see you at lunchtime.'

I left her, still in her obedient pose.

Angus looked quite cheerful. Well, the side of his face not covered by dressings looked cheerful.

'You don't look the same man today, Angus. What happened to that tear-stained, depressed young man of yesterday morning?'

'Och, dinna mention that, Doctor. I feel terrible ashamed of the way I was carryin' on, sobbin' and greetin' like a silly woman.'

The expression in his voice convinced me that he really did feel ashamed; that he'd somehow let the side down; that he'd broken some cultural taboo.

'Why, Angus? Do you think it's only women are entitled to cry?'

'Well, it is where I come from Doctor.'

'Scotland the Brave, is it, Angus?'

'I'll thank ye to no make fun of mae country, Doctor. We're maybe no as fancy as the English, but we have a bit of pride.'

'I'm not making fun of you, Angus. I'm trying to find out what your bravery's about. Hiding your true feelings is not bravery, is it?'

He paused to consider this, as if it were a new concept to him. I understood how deeply he'd been steeped in tradition.

'Sometimes it is.'

'Only if there's a good reason, Angus. Sometimes it's braver to drop your pride and ask for help, which is what you did. You're none the worse for it.'

'I hope you're right, Doctor. Not everybody would agree with you. Ma mate caught in the accident I caused will be none too pleased with me.'

I'd forgotten that aspect. Teamwork would be everything in an engine room. He'd obviously feel guilty about letting his mates down and causing an injury, which he had.

'He's all right, Angus. He got a bump on the head, but his thick skull saved him. Mind you, I heard that he's expecting a drink from you for compensation. The truth is, you shouldn't have been back at work in your state of mind, and that was my error. We're none of us perfect.'

'Well, when can I get back to work now to make amends, Doctor? I

69

dinna like this shirkin' about.'

'You won't be back to work this voyage, Angus. You'll be off sick for a month. Best to get reconciled to the fact. Anyway, I want to know why you're looking more cheerful; nothing to do with somebody called Barbara, is it?'

'Who's been saying anything about her?'

'My patient, Mrs Montrose, just mentioned you'd had a visitor called Barbara.'

He flushed a little and sipped from his glass of water to cover it up.

'Och, that's nothing. She's just a lass I talk to sometimes.'

Brave attempt, but his face told a different story. He knew he hadn't fooled me though.

'Not the same lass you got into a fight over was it?'

'Has someone been telling tales out of school, Doctor? That was just a wee altercation over language; nothing important.'

Again those erudite phrases spicing up his speech. There must be some explanation for his command of English, Scottish in flavour though it was. I promised myself to find out sometime. For the present I wouldn't push him any more about his potential romance.

'I'll believe you, Angus. Now how's your arm feeling?'

'Well, I can move it more than yesterday and the pain's nae too bad. D'ye think I can leave the hospital now, Doctor?'

Another patient wanting to leave the hospital; it must be catching.

'What's the hurry? You're being well looked after here. Another day or two will see your face healing well.'

'I just feel isolated from ma mates and I cannae see what's goin' on around the ship.'

'Just stay put for a while. I'll let you out as soon as I can.'

He seemed pleased by this idea and his face brightened.

'Perhaps you'd join me for a wee dram in the Pig when I'm out, Doctor?'

'What's the Pig, Angus?'

'Och, it's terrible ignorant ye are Doctor Vaughan. The Pig's the crew bar.'

'Right, I'll take you up on that. Start moving your arm a little more today; don't let it stiffen up. You'll never lift your pint if you do.'

He raised his small tumbler of water, and grinned at me.

70

'It was'nae a pint I was thinking of lifting, Doc.'

'So there are some advantages to being Scottish, Angus?'

'Och, aye Doctor.'

He certainly did look in better spirits. Something had cheered him up. Probably it had been Charity Box. I thought how lucky he'd been; he could easily have been seriously injured; even killed. If that had happened I think I'd have been feeling very guilty, so it was lucky for both of us.

John came into the room and broke my reverie.

'Mike, got a minute? I'd like you to look at this foot.'

'Sure; is this your new patient?'

'Yes, he looks like being a problem. Come and meet him.'

We entered the third ward. Sir Giles Underwood looked every bit the aristocrat he was. He was sitting up in bed reading a magazine. With his swept-back, grey hair and small, neat, silver moustache, dressed in smoking jacket with silk kerchief in place, he managed to look distinguished in spite of the humbling aura that hospitals tend to give to patients.

'I'd like you to meet my colleague Doctor Vaughan, Sir Giles.'

'Very pleased to meet you, Doctor Vaughan. Though I am a bit worried that John thinks that two brains are needed for my problem.'

'Well, doctors are naturally cautious. We always take the opportunity of a second opinion if it's available. It reduces the odds against making a mistake,' I replied.

'Not a betting man are you, Doctor Vaughan? I have a small penchant for gambling myself.'

In a typical genteel manner he was trying to provide a light veneer to the situation.

'I like a bet on the horses, but I won't be betting on your foot.'

'I hope not, but you'd better look at it first in any case.'

John pulled back the sheet covering the metal cradle protecting his leg. I wished he hadn't; I'd had a big breakfast.

A large area of the sole of his foot had become a deep ulcer, so deep that the shiny white tendons and ligaments could be clearly seen. Surrounding this, and extending up into his leg, was an angry red area of skin. The rest of his foot was white, ominously white. Neither was I prepared for the stench. Prior to lifting the sheet the room had smelled heavily of pine deodorant. Without the sheet, the deodorant lost the olfactory battle hands down. This was rotting flesh; no doubt about it. After the minimal amount of fingertip prods, unnecessary except to provide a gesture of professional expertise, I pulled back the sheet and turned to John. With his eyes he said 'Say nothing, we'll talk later.'

'Well, Doctor Vaughan, what is your professional opinion?' Then, noting my hesitation, Sir Giles added; 'Sorry, you will, of course, need to confer with your colleague first. I do understand these matters.'

'Yes, thank you, Sir Giles. I would like to discuss it first with John.'

'Naturally, we'll be meeting later then?'

'Of course.'

John and I returned to the small consulting room. 'What do you think, Mike?'

'No doubt about it; gangrene... and from the feel of the leg, and the smell, it's probably gas gangrene at that, and it looks to be spreading.'

'Yes, I drew a line around the inflammation yesterday, and it's spread above it already.' He looked concerned. His normally relaxed face had grown a few worry wrinkles.

'What's the story, John?'

'He's been doing a tour of the States with his son, trying to get over his wife's death. He's been diabetic for years and smokes 60 cigarettes a day. He says he got a blister on his foot walking, and was given a course of penicillin by a doctor out Mid West, but it's got steadily worse since.'

'Why didn't he get another opinion before boarding ship?'

'Well, his son, Rodney, says that he kept trying to get him to do just that, but he's evidently a stubborn old goat and decided he'd wait till they got back home. He's been sitting in a hotel room in New York for days, deadening the pain with Scotch. The Hotel Manager almost kicked them out because of the smell.'

It said a lot for Sir Giles's charm that he'd avoided eviction from the hotel. The odour from his foot must have severely affected the atmosphere.

'That I can understand! Anyway, he needs an amputation, and soon.'

'I thought that we'd step up the antibiotics first; see if massive doses of intravenous penicillin will hold it.'

I thought that was very wishful thinking. I'd met gangrene like this before. I couldn't imagine anything short of a visit from Jesus curing

72

this foot.

'No chance,' I said, 'if there's no circulation to his foot; the penicillin won't even reach it. It'd be as much use as farting against a hurricane! We'd better get the Captain to evacuate him by helicopter.'

'You must be joking, Mike! Have you any idea how far we are from land?'

'I reckon we must be a third of the way across by now; that would put us 2,000 miles to the UK and 1,000 miles to New York.'

I thought this was a pretty fair guess and John didn't disagree. He looked as if he'd already done the calculation, probably several times in the past as well.

'Do you know the range of a helicopter?'

'No, I've never thought about it.'

'Five hundred miles, maximum, and then he's got to get back. We don't keep helicopter fuel on board.'

This was outside my sphere of experience. I'd dealt with evacuation on land in the army many times, but these distances were huge by comparison. I felt again like a complete novice.

'Then it looks like you'll have to amputate, John.'

For once he looked less than confident. 'I've never done one.'

This was a blow. I'd assumed from his previously confident manner that there wasn't much he hadn't done. I shouldn't have been surprised; emergency amputations don't crop up that often.

'Neither have I. What about the passengers? It could be that there's a specialist surgeon travelling on board.'

'I've checked that. All the doctors listed are either doctors of philosophy or theology. Not much use to us; I suppose they could pray for him.'

I thought that if he'd already looked for a surgeon, he must be near to my way of thinking.

'Well, we'd better prepare for one of us to do it.'

It wasn't a pleasant thought. We'd both done basic surgery, but I'd lost my stomach for it, and from the look of John's face, so had he.

'Look, perhaps if we keep his leg cool and step up the antibiotics there's a chance it'll hold until we get to Southampton. It'll be a hell of a risk operating on him with his diabetes and lousy circulation. He smokes so much that his heart is bound to be dicky as well. He mightn't survive the operation.'

His reasons for not operating were equally good reasons for operating as the diabetes would make the gangrene more rampant. I suspected he agreed with me but had to go through the motions of presenting the opposite view.

'I think he'll die anyway if we don't operate soon. I've seen gas gangrene before. It spreads like wildfire. Anyway, if we do it today we'll get away with a below-knee amputation. Tomorrow it'll need a much trickier above-knee job.'

I could see he agreed with me. Probably had all along; but he carried the ultimate responsibility, as senior doctor, for the decision, and was therefore more hesitant. 'OK; you're right, but let's get an X-ray first to confirm the gas gangrene. It could be useful evidence if anybody decides to sue us.'

Within half an hour Terry had X-rayed the leg. Evidently even his stoical stomach was disturbed: 'Ye could 'ave warned me, Sir! I'd have skipped me breakfast if I'd known. The film's ready for you now.'

He clipped the X-ray film onto the viewing screen. Sure enough, lots of little gas bubbles could be seen spreading up from the foot, under the skin. Thankfully they stopped well short of the knee.

'Well, that clinches the diagnosis. We'd better go and tell him.'

John's nod of agreement was slow in coming, not, I suspected, because of doubt, but because his mind had moved on to contemplating the details of the task ahead.

With unanimity at last achieved, we revisited Sir Giles. He was sitting up and appeared to be expecting us.

'Well gentlemen, you appear to have made a decision.'

John broke the news to him, explaining the pros and cons of operating. I admired the way he did it. His condescension and arrogance had disappeared and he performed the difficult task with artistry, neither being over-sympathetic, having regard to the man's pride, nor hard and factual. This was a new side to John, showing a depth of understanding I hadn't expected.

Sir Giles appeared not to be in any way disturbed or upset. He had clearly been well schooled in keeping up appearances. 'Well, I don't appear to have much choice. It's either lose a leg or die before I've had a chance to finish the vintage port I've laid down. It's a very good port, so you'd better go ahead. You've explained the reasons for your decision very clearly. Thank you.'

I added to John's reassurance that we'd given every possibility full consideration.

'Well, I suppose you chaps must meet this sort of problem a lot?'

'Oh yes,' I assured him, '... happens frequently. John and I can't decide who's the most experienced in these things.'

I was sure he knew I was lying, but seemed prepared to play along with the subterfuge.

'So you'll be drawing straws for the job, eh?'

'Something like that.'

'When will the great event happen?'

'Well, you've had breakfast, so it'll be four to five hours from now, once your stomach's empty.'

'Look forward to seeing you later then.'

As we left he picked up his magazine. When I looked back from the doorway, his face was hidden.

On returning to the office, John and I thrashed out the details.

'You've got a nerve telling him we do an amputation most voyages!'

'Well, it was worth a try to make him think we're both experts. At least we've both seen an amputation done.'

'I suppose so. Anyway. which one of us "experts" is going to do it?'

'Well, what are you like at anaesthetics?'

'Not bad; I did a few months' gassing in the RAF.'

'That settles it then; anaesthetics is not my strong point. You gas him. I'll chop.'

John flinched: 'You could have phrased that better!'

'I suppose so. Anyway, where's the operating manual you told me about? I'd better get reading.'

I felt easier now the decision had been made.

John pulled a huge tome off the shelf. It had, thank God, all the details and diagrams of the operation, from start to finish.

'OK, I'll spend half an hour reading this and checking the instruments. We'd better meet up after crew surgery.'

'Fine, I'll go and tell Sister what's happening, and check the anaesthetic kit.'

I settled down with a cup of coffee and the manual.

75

The reading didn't take long. By and large it was probably easier than reading the instructions for erecting a 'flat packed' wardrobe. Only one big difference: you could live with a lopsided wardrobe.

Now check the instruments. Everything was there, from scalpels and sutures to a whole range of retractors, and the saw. I'd used everything except a saw before, except for woodwork, of course. Better check the teeth. Clearly this operation had not been done aboard for years, as the teeth looked and felt blunt. My mind ranged through the alternatives; carpenter's saw - too damn greasy, and I didn't know if it could be sterilized enough; butcher's saw - that's it - they cut bone.

'Janet, get the butcher for me. Ask him to bring his saw down.'

'Anything you say, Doctor. Leg of lamb as well, d'you think?'

'For God's sake, Janet. Just get the saw.'

I knew I shouldn't have snapped but I was beginning to feel edgy. It would be all right, but I had to prepare my mind.

Within minutes the butcher arrived looking breathless and uncomfortable. He'd evidently been told by Janet that it was an emergency and he hadn't had time to remove his apron, which was covered with blood. He was carrying half a dozen saws in his beefy arms, and must have wondered why they were needed in the hospital in such a hurry. His reddened face and neck told me he was embarrassed, but he tried to cover it up. 'What's this, setting up in opposition Doctor?'

As I explained to him the reason for borrowing his saws I tried to avert my eyes from his bloodied apron, which was too gory a reminder of the task ahead.

He didn't look too happy about the new use for his precious tools, but surrendered them willingly enough.

'You can have them back tonight. Keep this to yourself - I don't want rumours going around that there's a massacre going on in the hospital.'

He departed, relieved and somewhat placated.

CHAPTER 7

I was now looking forward to crew surgery, to give me something routine and less macabre to think about.

Terry appeared with the bundle of notes. 'All lined up, ready and waitin', Sir. I've dealt with some of the minor stuff and asked some to come back this evening, seeing as how you're goin' to be busy like.'

'Thanks, Terry, I appreciate that. Who's first?'

'Well, bit of a tricky one for you, Sir; it's Charity Box, said she couldn't wait till this evening, and she might take a bit of time.'

She entered my office hesitantly, as if trying to weigh me up before speaking. Millie's description of her had been pretty good. She did have a pretty face, behind a layer of make-up, and her skirt was too short for a peaceful life in a ship filled mostly with men. She struck me as bouncy; short and plump, with bouncy, curly hair and bouncy breasts and hips. Most of her sturdy, well-shaped legs were visible.

'Please sit down, Charity ... sorry – Barbara.'

'It's all right, Doctor, I know everybody calls me Charity but I'd rather you didn't. I'm not really proud if it, you know.'

I really must keep my mind on the job, I thought, *that was a crass mistake!*

'Yes, I do understand; it was a stupid slip-up. How can I help you, Barbara?'

'I'm not sleeping, Doctor; haven't been for weeks. Now I'm so tired I can't work properly; I keep making mistakes – I turned a blue-rinse job platinum blonde yesterday and she's after my blood. Says I've ruined her cruise and she's going to tell the Captain. And I dropped the scissors on someone's foot and got shampoo in a woman's eyes, and ...'

She was rattling on with her story as if she'd been bottling it up for a long time. With the cork out of the bottle it was all streaming out in a bubbling gush.

'Steady on, Barbara. Slow down a bit. You're making yourself sound like a disaster area.'

'Well I am, and I'm going to get the sack, and I wanted to stay 'cause I really like the job, and I don't want to leave the ship, not yet anyway: and I just don't know what's wrong with me.'

'How long have you been at sea, Barbara?'

'This is my third voyage and I really like it. I was working in a stuffy old job before, and I was hating living with me mam and dad, so this job is just right for me. Don't let them give me the sack, Doctor.'

I wondered why she'd hated living with her parents. Perhaps that was a clue to her sense of insecurity.

'Well, Barbara, that's not my department, but if I could understand your problem, I'd be in a better position to help you. I still don't know why you're not sleeping. Perhaps you're seasick?'

I thought that unlikely, but had to start somewhere.

'No, not me; stomach like an ox, me mum says I've got!'

Her face brightened with the mention of her mother, suggesting that she had an affectionate bond with her.

'Well then, something must be on your mind. What do you lie in bed thinking about?'

'The horrible things that people say about me. They've got no right!'

'What sort of things?'

'Nasty things, like saying I'm a whore - and I'm not.'

'Is there anyone in particular saying this?'

'No, it's all the lads; they keep jibing at me and make sly remarks to each other, so's I can overhear them. I can't even enjoy a drink in The Pig any more.'

'Well, tell me how it started.'

Her manner suddenly stiffened. She had begun to open up to me: now she was on the defensive, but there was anger in her eyes.

'What d'you mean, how it started?'

I'd obviously said the wrong thing but I had to continue;

'Well something must have happened, or you must have upset someone.'

'There you are, you believe I'm a whore as well. You all gang up together you men, particularly you officers.'

I'd gone from bad to worse. Dug myself into a deeper pit.

'Wait a minute, Barbara. I didn't say that.'

'Yes you did! You said I must have upset someone. What about them upsetting me? Why have I got to be in the wrong? Just because I'm not important and don't wear a posh uniform, I'm in the wrong. Well I'm not; and I'm not saying any more to you. Angus said he thought I could trust you, but he was wrong. You're the same as all the rest!'

'Barbara, wait, you haven't given me a chance yet.'

Too late; in a flood of tears she'd vanished; the only evidence left of our interview was the eye chart, still swinging violently from the hook on the door she'd slammed shut behind her.

Ah well, I consoled myself, *you can't please everyone all of the time.* But somehow she'd managed, in one minute flat, to make me feel heel of the year. I'd obviously underestimated her sensitivity, but she was being exceptionally defensive and it had something to do with officers. I hoped I'd get another chance to talk to her. All I knew of her was her reputation; I might have lost the chance to learn the rest.

My confidence was partly restored by my next patient, the eye operation from the day before. His eye was now near perfect, apart from the tiniest of scars on his cornea, which was healing well, and he appeared to have forgotten the trauma to his ear-lobe.

The remainder of the crew surgery had miraculously disappeared, no doubt persuaded by Terry, who was trying to keep the morning's work light, ahead of the operation. He'd probably treated half of them himself. Time now to take a walk.

The cold but fresh air that greeted me on the promenade deck was a sudden reminder of how cocooned I'd been in the air-conditioned ship. I had hardly given a thought to the outside world for days. After only a short time my previous life seemed light years away. I should have been relieved that my memories had been squashed, but instead I felt sad that Alice could be so easily blocked out. I sniffed the air, expecting the smell to recall memories of our seaside visits together, but the familiar odour of seaweed was missing; just a slight tang of salt was all the wind carried. The bracing sharpness of the wind was welcome, helping as it did, to clear my head. It was cold, so my thick uniform jacket felt comforting. I fingered its impressive brass buttons and the rank insignia on the lower sleeve. Three thick gold bands on a bright red background. The red background indicated the medical department. It had been the same in the Army Medical Corps; red epaulettes. Red for blood I supposed. What a gory image to display! Was that how people viewed us - up to our elbows in blood and gore?

Well, I reflected, *that will be true in a few hours time!*

After pacing the almost empty deck for ten minutes, I tired of the exercise so leant on the ship's rail. The bleakness of the view led me to wonder why sailors became addicted to sea life. Nothing to see except miles of grey water, the only relief being the light-white flecking provided by the wind. Nothing to hear except the hypnotic rushing of the bow-wave - no seagulls this far out from land.

Perhaps that's it! I thought, *like a blank canvas to an artist, allowing your head to fill in the foreground.*

I wondered what foreground I'd paint.

'Penny for your thoughts, Doctor Michael.'

The only person who had addressed me as such had been Susie. The voice sounded right. When I looked round I was proved to be correct. She'd crept up on me unawares. as she had on John in the bar. This time the wind had prevented her perfume giving me a warning of her closeness.

'You startled me, Susie. I've been deep in thought, miles away.'

'Further than the horizon, Doctor?'

'You're near to the truth, but I had just begun moving closer.'

'That's a healthy sign. Too much meditation isn't good for a chap.'

I wondered how she'd come to appear on deck. The weather hadn't attracted many others.

'I'm surprised to see you outside in this weather. I thought I was the only one who enjoyed a bracing breeze.'

She pulled her shawl tighter around her shoulders as she leant on the rail, close enough to me that her hair, blown by the wind, was flicking my face. It didn't seem to bother her: nor me for that matter. Now I could catch her perfume, but I noticed, with relief, that she had changed it.

'Well, Michael, I was looking for you. The hospital told me you were taking a walk.'

'Do you have a medical problem then, Susie?'

'I could have, if it would make you feel more comfortable.'

I was struck by her extreme confidence. She had every right to believe that she was attractive. But if as she seemed to imply, she was attracted to me, she could well have afforded a slower, less direct approach. Resisting her would be difficult enough anyway. Again I was feeling uneasy in her presence. Not unhappy, just uneasy. I was stumped for a way to continue the conversation, but she perceived my difficulty: she was probably even prepared for it, as she didn't let me flounder in my thoughts for too long.

'You think I'm giving you the "come on", don't you?'

'I haven't decided on that, we've only met once. To be honest, you baffle me.'

'Well, I've known you a bit longer than you think. I watched your late arrival from the boat-deck. Had a good laugh like the rest at first. Then I became curious.'

I remembered the row of faces peering down at me as I boarded from the launch. Obviously hers had been one of them.

'Curious about what?'

'About why you'd get yourself into such a pickle. I wanted to find out if you were a complete idiot: or if there was something different about you. That's why I introduced myself in the bar.'

'And?'

'I thought you were different enough to get to know.'

'You don't think I'm a "complete idiot" then?'

'No. Just a bit detached from reality.'

If she was right, I didn't want her to learn the reasons for this detachment. I wasn't yet ready. The problem now was how to steer the conversation away. Better try the abstract approach.

'Don't you think that reality is a variable concept, depending on how you see it?'

'That's just theory, Doctor. You have the look of someone avoiding reality, as I see it anyway.'

I could tell the abstract approach wasn't going to work. I would have to counter-attack.

'You had the look of someone already involved – with John.'

Her head turned abruptly away so that her hair was now blowing full into my face. I edged away and allowed the silence to continue. From the back of her head I couldn't tell whether she was angry, crying or sulking. I didn't understand why I'd spoken those words. Partly in defence perhaps, but partly maybe from jealousy. I'd remembered everything Pete had told me about her and John, about their whirlwind romance. I think I was also afraid of being used as I guessed that John had been. Eventually she turned to face me again. There were no tears in her slightly asymmetrical eyes, just anger:

'You don't think much of me, do you?'

There was now no avoiding the truth.

'I'm very attracted to you, Susie, but I think you're a flirt.'

'Perhaps you are a fool after all. Do you always judge a book by its cover? I'd have thought a doctor would have more brains!'

Again she marched off with her head held high. This time there was no one but me to watch her proud departure.

Ah well, I thought, *I've ruined that relationship. Perhaps it's just as well: she could be a lot of trouble.*

But I felt sad, and the air was colder. I went inside.

There were still several hours left before the operation so I decided to visit Pete on the bridge. He was busy drawing lines on charts and taking readings from various meters, but he stopped when he noticed me.

'What's this, Doc: taking up navigation?'

'Not me: couldn't tell the pole-star from the man in the moon!'

'Don't need that stuff any more: all done by satellite now. Gazing up at the stars is only for lovers nowadays. How's your love-life by the way?'

He seemed to have a keen interest in that subject, but I wasn't to be drawn.

'Bit early for that. I was just having a look around: I've got some time to spare.'

'I heard you're operating later. Shouldn't you be sharpening the knife up, or something?'

'No: done all that.'

I decided not to tell him about the saws.

'Well, if you've time on your hands you can join me on an inspection. Might as well get used to them now, you'll be doing a lot of them – part of your duties. Anyway, got something to show you.'

He handed over the care of the bridge to a colleague, donned his hat and led me off to the public rooms.

'Should be wearing your hat for an inspection really, but you'll get away with it. No one expects the quack to know the ropes. Better wear it when the old man's on inspection though - he's different.'

You can say that again! I thought.

We took our time checking the rooms. He wasn't built for speed and he had to slow me down on several occasions.

'Hang about, Mike. This is not a march - you're not in the army now.'

His pace was better suited to the job at hand, giving more time to take things in. He made several notes on his pad about bits of worn carpet and stains on seats.

'Always carry a clipboard and pad on inspection, Doc: makes 'em think you mean business.'

We stopped at one of the bars. He introduced me to the bartender and then asked to inspect his cocktail glasses. I could see that the man didn't like the idea, as it wasn't a scheduled inspection. But he needn't have worried. Pete's attention was only half on the glasses and the slight smearing, if any, didn't hinder his view of the opposite side of the room. He held one up to the light.

'See anything, Doc?'

'Looks pretty clean to me.'

'Not the glass, idiot - over there, in the corner, next to the rubber-tree plant.'

There were several small groups of people taking early drinks and in the corner was a stunning-looking girl. I now knew him well enough to guess that she was the focus of his attention, through the glass.

'Yes: a fine pair of boobs!'

'And the rest ... there's not much missing on that little corker: but who's sitting with her?'

Sitting opposite her, half-hidden by the rubber-plant, was a uniformed figure. The arm that dropped into view carried an insignia on the sleeve. Three gold bands on a red background. There were only two doctors on board, and it wasn't me.

'Looks like John's having a good time: and he told me he was off to check the anaesthetic equipment!'

'He's been seeing her for days, but he's not been advertising the fact. He's been taking her to quiet spots on the ship, hoping to escape attention, but not much escapes my beady eye.'

'Who is she?'

'One of the passengers on his table in the Second-Class restaurant.'

That explained John's generosity: why he'd offered me the First-Class restaurant.

'The sneaky blighter! That's why I'm eating in First Class.'

'Of course, Doc. Didn't think he was being kind, did you? He likes eating top-class food, does John - usually.'

So this is what Pete had wanted to show me. There was no point asking him how he knew they were there; he probably had a network of informers. There seemed to be no malice in his nosiness, rather he seemed to take pride in being well informed. It would be more interesting to learn why he'd bothered to show me his latest discovery.

'Is this why you brought me on an inspection, Pete?'

'Well, just thought you'd be interested; especially with you and Susie taking a liking to each other. With John occupied elsewhere he won't be so jealous. Make it easier for you.'

I was beginning to feel that I was in a goldfish bowl. There didn't seem to be any privacy in this little floating city. I wouldn't be at all surprised if he already knew of my talk with Susie on deck only minutes before.

'There's no romance developing between me and Susie, and I'm not looking for one.'

'Why not? There's nothing stopping you. Captain told me you're not married: broken engagement or something isn't it?'

I was pleased to hear that the Captain had kept to his word, although he'd have to give out some information to his senior officers. He'd probably been rather vague about it, pretending to know very little about me.

'It wasn't that: I just think she's a flirt, playing me along, like you told me she'd done to John.'

'I didn't say she'd played him along: just that their fling had broken off suddenly. I wouldn't judge her too harshly. I think there's more to her than shows. Anyway, that's your business.'

I wouldn't have thought it was 'my business' from his previous comments. I wondered how much he did know about her, but I didn't want to show any further interest by asking him.

By this time the barman seemed to be wondering about the results of our inspection. He was looking a little on edge. 'Everything all right then, Chief?'

Pete looked rather surprised at the question; and then seemed to recall the 'inspection'.

'Oh ... yes ... very good: very clean glasses, Joe, credit to you.'

Looking rather relieved, Joe offered us a drink.

Pete hesitated momentarily, but then replied: 'No thanks Joe, too early in the day for us working chaps to start drinking. I'll be around later though.'

The inspection over, we sauntered back, Pete taking in the details of the passengers, now gathering in force for pre-lunch aperitifs.

'Sun's almost over the yard-arm, Mike. Care for a drink before your operation?'

'You've just turned down a drink.'

'Ah yes, that's different. Not done to be seen drinking too early.'

'I think I'll miss this one out. I'd rather have one afterwards.'

'See you around then.'

I could easily have accepted his offer of a drink, but I wanted to have all my faculties intact for this afternoon's task. I decided to visit Sir Giles, to check that he was well prepared and had had his premedication, though I was sure that Janet had this in hand.

I had expected to find him alone, perhaps engaged in writing a few last letters, in case he didn't survive the operation. Instead, on entering the ward, I found myself interrupting an intimate scene. Sitting alongside his bed was Millie, her face uplifted and looking intensely into his, both of her hands clasped one of his with knuckle-whitening firmness. So all-absorbing was their concentration on each other, that it was some moments before my presence was noticed. It was Sir Giles who first turned to me.

'Ah, Doctor Vaughan. I hadn't expected to see you so soon.'

Embarrassed, I fumbled for a reply. 'Just doing a final check-up: didn't realize you had company.'

'Oh. Mrs Montrose just called in to wish me well.'

Millie looked up at me. 'You don't mind me visiting your patient, do you, Doctor?'

I should not have been surprised at this extension of her social activities, but I was a little taken aback at the enthusiasm she was showing for her current project.

'Not at all, Millie. I'll leave you two alone; I've a few things to see to.'

I departed immediately to avoid further disturbing their intimacy. Whatever Millie was up to, it didn't seem to be doing Sir Giles any harm.

In the Treatment Room I found Janet preparing an injection.

'Is that Sir Giles's premedication?'

'Yes, I'm waiting for Millie to leave before giving it to him. She's been with him most of the morning. They look like a pair of lovebirds. I don't like to disturb them but I can't wait any longer if he's to be ready by one o'clock.'

'Give them another five minutes, Janet, he seems to be getting a lot of moral support from her. Has his son, Rodney, been in?'

'Yes, about an hour ago. He seemed very upset and worried, but Sally had a long talk with him.'

'I thought Sally was in bed.'

'You're joking! Sally wouldn't miss this operation. She had two hours sleep and has been buzzing around ever since: checking the theatre, instruments, anaesthetic – the lot. This is her little kingdom. By the way, her face was a picture when she came across the butcher's saws!'

Janet was a pleasure to have around. She could always see the humorous side of life, even if her humour sometimes jarred. She was also thorough and could be relied upon to remember things I'd forgotten.

'I've repeated Millie's ECG, as you asked, Doctor. Would you like to see it?'

I'd forgotten my promise to let Millie out of hospital if her tracing was all right, and she hadn't mentioned it either, which was a bit out of character.

'Yes please, Janet. How is her pulse today?'

'Still fibrillating, but steady at 90 to 96 per minute.'

I studied the ECG: it was unchanged. With no signs of any serious developments I had no reason to keep her in the hospital any longer.

'When you break up the lovebirds, could you tell Millie that I'm happy for her to return to her cabin?'

'Certainly, she'll be pleased at that.'

She set off with the injection for Sir Giles.

Time enough left now to do some paperwork, so I settled down in the office with a cup of coffee and the files I had to complete.

John called in to discuss some final details. He was his usual self again and now seemed eager to get started. I couldn't match his enthusiasm but felt that I would be very pleased to have the operation over and done with. It was quite a relief to have him taking charge again. He left me, on his way to do a final check on the 'gas machine'.

My paperwork didn't get completed. No sooner had John left than Patrick's head appeared around the door.

'Captain sends his compliments, Sir. Asking if he could see you for a few moments? He's just outside.'

It was unlikely that I'd tell the Captain I was too busy with paperwork to see him.

'Of course, Patrick; ask him in.'

The tall figure entered, removing his cap in a courteous gesture. The same impassive face that I'd met in his cabin confronted me.

'So kind of you to spare the time for me, Doctor. I realize you are going to be very busy.'

'It's a pleasure to see you any time, Sir.'

In front of God, I thought, *even creeping is justifiable.*

'How can I help you?'

'Well, I wanted, of course, to check that you are all prepared for this operation you are about to perform. I trust that my Chief Officer has arranged to stabilize the ship as much as possible?'

I couldn't remember Pete mentioning this, but I didn't want to get him into trouble.

'I'm sure he's arranged that with John, Sir.'

'Good. There was also another little matter I wished to discuss with you.'

I wished he'd get on with it. Waiting for his ponderous words was unnerving. I hoped it wasn't another misdemeanour of mine he wished to discuss; perhaps not wearing my cap for inspection. But, as far as I could tell anything from his face, he didn't appear to be in a reprimanding mood.

'Please do, Captain.'

I was aching for him to sit down so that I could do likewise; but he maintained his rigidly vertical pose.

'You remember I mentioned a little problem that I had, when we first met?'

The memory of our conversation and his fleeting wriggle of discomfort came back to me.

'Certainly, Sir. You promised to consult me about it some time.'

'Well, now is that time, I'm afraid. The "little problem" has become rather acute.'

It took him an age to explain that he had a pile, which had been troubling him for weeks, and that this morning it had become agonizing. It would have taken a wizard to deduce, from his expression, that he was in pain. However, the nature of his problem explained his refusal to sit down.

'Well, Sir, the only way to proceed from here is to inspect the area.'

'Would you, Doctor?'

'Of course, Sir. It's my job.'

I ushered him into the treatment room, feeling relieved that the problem was relatively simple. I then pointed to the examination couch and explained that he would need to lie down on his side and expose the area. While he was adjusting himself, I quickly sought out Janet to explain what was going on and ask her not to disturb us. On my return, I found him lying obediently, with the offending pile well exposed.

It was indeed a large swelling, not exactly a pile, but a large blood clot beneath the skin which must have been acutely tender. There was a simple operation to put it right, and it would be humane to do it immediately. I explained that I would have to incise it, but that I'd freeze the area first to deaden the pain.

'If that is what is necessary, then please proceed, Doctor.'

I set about preparing the instruments, thinking how much easier it was to converse with him in this position. I had the temporary advantage of being taller than him.

I sought for a topic of conversation to keep his mind off the impending incision and, out of the blue, Barbara Box's plight came to mind.

'Had an interesting problem this morning, Sir. Barbara Box was here crying her heart out because she thinks that she's about to be sacked. I wondered if you knew anything about it?'

'Ah yes, a hairdresser - known as "Charity". Rather a flighty piece, don't you think?'

'Well, I felt rather sorry for her actually. I wondered if maybe she's been misjudged. Something she said made me think that she's being victimized. She seems a nice enough girl underneath.'

'I don't know about that, Doctor. It seems to me that she's caused a lot of trouble on board. She'll probably have to go, for the good of the ship.'

I felt disappointed that his reaction was so automatic and authoritarian, but it was unfair to pursue the matter with him in such a position. Well, a little bit unfair.

'Perhaps we could talk about it another time, Sir. I'm ready to start now. First I'm going to freeze the affected area with a spray - it'll feel a little cold.'

I picked up the spray of ethyl chloride. By aiming the tip of the bottle at the offending object and pressing the nozzle, I was able to direct a thin jet onto the 'pile'. The liquid freezes on impact, so the dark blue swelling gradually turned white and frosty. As soon as the whole surface was thickly white, I dropped the bottle, lifted the scalpel and plunged home. He shouldn't have felt anything, well - hardly anything.

It was very satisfying watching the purple clot slither out of its capsule, leaving a flat area underneath. Now, one quick stitch to close the gap, and the operation was over.

'All finished, Captain.'

'Thank God for that!'

He pulled up his trousers and eased himself off the couch, relieving me of my temporary height advantage.

'I hardly felt a thing.'

He wriggled slightly and for the first time I witnessed his impassive face crack into a smile; a thin one, but a smile nonetheless.

'The pain has completely gone, Doctor. Thank you so much.'

He retrieved his cap and made his way out. But, at the door, he paused and turned to me.

'I'll speak to you about Charity Box tomorrow.'

With that little operation out of the way I felt I'd warmed up for the big one. Almost the entire medical team had gathered in or around the theatre.

Sally was to the fore, organizing everyone as to what they'd do. Janet would help John and Sally herself was to assist me. All the instruments were sterilized and everything laid out in readiness. Terry was standing by as an extra pair of hands for the crucial stage and Patrick was in reserve to fetch and carry and answer the telephone. Nothing had been overlooked.

It was now time to scrub up and don gowns, gloves and masks. Sally, Terry and myself were now 'the untouchables', barred from contact with anything but sterilized towels and instruments.

It is at this point, of course, that one's nose invariably starts to itch, but it must remain itching, unless there is an unsterile colleague in the room willing enough to scratch it for one. Janet obliged by rubbing it with a tissue, but not without adding, with a cheeky grin;

'Anything else itching, Doctor?'

At this stage the humour was appreciated; everyone was looking serious, waiting for Sir Giles to be wheeled in. John was studiously checking the gas flow metres for the umpteenth time and Sally, with hands held tightly to her chest and her eyes watching the clock, was struggling to contain her impatience to get started.

At last he arrived, wheeled in on a trolley by Patrick, who was simultaneously holding a deep conversation with him:

'There you are, we've arrived, Sir Giles; before you know what's happening, it will all be over and done with.'

Even in his premedicated, drowsy state, Sir Giles was able to mumble a reply;

'What about the new peg-leg, Patrick?'

'Ah well, I'll be seeing the carpenter about that for you, Sir. We'll have you looking just like Long John Silver.'

A weak smile was his only response.

By this time John had a needle into a vein in the back of his hand and was slowly injecting Pentothal. Very soon after that, Sir Giles's eyelids had closed and, with a deep sigh, he became unconscious.

I organized his transfer to the operating table and John placed the rubber mask over his face. Sally covered his body with sterile green towels so that only the bad leg was exposed.

The unconscious, aristocratic Sir Giles was now a mere case. For the time being his personality was gone; he was a body with a bad leg.

90

I tried to recall the long hours I had spent in training, as a student, in the operating theatre, part of a team of detached professionals, working almost automatically with no apparent thought for the enormity of the responsibility. The conversation had always been about anything but the patient: holidays, gardens, sex: anything that wasn't serious. With luck, the anaesthetist would be a good raconteur with a huge repertoire of jokes, mostly dirty. I'd soon learnt to squash my squeamishness, except for that first incision, when the skin parted, showing the white fat underneath for a fraction of a second, before the blood welled up to cloud the picture. I'd never learnt to detach myself from that first incision and always felt it mentally, as if I were the person beneath the green towels. From then on, the operations had been pure mechanics, and I could enjoy the jokes.

Looking around me now, I wondered if the others were feeling like me, searching for their detachment. All that showed of their faces were the eyes above their masks. It creates a strange intimacy, depending on eyes for communication. Sally was still busy with the towels but I could tell that, for all her efficiency, she was struggling to retrieve that old professional hardness. She clipped the last towel in place to her satisfaction, then handed me the antiseptic swabs.

'Time to get started, Doctor.'

I sterilized the skin with the pink fluid, then looked at John, who nodded to me;

'OK: ready this end.'

First I had to draw a line on the skin, over the calf muscle, planning for an area of flesh that would be long enough to flap forwards over the stump of bone when it had been cut. A lot depended on this. If the gangrene had not left enough healthy tissue the job could not be done, and I'd have to cut the bone above the knee.

I drew the curved line with a crayon, then took the scalpel that Sally had ready in her hand. This was it. Follow the line of the crayon mark, now cutting the skin. Blood is always a nuisance in an operation, but this time it was a joy to see it oozing out along the scalpel line. It signified that the flesh underneath was healthy. The muscle too bled, as I cut through it to find the underlying arteries and nerves. As quickly as possible I then clamped off the blood vessels, tied and cut them.

Instruments were appearing in my hand as if by magic, through

Sally's intelligent anticipation. This was going better than I had hoped.

I now had a healthy flap of skin and muscle hanging down: healthier than I had expected. Now for the bit I wasn't looking forward to.

Sally dumped a huge parcel onto the operating tray, opening it up to reveal half a dozen sterilized butcher's saws.

'Exactly which of these do you want, Doctor Vaughan?'

For the first time I noticed a genuine smile reflected in the small amount of her face showing above her mask.

'The smallest one will do fine, Sister.'

She handed it to me. Terry was holding the well-covered dead end of the leg and moved his hand up the calf to provide additional support, to counter the force of the saw.

'All set, Terry?'

I recalled the last bit of woodwork I had done: sawing off the rotted leg of a garden bench so that it could be replaced with a piece of new timber.

Not much difference, I thought.

It was the same action. A couple of tentative backward strokes of the cutting edge to get a purchase, then the steady, regular, backward and forward movements, allowing the weight of the saw to do the work - as my Dad had taught me:

'Don't waste energy forcing it, lad. Just concentrate on a straight line. Nice and easy does it.'

Sure enough, the bone behaved in the same way as the wood, except for the sound.

Terry, meanwhile, was expertly and sensitively manipulating his end, supporting it enough to stop it falling, but not too much to jam the saw edge. He was nursing it in his arms like a baby, and when it finally came free, he placed it in the dirty bowl. I didn't like to see it there - it didn't look at all aristocratic.

'Patrick, could you take it out and put it in the freezer?'

'Right, Sir, straight away.'

He looked a bit flustered and upset, but picked up the bowl containing the leg and rushed out with it, as if every second counted.

No doubt he'll soon be steadying his nerves in the galley, I thought.

The rest of the operation was pure needle-work - trimming the loose flap of flesh until it was the right size to fold up over the stump of bone and then stitching it to the healthy flesh over the front of the leg. It was as good as I could make it and looked the right shape to fit eventually into an artificial leg.

'OK, John, you can wake him up now.'

'My pleasure, Doctor Vaughan.'

This time he was using my formal name, with a warm tone to his voice.

There was a tangible sense of relaxation in the air as we busied ourselves getting Sir Giles back to consciousness and into his bed. He was no longer 'a case' and we were now looking forward to seeing him as an aristocrat again.

With the operation over and the patient conscious, the time was ripe for refreshment. The nurses took it in turns to sit with Sir Giles, whilst the rest of us gathered in the small Galley. Patrick had had the foresight to collect some cans of ale and a bottle of wine so that we could join him 'steadying his nerves'. It felt like a holiday with everyone smiling with relief - including Sally. I hadn't realized that they'd all felt as tense as I had. I think the patient had won their hearts during his short stay with us. There was a lot of mutual congratulations going on, but the best comment came from John;

'I'm proud of you, Mike.'

... and the second best from Sally;

'So am I.'

Now I really had been blessed by the Pope!

A plate of sandwiches arrived - beef sandwiches - none of us touched them.

Then Janet entered the Galley: 'Before you drink too much, Doctor Vaughan, I thought I'd better tell you about Millie.'

'Why, Janet? Has she taken ill?'

'No, but she says she doesn't want to leave the hospital yet. Think's she "ought to play it safe and stay another day or two".'

Now I wonder why?

CHAPTER 8

For the next few hours I was walking tall. I'd done a major operation before, but only under the supervision of a consultant, ready to take over if it went wrong. This had been my first solo job. I was also feeling very pleased at being accepted again in my own right as a doctor, and I could feel the old enthusiasm returning. Gone was the diffidence and drying-up sensation that had taken hold of me in my old practice. However, living in the clouds does not last long, and routine soon returns to puncture the euphoria.

Janet and I were ploughing our way through a large passenger surgery. Nothing had been straightforward. It had either been a problem with an American medication that I hadn't heard of, or a language problem with Latin American passengers.

'Who's the next passenger, Janet?' I asked wearily.

'Well, he shouldn't be here really, but Julian, the waiter, asked if you could fit him in. He couldn't see you this morning, and he seems very upset.'

Oh God, I thought, *I hope his discharge hasn't recurred.*

Janet showed him in. Again, he looked very ill at ease and embarrassed.

'Well, Julian, how can I help you? Not the old problem is it?'

'Oh no, Doctor, that's almost cleared up already, and I'm very grateful.'

'Well, what is it?'

I was feeling a bit irritated by his coyness. There were still a lot of passengers to deal with.

'Well, Sir, I'm on the bridge tomorrow, and you're the only person I felt I could talk to about it.'

'What do you mean, "on the bridge", Julian?'

'You know, Sir, I'm on a charge before the Chief Officer, for reprimand.'

This was a new expression to me, but I presumed it was the same as being charged for a misdemeanour in the army.

'Why, what have you done?'

'It was an accident, Sir, but this lady passenger has complained about me to the hotel manager, saying I did it on purpose.'

This was like drawing blood out of a stone. He was shifting from foot to foot again, and looked like he was going to take an age to give me the facts.

'Exactly what, Julian, does she say you did on purpose?'

I was trying my best to be patient.

'She says that I threw a flaming crêpe Suzette over her ... er ... Bottom, sir.'

I instantly recalled the fat lady from my first passenger surgery. She'd said that she was going to sue somebody over her burnt behind, and I remembered being puzzled at the time about how it had happened.

I looked through my old notes and pulled out the relevant card.

'Was it a Mrs Myers?'

'That's right, Doctor, only it isn't Mrs, it's Miss. She was on one of my tables in the restaurant. I was getting on with her very well until this happened.'

'You'd better tell me how it happened then.'

'That's the trouble; it's difficult to explain, and I don't think I can tell the Chief Officer.'

'Well you'd better have a try, or you'll be in trouble. What you did could have caused a very serious burn.'

I could tell his mind was working overtime, trying to decide where to start. His shuffling was getting worse.

'Sit down, Julian, it'll make it easier.'

I'd been hoping he would be a quick problem, but as it wasn't, we might as well be comfortable.

'Well, like I said, I'd been getting on very well with her, chatting away every meal-time; always making a joke about something, she was getting very personal.'

'Do you mean she was chatting you up?'

'Well, in a way, but I suppose I was leading her on a bit.'

This seemed reasonable; if he was going to make good tips he'd have to be friendly. I'd never met a successful waiter who didn't use flattery as a stock in trade.

'Hoping to get a big tip at the end of the voyage, then?'

'There was that, yes, but it was more than that; we'd arranged to meet out on deck, later.'

'So, you'd taken a liking to her?'

'That's right, Doctor. I know she's big, but I like women like that. My mother's very big, and she reminded me of her.'

It seemed odd that he had to defend his preference; that fat women had become so out of fashion that he felt abnormal for liking them. But he still hadn't explained the accident.

'Right. we've got that straight, but how did she get burnt?'

'Well, they'd had a lot to drink, her and her girlfriend that is, and they were ordering everything on the menu, just for the hell of it. They persuaded me to do them a crêpe Suzette. By this time everyone else had left the restaurant, but I agreed to make it for them. I'd got to the crucial stage, with everything flaming, and was just about to serve it, when her friend decided to pinch my bottom. That's when I tipped the tray.'

'But didn't she realize that it was an accident?'

'Well, I doused the flames with water, as quick as I could, and apologized, of course, but her friend insisted that I'd done it on purpose. Nasty bit she is. I think she was jealous that I wasn't giving her so much attention.'

'Haven't you spoken to her since?'

'No, they moved to another table.'

I could see his problem. He'd have difficulty in getting that story out on the bridge, especially with his coy disposition. It seemed an unlikely story, but I'd heard of stranger behaviour when jealousy was involved.

'Well, I can't promise anything, Julian, but I'll try to explain the situation to the Chief Officer for you.'

'I'd be grateful, Doctor.'

I decided that I'd have a talk to Pete later in the day, as he would be dealing with Julian on the bridge.

Poor Julian, I thought, *his budding romance going up in flames - literally!*

Mr and Mrs Sinclair, from Texas, were the next two patients to be brought in by Janet. They appeared to be in good temper and very solicitous of each other.

'Well, how are you getting on with your tablets?' I asked.

'Surprisingly well, Doctor,' replied Mary Lou.

She clearly had not expected too much from an English doctor.

'By the way, did you contact our doctor back home?'

'I certainly did. He confirmed that I'd given you the correct medication, and said that you are two of his favourite patients. He sends his regards to you both.'

What he'd actually said on the telephone was; 'Sure, I know Howard and Mary Lou. Are they still feuding? It's been a life-long habit with them; probably keeps them going! Best of luck.'

Mary Lou nodded a grudging acknowledgement of her doctor's greetings.

I checked them over and as their hearts and lungs seemed to be in good order. I reassured them and they left fairly satisfied. On his way out Howard paused at the door;

'Tell me, Doctor. I heard you did an amputation today. Is that right?'

'Certainly is, Mr Sinclair.'

'Just curious; d'you still use tar to seal the stump?'

Mary Lou dragged him from the room: 'Howard Sinclair! You old fool!'

I was not prepared for the next patient. To be exact, I felt rather embarrassed when the large Miss Myers entered, having so recently heard of Julian's escapade with her. I found myself trying to imagine what Julian found attractive in the lady. She wasn't my cup of tea, but she had a certain comeliness, and her face was very attractive when she smiled. She was smiling now which I found very surprising when I remembered her attitude during our previous encounter.

'Good afternoon, Miss Myers. Have you come to have your burn redressed?'

'No, that seems to be improving slowly. I called about another problem I wanted your help with.'

Her smile sweetened. 'Do you know anything about animals?'

Well, I knew how to feed cats and dogs, and I'd learnt to avoid horses after being thrown off the back of one, but their treatment was a mystery to me. At Medical School I had been amazed at the veterinary students' ability to learn about so many species. The human species had been plenty for my intellect, but I wasn't going to admit to complete ignorance;

'I know a little, Miss Myers. Why do you ask?'

'My little Pekinese dog has become very sick. He's travelling with me; in the kennels, that is.'

I turned to Janet for help, and quietly asked; 'Do we usually treat animals?'

'Part of the job, Doctor. At least to show willing.'

Turning back to Miss Myers I asked her what, exactly, the problem was.

'Well, poor little Pepe has been vomiting for the past two days, and the kennel girl doesn't know what's wrong.'

If the trained kennel maid doesn't know what's wrong, there's fat chance of me finding out, I thought. *Still, better show willing and at least have a look.*

'All right, Miss Myers, I'll have a look at Pepe. I'll meet you at the kennels when I've finished; in about half an hour.'

'I just knew you would help.'

With her winsome smile, she reminded me of a large version of a little girl who'd just won her Daddy over.

The remaining patients were far less difficult, but when I'd finished I felt more like soaking in the bath than meeting Miss Myers, and her little Pepe. However, an appointment had been made, so I found my way to the kennels, at the top of the ship.

My little 'patient' did look sick, and his eyes were looking up in that sad, appealing way that animals have when they want, or need, something. I hoped he didn't realize I wasn't a vet. His owner looked even more sad, as she cuddled him in her lap.

I thought quickly and decided the only vaguely medical action I could take was to use my stethoscope. I approached him to place the bell end onto his chest. At this point he must have realized that I wasn't a vet, and showed his distaste for my medical profession by attacking my hands with his very sharp teeth.

'Naughty Pepe! Don't do that to the nice doctor!' admonished Miss Myers ineffectually.

I wished she hadn't told him I was a doctor.

She wasn't being very useful in controlling the beast, so I persuaded the kennel maid to hold him. Now I was able to listen to his heart.

There was something strange going on in this little chest. The 'lub-dub' was very audible, but I had to wait an age before the next sound arrived. The heart rate couldn't be more than thirty per minute. I checked it with my watch; definitely thirty per minute.

One of the few facts I knew about the animal kingdom was that the smaller the animal, the faster the heart rate. This Pekinese had the heart rate of an elephant!

I retrieved my stethoscope, licked my bleeding knuckles, and tried to look wise.

A thought came to me; 'Is little Pepe on any medicine?'

'Oh yes, but only a tiny little heart tablet; Digoxin the vet called it.'

'How many is he having?'

'Well, the vet prescribed one per day for his heart failure, but I thought I'd better increase the dose because of the stress of travelling.'

'So how many is he taking?'

'Oh, four, maybe five, per day, the tablets look so tiny.'

There was now, thankfully, no need to look any further. The poor animal was being poisoned. I remembered patients with overdoses of Digoxin. It slowed down the heart rate too much, and made them vomit. It also made their vision turn yellow, so perhaps that was why Pepe didn't like the look of me.

'I think I know how to cure him. Just go back to your cabin and I'll sort his treatment out with the kennel-maid.'

I wasn't going to let her know my trade secrets; besides which, it might offend and upset her if I told her she'd poisoned Pepe!

Once she'd left, I instructed the kennel-maid to stop his tablets, and let me know how the 'patient' was in the morning. We could warn Miss Myers about the tablets at the end of the voyage.

As I made my way to my cabin I realized how lucky I'd been to have found something I could cure. I couldn't pretend to liking Pekinese dogs but, until he'd bitten me, he had looked quite appealing and vulnerable. I hoped Miss Myers would be grateful when he recovered. With that thought, the germ of an idea began to grow.

Wallowing in a warm bath was becoming my favourite part of the day. Not only was it peaceful, but it allowed time to reflect on the day's events. So much had happened, most of which I felt good about.

99

Mainly I was pleased about Sir Giles as I was reasonably sure that he would make a good recovery. John would look after his treatment, and I felt certain that Millie would be looking after his spirit! Somewhere in that woman, I suspected, was a bit of magic. A man would have done well to have her as his wife. I wondered if she had ever been married; something made me think not, and it was not just the absence of a ring. It had to be in her face, in the little lines, or absence of little lines, that tell everything about our past.

Then I realized that it must show in my face too, and that perhaps there was no point in trying to keep secrets. Probably my recent heartbreak was clear for all to see; perhaps even Susie had seen it, but not recognized it as such. Not that that mattered, now that I'd managed to upset her; but I still wished that I could talk to her again.

There was time left for another five minutes, wallowing, so I turned on the hot water to top up the heat. This was, of course, an invitation for the telephone to ring. It didn't stop quickly, so I dripped my way to the phone.

'Hello, Doctor Vaughan.'

'Mike, it's me, John. Not taking a bath were you?'

'No,' I lied.

'Good. Just wanted to check on this evening's arrangements. How are you getting on with your first-class table?'

'Pretty good, why?'

'Well, I thought you might as well carry on there, now that you've settled in with them.'

I remembered the pretty girl on his second-class table, and couldn't help baiting him;

'No, John, that's not fair. It's your turn tonight and you are the senior doctor after all.'

'No, after your operating you deserve first class. By the way, Sir Giles is doing very well, sitting up already. Cracking good job that.'

'That's really good news. But you shouldn't underestimate what you did! It was your anaesthetic that kept him alive. You deserve a reward as much as me.'

I knew I'd give in in the end, but I'd make him fight for it first.

'Look, Mike, I've been thinking. Perhaps we should take first class on alternate voyages, rather than alternate nights; less disruption that way.'

'I don't like that idea much, it could get a bit boring, John.'

There was a pause. I could hear him sniff, and imagined him flicking his forelock. Then came his reply;

'Mike, as you said, I'm senior doctor and I've decided! You're dining first class!'

The phone went dead.

By now I'd drip-dried so I resisted the temptation to return to the warm bath. Besides which Gwilym had quietly arrived and was hovering about.

'You know it's Captain's cocktail party tonight, Doc? Best bib and tucker for that!'

I had forgotten about it. It was the 'grand occasion' which John had described in the Princess Room; the opportunity for all the first-class passengers to dress in their finery, shake hands with the Captain, and drink champagne. All officers were expected to attend, to mingle and chat.

'Yes, thanks Gwilym; just getting ready. D'you know where the polish is? My shoes need freshening up.'

'No problem. I'll do them for you now.'

I hadn't expected him to volunteer for the task, just to find the polish; but he seemed happy enough brushing away, spreading the black polish evenly over my shoes and the carpet. I could imagine what Alice would have said if I'd dared to do that over her immaculately cleaned rugs. He was taking his time over the job, as if he wasn't very eager to leave, perhaps waiting for the right time to say something.

'Young lady called to the cabin this afternoon, Doc. Looking for you she was.'

He paused.

'Tell me more. Did she leave her name?'

'No; but I recognized her. She works on board. I've seen her talking to passengers a lot.'

I was surprised that he didn't know her name as I'd have expected him to know everything via the ship's grapevine. Perhaps he was just holding out on me.

'Well; did she leave a message?'

'She gave me a note for you; I thought I'd better deliver it personally. Didn't like to leave it lying around.'

I suspected he was less concerned about the note getting lost, than about trying to discover what it said.

He pulled out the note from the inside pocket of his steward's jacket and handed it to me. I placed it on my desk to read later. I was curious all right, but not curious enough to read it in front of Gwilym.

'Don't you think you'd better read it, Doc? Could be urgent.'

I wondered how long it had been lying, urgently, in his pocket.

'No, I'm sure it can wait until I've finished dressing, Gwilym.'

'If you think so, Doc.'

He looked disappointed, and suddenly lost interest in my shoes, giving them a cursory buffing with the tea-towel that always hung from his arm.

'Bring your tea in the morning then, Sir.'

He departed; thwarted.

Now, in privacy, I could open the note. Inside the small sealed envelope was a card bearing the picture of a tearful teddy bear. The message inside read;

Sorry for the tantrum. See you after dinner?

... and was signed, Susie.

She was leaving it to me to track her down, if I was interested. It was a clever tactic; by looking for her I would be demonstrating a degree of commitment. Now I had to decide if I was prepared to give that commitment. She'd put the ball into my court.

As I finished dressing I tried to analyse my feelings. The physical attraction was there, without doubt; but something was holding me back. Too easily my guilt over Alice came to mind. I couldn't continue letting that paralyse me emotionally; perhaps I was using it as an excuse, hiding behind a dead woman's skirt, like a cowardly little boy behind his mother. The truth was that I was afraid of being hurt. I'd been kidding myself that I was being noble and loyal to Alice; but it wasn't that, it was sheer funk! Susie scared me. The very aggressiveness in her manner that attracted me, also scared me. She had the ability to pierce through my armour, to reach the bits I wanted left undisturbed. It wasn't only her karate-type conversation that gave her this ability to pierce. Her oddly asymmetrical eyes played an equal part. It was as if her healthy left eye had overcompensated for its weak partner by becoming uncannily sharp. But perhaps I was getting it out of proportion.

102

In essence Susie was simply an attractive girl, with the gumption to look for what she wanted. She also had a squint; a simple clinical condition described as strabismus in the textbooks. As a doctor, I should not be attaching undue significance to a simple squint.

What I needed was a drink.

I turned down the first drink I was offered at the cocktail party – champagne had never appealed to me - all fizz and tickle. Scotch and water had a substance, but I had to search to find one. I spotted a wine waiter carrying a tray of drinks of the right colour and headed his way; which was not easy in this room crowded with elegantly dressed passengers. Easing my way through this sea of splendour I should have been impressed by the array of fashion surrounding me, but it was the overwhelming assault of heavy perfumes that struck me. From the evidence of the wealth around, it was a safe assumption that each of these perfumes was expensive and designed to be subtly arousing to the male libido, but *en masse* they were more likely to produce a mighty sneeze.

I arrived just too late for the last scotch on the tray. Pete had beaten me to it.

'Hi, Doc. Where's your drink?'

'You just took it, Pete! I'd had my eye on that scotch from the other side of the room.'

'Sorry about that; timing's everything. Don't worry though, I'll get you one.'

He grabbed the waiter's arm. 'Doctor wants a scotch.'

'Straight away, Chief.'

There was no hesitation in the waiter's response. He headed straight for the bar to get my drink.

'You've got a winning way with the staff, Pete!'

'Nothing to it! I just happen to know that he's coming to see you tomorrow; his ulcer's playing up.'

I wondered if there was anything on board he didn't know about. His next remark proved that I was right to wonder.

'Heard that Julian's been to see you, trying to get off his logging. He probably thinks that you're a soft touch, being the new quack.'

Medical ethics were taking on a new perspective. What Julian had said to me was confidential, not even Janet had witnessed it as she'd diplomatically left the office during our talk. Julian himself must have let it slip. Whatever, as I'd planned to speak to Pete about him, this was a good opportunity.

'I don't know where you heard that, but I wanted to talk to you about it anyway. He's told me the whole story, and I believe it was an accident. He couldn't have done it on purpose.'

'That's his story, Doc. Passenger says he burnt her bum on purpose. Her word against his. Serious offence damaging a passenger, you know. Not good for business!'

I could imagine that, two hundred years ago, Julian would have received twenty lashes, and that would have ended the matter. Times have changed. No lashes, but he could end up losing his job. With Miss Myers' and her friend's evidence against him he didn't stand a chance.

'Can I ask a favour, Pete?'

'Depends.'

'Put his logging off for a day. I've got an idea.'

'It had better be a good one. Captain doesn't like these things delayed.'

'It's a good one,' I lied.

I rated my chances of pulling it off less than 50 per cent, but it was worth a try.

'OK, as you're a friend I'll give you 24 hours – don't let me down. Anyway, we'd better start socializing now.'

He headed off with practised ease into the nearest group of passengers which, I noticed, just happened to include a very attractive girl in an expensive, but almost transparent, dress.

I looked around for some familiar faces to join. From my vantage point on the raised perimeter of the room I had a good view.

The sea of colourful dresses and flamboyant American tuxedos was dotted with the occasional black and white of the officers' uniforms. A small band was playing quiet mood music and the party had reached the stage where the champagne had started to work; the quiet hum of conversation was being punctuated by the booming laughter of the extroverts amongst the crowd. One of these voices was head and shoulders above the rest, as was its owner, a massive Texan dressed in a bright tartan tuxedo.

'Doctor, come and join us.'

His voice had been hurled without difficulty from the other side of the room, so that it had the momentary effect of surprising the other guests into silence. In unison three hundred, or so, heads turned first towards him, then towards me, the object of the invitation. If I'd been waiting for a stage entrance, he'd provided it. As it was he'd ruined my ambition to quietly mingle until I found a group in need of my conversation.

My moment of enforced limelight soon vanished, as the heads returned to their previous positions and the background hum resumed. I made my way across to meet the huge man whom I'd instantly assumed to be Texan. He looked bigger than John Wayne and I could imagine his booming voice hurling instructions across a ranch the size of England.

If my arm had been a pump handle, he would have flooded the room before he'd finished greeting me.

'Sinclair's the name, Sir. Howard Sinclair Junior. You've been treating Ma and Pa, and they're mighty pleased with you, ain't you, Pa?'

Howard Sinclair Senior nodded briefly in agreement.

'Sure, Son.'

'Don't you mind Pa, Doctor, he's never much good at praising; but a grudging thanks from him is worth a cart-load of fancy words from anyone else. Ain't that right, Pa?'

'Sure is, Son.'

I was pleased to find a fan, albeit a grudging one, but the topic of conversation was soon exhausted so I took my departure; being careful to avoid any further hand-shaking.

To my surprise I spotted Sally. I hadn't thought of her as an officer, with similar entertainment duties as myself. The company had not designed a formal uniform for lady officers so she was wearing a light-blue cocktail dress. This was a definite improvement on the Sally I knew in the hospital, and she was prettier than I'd imagined her dressed up. The smile on her face was still thin, but she had a sensuality that the hospital uniform denied her. Standing next to her was another attractive girl that I vaguely recognized. It was with a slight shock that I recognized Janet. We'd worked quite closely together, but I'd never really looked at her as a woman. Wearing a body-clinging black dress, and with her auburn hair let down from her customary bun, she looked far less plump and frumpy that the girl I was used to. Her chubby face carried a broad grin and her eyes sparkled with fun.

'You look rather surprised, Doctor!'

'It was just a bit of a shock seeing you here. After all it's the first time I've seen you with your clothes on.'

'Oh, is that what you've been up to, Doctor Michael!'

The familiar voice came from over my left shoulder. Susie had managed to creep up again.

'Hello, Susie: have you met Sally and Janet?'

'Of course, we've all been at sea together for a long time.'

I felt awkward meeting her so out of context, and I still hadn't decided whether or not to look for her after dinner; well, not quite decided.

'Now tell me what you and Janet have been doing without her clothes on?'

She was up to her usual teasing, but there could just have been a hint of jealousy in her voice. I decided to leave them to talk amongst themselves. Sally was beginning to look a bit frosty; possibly she didn't like Susie.

'You'd better ask Janet to explain,' I suggested, 'I've just seen some people I want to meet.'

It wasn't a lie, the family from my restaurant table were standing nearby. I joined them. The father greeted me;

'Nice to see you again, Doctor Vaughan, looking forward to having you dine with us tonight. My son's bursting with questions to ask you. You don't mind do you?'

'Not at all,' I lied.

I wondered how many questions there were left, after our first dinner together.

I could tell his son was very keen to strike up a conversation with me; in contrast to the teenage daughter whose attention was firmly fixed on a young engineering officer standing nearby. His attention, in turn, was only half on the male passenger he was conversing with. Mother was trying, in whispers, to persuade her daughter to be polite and say 'hello' to the doctor.

Her obedient 'nice to meet you again, Doctor' was even briefer than her first greeting had been, and did not involve turning her eyes away

106

from the young engineer: which didn't please her mother. The budding medical student could contain himself no longer.

'I'd like to have a job like yours someday! What qualifications do you need to be a Ship's Doctor?'

I thought for a while before replying. 'Well, from my experience, I have found that you need to know a little about everything.'

'Everything, Doctor?'

'Yes, including a little bit about veterinary medicine.'

'You treat animals as well?'

'Naturally, there are a lot of animals on board, you know.'

'That sounds exciting!'

'It certainly is!' I said, remembering little Pepe.

'You must have a lot of qualifications.'

'Well, yes, I suppose I have.'

It was nice to be able to show off, sometimes.

Further conversation was prevented by the arrival of Julian bearing a trayful of colourful canapés. He seemed to be entering my life quite a lot recently. Whilst he offered his wares around, he leant over to whisper in my ear;

'There's a lady on the other side of the room would like to speak to you, Doctor.'

'Oh, not a medical problem in the middle of the cocktail party, Julian?'

By now I was enjoying the atmosphere and looking forward to mingling a bit more.

'Well, it's not exactly a medical problem, but she wants to speak to an officer.'

'Well, why did you pick on me? There are 30 or 40 officers in this room.'

I could tell he was a bit embarrassed now at disturbing me. He was beginning to shuffle again.

'I'm very sorry for bothering you again, after all the help you've given me, but I thought you'd be the best one to talk to her. She seems sort of odd.'

In my experience 'sort of odd' could mean a multitude of things, but somebody would have to see her, so it might as well be me.

'You did the right thing, Julian. I'll speak to her. Where is she? Just point her out.'

'She's over by the far starboard pillar, just aft of the band. You can't miss her, she's wearing a long white dress and there's a big metal thing dangling from her neck.'

I didn't ask him any more details about the 'dangling thing'; he looked as if he'd had enough excitement for the evening. I'd soon find out for myself. I excused myself from the conversation and threaded my way back across the room, which by now was even more crowded.

I found her easily enough. Julian was right, I couldn't miss her. For one thing she was alone. Standing next to the pillar she gave the fleeting impression of a Grecian priestess, and the 'dangly thing' around her neck was a large Celtic cross. For a woman in her early fifties her face and figure had a youthful appearance, but the fanatical look in her eyes prevented her being attractive. I approached her quietly, not sure what I was dealing with.

'Excuse me, I'm Doctor Vaughan. I understand that you wanted to speak to an officer.'

She gave me a wary glance, but wouldn't grant me her full attention which seemed to be preoccupied elsewhere.

'Are you a senior officer?' she asked sternly.

She was a little taller than me and had an imposing presence. I felt distinctly ill at ease.

'Yes, I am, Ma'am. I'm sorry but I don't know your name.'

'That doesn't matter! Come with me, I want to talk privately.'

She turned abruptly and marched off, confident that I would follow. I felt I had no alternative. Whatever was on her mind, it seemed to be important and could well be serious; so it was partly sense of duty and partly curiosity that urged me to follow her. She led me briskly, without talking, on a long march to her cabin which was right at the forward end of the ship, in fact as far forward as passenger cabins go. She opened her door and gestured me in impatiently.

It was a tiny cabin with just a single bunk and a small vanity unit. On the bulkhead above her bunk was a large hand-drawn map of the world. In this tiny space, I felt cornered and was beginning to wonder if I was to be involved in a forced seduction scene, but her next words banished that idea from my mind.

'We are, all of us, in serious danger unless you listen to me quickly.'

108

I'd heard of hijacked ships in the past and wondered if she was about to pull a gun on me. I think I was beginning to perspire.

'What do you know about nuclear explosions?'

There was a lot I didn't know about nuclear explosions, but I knew the basics and she seemed to want a reply;

'Well, I do know that they kill a lot of people,' I hazarded.

'Exactly! Now look at the map.'

She pulled down the beautifully hand-drawn world map from the bulkhead. She must have drawn it from memory, because I could tell that some of the contours weren't exact. There were red lines superimposed, much like isobars on a weather chart.

'These red lines show the nuclear fall-out zones. We are here.'

She drew a small cross in the middle of the Atlantic ocean, presumably representing the exact position of the ship.

'It is imperative that the Captain diverts the ship to avoid the fallout zone we are heading towards.'

I must admit that I was impressed. Her drawing had the hallmarks of a scientist, being dotted here and there with mathematical sums involving calculus signs, which had left me completely baffled at school. By this time, of course, I'd deduced that she was mentally deranged: at least I hoped she was. The only way forward was to humour her.

'Excuse me, Mrs ... er ...'

'Franik, Eliza Franik's my name. That's not important!'

'Well, Mrs Franik, I'm puzzled. Where exactly is this nuclear fallout coming from?'

'Russia, of course!'

'I haven't heard anything about it.'

'You wouldn't, it's being kept secret, to avoid panic.'

'Then how did you hear about it?'

'God has given me the sign, and is directing me.'

Now the picture was becoming clearer. She was having hallucinations, probably a schizophrenic illness. As far as I knew there were no psychiatrists on board. Her single cabin indicated that she was travelling alone, so with no friends or relations to give us her background, I would have to ease it out of her slowly, first, hopefully, gaining her confidence. I would have to go along with her story.

'Could you tell me why God has given you this message?'

'It's obvious, young man. We are his chosen people. He is guiding us to safety, to restart the world after the holocaust. Have you never heard of Noah's ark?'

I mentally pictured the wooden-planked boat that Noah had stored his animals on and couldn't help comparing it to this 76000-ton colossus of a ship we inhabited. At least we had a few animals on board, including Pepe, but I couldn't imagine God expecting him to father a new generation. However, this wasn't solving the problem.

'I think I understand the seriousness of the situation now. How do you think I can help?'

'By telling the Captain, of course.'

'Haven't you spoken to the Captain yourself?'

'No; nobody will let me near him. The bedroom steward keeps on putting me off, telling me he's too busy. That's why I came to the cocktail party. I had to find somebody.'

There was no doubt that if you accepted her basic conviction about an impending disaster, her logic was sound. I wondered briefly whether Noah had been written off as schizophrenic. That was the trouble with psychiatry; patients often make you wonder about your own sanity. Coming back to the basics though, I'd have to find a way of getting her to accept treatment.

'Mrs Franik, as soon as I leave you, I'll speak to the Captain. In the meantime, we're going to need rest to face the ordeal ahead of us.'

'What are you suggesting, Doctor?'

'Just that, after all your hard work on these charts, you could do with something to help you sleep, to enable you to recover your strength.'

If I thought she was going to be a pushover, I was wrong. Her eyes hardened and she clutched her Celtic cross with both hands.

'God has warned me of people like you, trying to keep me from his chosen task. The devil has many forms. Get out of here! I'll sleep without your evil potions.'

The situation seemed irretrievable, but I had to try; 'Please believe me; I'm on your side. I'm a doctor so I look on you as someone needing help. If you want me to speak to the Captain I will, as soon as possible.'

Her eyes softened a little, but suspicion was still there. Then she thrust her metal cross at me.

'Before I trust you, you must pass the test. Touch my cross.'

110

I half-expected my hand to be burnt off, but I touched the cross, with as much fervour as I could muster. She seemed satisfied.

'Very well, you are a good man. Now find the Captain.'

Once outside her cabin I heaved a sigh of relief. I'd known schizophrenic patients who could be violent, but happily she'd shown no such signs. Mostly I'd found that people with that sort of illness are very pleasant once the acute episode is over, but curing the acute episode required drugs, and persuading her to take them was going to be very difficult. She was clearly an intelligent woman, and although her hallucinations were distorting her perception of reality, they were not affecting her powers of reasoning. If her behaviour became severely disturbed, the last resort would be to physically force treatment on her through an injection, but that felt barbaric and reminded me of the dark days of psychiatry in the old asylums. The alternative was to persuade her, using her own perception of the problem to my advantage, but first I'd have to think it out.

Back in my cabin I rang the hospital to check that the tablets I needed were in stock. They were; so that was the first hurdle over. Next I rang the bridge to find out if there was any other information I could find out about Mrs Franik. Pete answered. I was surprised to find him there but presumably he'd had to leave the party early for his watch. I asked him if he knew the lady.

'Of course, Doc. Mrs Franik has been quite a celebrity since the start of the voyage. What do you want to know?'

'Well, what has she been doing, for a start?'

'To start with she insisted on moving to the most forward cabin available. Daft really; it's one of the worst cabins; moves a lot in rough weather. But she insisted, because she reckoned it was the nearest cabin to God, who was at the front of the ship.'

So far that matched up with my findings, so her delusion about being in touch with God had been consistent. He proceeded; 'Next, I'm getting reports that she's spending most of the day in a yoga lotus position at two deck, forward square, making mumbling, chanting noises; but she wasn't doing any harm and the other passengers seem to have dismissed her as either a crank, or part of the ship's entertainment. Didn't seem any point in disturbing her: there's always an odd-ball on board. You get used to them.'

111

I tried to imagine the bemused glances that Mrs Franik in her lotus position must have attracted, but as most of the passengers would be first-timers and American, they might well have dismissed the scene as some quaint British nautical custom.

'She hasn't actually caused any problems then, Pete?'

'Not really, apart from trying to get onto the forward mooring deck, which is banned to passengers, of course; pretty dangerous place.'

'She tells me she's been trying to see the Captain.'

'Lot of people try that, Doc, wanting autographs usually. But I'm sure the old man would see her, if she insisted.'

'That might help at some stage; she's become a medical problem, and I might need some backing up. Do you know if she has any relations or friends on board?'

'None; I checked with the purser. Not even a "next of kin" listed.'

That's what I had feared. Not even a chance of discussing her past history with someone.

'OK, thanks, Pete. I might need your help later.'

'Any time, Mike.'

I was grateful for Pete's information. As usual, he had all the facts at his fingertips. There were definite advantages to his professional 'nosiness'. For one thing I might well need his help. In general practice, I'd found that psychiatric problems were often the most taxing, not least because they usually demanded instant attention and would not be put off. The more bizarre cases, like this one, could be handed over to a psychiatrist, but not on a ship. I'd have to find the answers myself.

I reflected on how fashionable delusions are. The common conception of an insane person is of someone dressed up as Napoleon: but not Mrs Franik. She was right up to date, and her hallucination was uncomfortably near to the possible. A nuclear holocaust; no medical protection against that, no vaccination, no antinuclear pills.

That's it, I thought. *Antinuclear pills!*

I rang Mrs Franik's cabin. She took an age to answer, being no doubt in a deep state of meditation.

'Mrs Franik here; who is it?'

'It's Doctor Vaughan. We met a few minutes ago.'

'Yes, what do you want?'

'Well, I've spoken to the Captain and he agrees to see you. He is very concerned about your information and has ordered everyone to take antinuclear pills immediately. Shall I bring yours along to you?'

There was a long pause. I prayed that her mind hadn't retained enough logic to see through my bit of fiction.

'I will take that instruction only from the Captain, in person.'

At best she hadn't turned the idea down; but now I would need to involve the Captain.

'Very well, Mrs Franik, I'll arrange that as soon as possible.'

There was time enough to catch the Captain before dinner, so I returned to the cocktail party. He was just finishing his speech to the passengers, through the stage microphone;

'... and in conclusion, ladies and gentlemen, on behalf both of myself of all the officers and staff on board, I would like to wish you a very happy and enjoyable voyage.'

In response there were a few isolated pockets of clapping from those able to put their drinks down, then the chatting and drinking resumed.

I interrupted him as he left the stage.

'Ah, Doctor, nice to see you again. Have you enjoyed your first cocktail party?'

'I missed a lot of it, Sir. I have a problem patient and wanted to talk to you about her.'

'You have collected a lot of problem patients for your first voyage, Doctor. How can I be of help?'

He led me to a quiet corner, away from the party atmosphere, where we could talk. Thankfully he sat down and gestured for me to join him.

'The problem is rather unusual.'

He gave me his full attention, lowering his spectacles in his unnerving way. 'I'm all ears, Doctor.'

I explained Mrs Franik's problem in detail to him, describing the nature of her delusion and my plan to substitute sedatives for antinuclear tablets provided he could back me up in the subterfuge. He listened intently, but maintained his silence some moments before replying;

'It certainly is an unusual problem. Can't say I've ever been threatened by nuclear fallout before. Isn't your plan a little deceitful though, Doctor?'

'Well, I have thought of that, but the alternative is to allow her to get worse and possibly put herself, and others, into danger. She has already tried to get onto the forward mooring deck. I consider the deceit is justified.'

He replaced his spectacles, a sure sign that he'd made a decision. 'You seem to have reasoned it out well. Shall we meet in half an hour, in the hospital?'

'Right Captain, I'll get it organized. Thank you.'

'Thanks are not necessary for doing one's duty, Doctor.'

With that he rose to his full height and departed.

The cocktail party was in the dwindling stage as people sauntered off to dinner looking relaxed and happy. I wondered how happy they would feel if they'd been aware of Mrs Franik's scenario.

My next task was to persuade her to come to the hospital. I'd rather deal with her there, as she'd need to spend the night in hospital after her sedation.

Back in her little cabin I sat down to talk to her, I think she'd expected the Captain as she'd added to her finery a tall conical hat made out of silver wrapping paper, as if preparing herself for her ultimate moment of ceremony. She addressed me; 'What news are you bearing?'

'I'm pleased to tell you that the Captain will meet us in the hospital where the antinuclear tablets are to be distributed.'

The look of suspicion returned to her eyes. 'Am I the only one taking these tablets?'

I thought quickly. She would, of course, expect everyone to be taking antinuclear pills, not just herself. I'd have to sort this problem out later.

'Of course not, the entire ship's company and passengers will be taking them.'

'Good, then I agree. Lead me to your Captain.'

I was beginning to feel that I was in a science fiction film. She carefully rolled up her chart and stood ready to go. I opened the door for her and she strode out. As we marched along the alleyway towards the hospital I prayed that no one would observe us, as we must have appeared an odd couple with me in uniform and her in long flowing white robes, large Celtic cross and silver conical hat. Hopefully, they'd assume we were off to a fancy-dress party.

Once in the hospital I explained to Janet what was happening and we sat her in one of the wards where she quickly set about mounting her chart on the bulkhead with sticky tape. I left Janet to stay with her whilst I raided the pharmacy. First I selected the ideal sedation for the patient, then searched frantically for some other pills that were both harmless and looked approximately the same. Luckily Terry arrived on the scene;

'You're making an awful mess of my shelves, Doctor.'

'Sorry, Terry. I'm desperate: I'm trying to find something harmless to match these.'

'How harmless do they have to be?'

'Completely harmless, the Captain and I will be taking them!'

He gave me a quizzical look, but quickly shrugged it off and vanished into the back store. Within minutes he returned with a large bottle of tablets.

'These old vitamin pills should match. Haven't used them for years.'

He poured a few out onto the bench, next to the sedatives. They were a pretty good match for colour, although a little larger.

'They're not quite the same size, Terry.'

'Aye, but a man on a galloping horse wouldn't notice the difference! They're the best I can do.'

I explained to him how unlike 'a man on a galloping horse' the patient was; indeed I told him the whole story to stop him wondering about my sanity. His face didn't show any signs of surprise. He picked up a handful of each of the tablets and, holding them away from himself, examined them.

'At a distance they'll pass muster, Sir. Met a case like this in the Navy. You'll need to keep her attention on something else, when you give them to her. I'll hang around in case you need my help.'

'Thanks Terry, I'd appreciate that.'

I was pleased to have him at hand. His laconic but practical approach to problems was a calming influence. I could tell from his semi-raised eyebrows that he saw the humour in situations, but the lines around his mouth and eyes added a suggestion of sadness, as if he'd been dealt some undeserved personal tragedies that had taught him the irony of life. The way he used his hands portrayed a sensitivity and caring that had survived any hardening influence from his experiences. He was now preparing some little tablet pots.

'How many sedatives are you giving her, Sir?'

'Four should do the trick.'

He placed the four sedative pills into one of the pots and made a tiny red mark on the side to distinguish it from the others. He noticed me watching him:

'Better safe than sorry. Can't have the Captain taking them by mistake.'

I had a flashing image of the Captain fast asleep on the bridge and Mrs Franik still raging in the hospital.

'I agree, Terry, good thinking that.'

'Exactly what might I take by mistake?'

The Captain's voice was unmistakable. He must have been standing behind us for some moments whilst Terry and I were fully absorbed in the tablets. I looked up at him;

'You've arrived early, Sir. There's been a small complication. The patient insists that we also take the antinuclear pills.'

'That doesn't sound like a *small* complication to me! What are you proposing that I swallow?'

'Just harmless vitamin pills. Terry's counting them out for us.'

'And Terry will ensure that I receive the correct pills?'

'Aye, Captain. I can't afford to put you to sleep by mistake,' replied Terry with a well-camouflaged smile.

'Very wise of you. Well, Doctor, shall we meet the patient?'

Mrs Franik was prepared for us, sitting cross-legged on the hospital bed, in full regalia; behind her, mounted on the bulkhead her chart proclaimed her story. Since I'd last studied it, she'd added a prominent skull and crossbones. She seemed to be impressed by the Captain's stature and authority, as she made a small nod of approval; but she was taking no chances. She thrust her cross at him as she had done to me earlier;

'Touch this,' she commanded.

I was surprised by the Captain's immediate obeisance to her order. Pausing only to lower his half-rims, he stretched out his arm and grasped her Celtic cross firmly, all the time looking steadily into her eyes. His performance was impressive; I thought he would have made an excellent Captain Cook, winning over savage islanders. But this was no ignorant savage he was winning over; this was an intelligent woman, temporarily deranged, and he seemed to appreciate that fact.

116

'Mrs Franik, it is my privilege to meet you. Doctor Vaughan has told me all about you. He tells me that you have had a profound experience. May I study your chart?'

She seemed very pleased by his recognition of her importance and instantly turned and removed the map from its flimsy mounting; then handed it to him with both hands, as if surrendering a prized possession. He placed it on the adjacent bed and studied it carefully, running a finger over the zone lines. After a full minute or two of silence he turned to her;

'I wish my navigators could produce such good charts. You have the ship's position absolutely correct. We are indeed heading into one of the danger zones. I will instruct my chief officer to detour the ship. Thank you for the information.'

'It is God's will that you should receive the knowledge.'

'Exactly so, Mrs Franik. It is also, I presume, God's will that we take the sensible precaution of using the antinuclear pills that we store on board for just this eventuality.'

She looked at him carefully, just a hint of puzzlement showing in her eyes, as if two strains of logic were fighting within her head. I prayed that the correct one would win. Eventually she replied; 'I agree, provided we all take them.'

'Naturally so, Mrs Franik, we are all at risk.'

Then turning to me: 'Doctor, could you please have the tablets brought in?'

I hurried out to find Terry, anxious to get the ordeal over. He was waiting outside, holding the three small pots in readiness.

'Could you bring them in now, Terry?'

'Aye, Sir.'

He gave me a few moments to return, then entered. 'Here we are then, Sir, the tablets you ordered. Shall I hand them out?'

'Please, Terry.'

He handed a pot first to the Captain, then myself, then lastly to Mrs Franik. The tiny red dot on her pot looked alarmingly obvious to me; I hoped she wouldn't spot it. Next Terry delivered three glasses of water, a detail I had overlooked.

We were just about to perform the ceremony of swallowing the pills, indeed they were tantalisingly close to our three mouths, when Mrs

Franik sat bolt upright, alarm flashing from her eyes;

'Who's he?'

'Who's who?' I responded.

'The man with the pills.'

'That's Terry, the medical petty officer. Why do you ask?'

'Why isn't he taking the antinuclear pills? How many more are there?'

With that she jumped off the bed and rushed out of the ward. I followed her as she raced around the hospital, opening all the doors and looking inside each room. Eventually she stopped and challenged me:

'Why aren't these others taking the pills?'

I felt the situation had got out of hand. During the rapid inspection of the hospital, she'd discovered Sally and Mary doing a duty hand-over; Millie and Sir Giles holding hands; Angus and Barbara Box doing something similar: and Patrick 'steadying his nerves' with a cigarette in the galley. They'd all looked startled by this rushing apparition.

There's many a slip 'twixt cup and lip, I thought, realizing how appropriate some aphorisms can be. Now I'd have to regain her confidence.

'Mrs Franik, everyone will be taking the pills, but it is important to start with key personnel on board, and you are one of those.'

For a moment she appeared to be placated, and I thought the battle was won; but she disappointed me.

'Very well, but everyone in the hospital must take them, now!'

This was a complication but I couldn't see any alternative to meeting her demand.

'If that's what you wish, I'll arrange it. Let's return to the ward.'

I returned her to the Captain's company then set about explaining the story, yet again, to Sally and Mary and asked them to pass it on and arrange for everybody to join us in Mrs Franik's ward. Next I asked Terry to prepare another seven sets of vitamin pills, including one for himself. I decided that we needn't move Sir Giles as she wouldn't notice one missing.

Ten minutes later ten of us were gathered in the tiny ward, each holding a small pot of pills and a glass of water.

'Everybody ready then?' I said, raising my pot.

'No!' replied Mrs Franik. 'Where's the man with the moustache?'

I hadn't counted on her mathematical brain.

'I'm sorry,' I replied, 'he can't be moved; he is just recovering from a major operation.'

'Then we'll go to him. He can't be left out: remember the Good Shepherd.'

I presumed she meant that even one sheep must not be lost.

Five minutes later eleven of us were gathered in Sir Giles's tiny ward.

'Are we ready then?' I tried again.

We all lifted our pots, but she hesitated; 'Are we all taking the same tablets?' she asked.

My heart sank. She'd spotted the flaw in the plan. I just knew she was going to compare the tablets closely. I had to think of a diversionary tactic. But it was Millie who came to the rescue. She left Sir Giles's side and sat next to Mrs Franik on the spare bed. Putting her arm around her shoulders she said: 'It's a terrible ordeal you have been through, and we're so grateful you've saved us from disaster. Don't worry any more. I'll have one of your pills and you can have one of mine.'

She delicately transferred one of her vitamin pills to Mrs Franik and then removed one from her pot in exchange. Next she put a hand on Mrs Franik's forehead, smoothing it as you would to ease a child's pain.

'There you are, you can take them now. All together.'

Millie raised her pot, we all obediently followed her lead, including Mrs Franik. Next we all gulped the pills down, following them with a swig of water. It felt like a toast at a party. It was in a way; we were toasting Mrs Franik's recovery.

Millie had saved the day; she'd remembered the common touch; seen through all the complicated delusions to the insecure child beneath. She had also shown gallantry, taking one of the sedatives herself; I hoped it wouldn't make her too sleepy.

We departed one by one from the ward, and I noticed the Captain guiding Mrs Franik back to her room.

'Thank you once again,' he was saying, 'I'm now going to make sure the ship is on the right course.'

'I'm sure it will be, in your hands Captain,' she replied.

Sally took over from him, settling her onto her bed, and sat down to talk to her, waiting for the sedatives to work. I went to thank Millie.

'You saved the day, Millie. I hope that sedative won't make you too drowsy.'

'Don't worry about that, Doctor,' she replied, smiling at me, 'I removed the same pill I'd just given her. It was the gesture that mattered.'

You're right, I thought as I walked off to find some supper: four vitamin pills weren't enough.

I caught up with the Captain who was waiting for the elevator.

'I'd like to thank you for your help, Captain. It was an excellent performance you gave. I could see she was very impressed by you.'

'It wasn't entirely a performance, Doctor. Her chart showed exactly the fallout pattern I'd expect from a huge explosion in Russia. The wind directions and strengths were correct, and she had the ship's position to the dot. I was seriously worried for a few minutes!'

CHAPTER 9

Dealing with Mrs Franik made me late for dinner, so that my guests had completed their first course by the time I arrived. Nonetheless they were pleased to see me and keen to enter into conversation. I would rather have had a quiet dinner; switching from the bizarre events in the hospital to light dinner conversation was a difficult mental gear-change, so for a time I must have appeared preoccupied. Surrounding me was the epitome of holiday atmosphere: the glamorous and glittering clothing, the buzz of light-hearted conversation speckled with laughter and the faint but distinctive smell of *haute cuisine* mingling with perfume and after-shave. Few would imagine that serious medical problems could occur against this light-hearted backdrop. Why should they? Even the ship's doctor was dressed up in his finery, about to enjoy his meal.

The medical student's father interrupted my daydream, as if reading my thoughts; 'I don't suppose many serious illnesses happen on a cruise ship, Doctor?'

I thought back over my first three days at sea; hardly a large experience to quote from, but enough to give me some indication. 'Well, Sir. Occasionally they do. There are 3000 people on board. By the law of averages some of them will get ill, even if they had stayed at home.'

He seemed somewhat puzzled by my logic; 'But surely they'd have stayed at home if they were likely to be ill?'

He had a point, but I remembered Sir Giles who'd been determined to travel, in spite of his rotting foot.

'Not everyone has that foresight. What's more, I suspect a lot of people think the cruise will make them better.'

The elderly, buxom lady on my left broke into the conversation; 'That's right, Doctor. My husband says his gout always gets better when

121

he's cruising. DON'T YOU, HENRY?'

'Yes, Dear.'

I would have liked to have brought Henry into the conversation, but it would have involved too much shouting. The poor man looked isolated in his deafness and I suspected that he had long ago stopped using his hearing aid. The battery-pack clipped to his tuxedo top pocket was switched off. He'd probably given up the battle to distinguish words from the background hissing of the inadequate device. Now he'd settled for his own quieter world of thoughts. No doubt his devoted wife would fill him in on the evening's events once they were back in their quiet room.

The Medical Student was in a more pensive mood, but still inquisitive: 'I hope you don't mind me asking, but have you ever had doubts about being a doctor?'

I wondered why he had picked this question. Perhaps he could detect a hint of disillusionment in me, or perhaps he had his own doubts about his chosen career. At our first meeting I'd dismissed him as a rather naïve youth, who hadn't properly questioned his dreams of curing the world's ills. That, I realized, was unfair, especially remembering my own missionary zeal at his age. In truth, that had not been my only motivation, as I had also been distinctly impressed by the relative affluence of my local general practitioner. Perhaps this lad's father had persuaded him into his career, aware, of course, of the golden pathway to fortune that a medical career provides in the United States. Father certainly seemed to be devoted to his son, even now watching him intently, evidently taking pride in his offspring's conversation with me; perhaps even hoping to experience, by proxy, a secret ambition of his own.

His wife appeared to have been delegated to the care of his daughter; an arrangement which daughter clearly resented as she brushed away her mother's fussing hands from their umpteenth attempt to adjust her décolletage, which was revealing a large area of her youthful cleavage.

I wished I had Alice alongside me. She could have easily managed to bring the ladies into the conversation. But she wasn't. I would have to cope on my own, and the young man's question needed a reply, whatever his reason for asking.

'Yes, there are moments when I've had doubts, but only after I've

122

made a mistake.'

Perhaps he was too young to be aware that mistakes can be made, perhaps life had been too plain sailing for him so far.

'But surely you wouldn't make a mistake? You seem to be so experienced!'

I was flattered that I gave that impression of competence, but it wasn't much help to the young man.

'I'm afraid that experience is inevitably partly gained from mistakes. They make a lasting impression on you and you try never to make the same mistake again. But there's always something to trip you up.'

I thought it might be helpful to warn him against too cosy a picture of the world, but I didn't want to disillusion him too much, so I added; 'However, by following the rules, and with luck on your side, your mistakes won't be big ones.'

The buxom wife interjected; 'Henry's doctor made a mistake once, prescribed him some pills for his cough; they gave him diarrhoea for weeks!'

The main course arrived.

After dinner I had no pressing commitments, except to check on Mrs Franik. The meal had left me feeling pleasantly replete and I looked forward to my short visit to the hospital. I had always found a paradoxical pleasure in dealing with the occasional out-of-hours patient, once the initial irritation of being disturbed had passed. I'd discovered, some years before, that the main hardship of my job was not dealing with patients, but worrying about the others, still waiting to be seen, and the constant fight against the clock. There had never seemed to be enough time to deal adequately with the problem at hand. This time factor, I felt sure, had led many good doctors into a state of disillusionment. The out-of-hours problems, however, were not bracketed by time, and so often provided those titbits of professional reward so essential for mental well-being.

The hospital was quiet when I arrived, and Sally had even found time to write some personal letters, which were neatly stacked alongside the blotting pad on her desk. She paused in her writing to acknowledge me.

'Good evening, Doctor. You're working late. Feeling energetic after your vitamin pills are you?'

I'd never considered vitamin pills to be much more than a placebo, a

123

modern alternative to the mysteriously coloured and strange-smelling potions prescribed to me in my childhood. I suspected that Sally felt the same.

'I think it's more likely that the bottle of claret at dinner has perked me up.'

She gave me her matronly look; 'Mustn't depend too much on alcohol, Doctor. It's an easily acquired habit at sea you know.'

'You're probably right, Sister, but I haven't come in for a sermon. I want to check on Mrs Franik.'

I wondered how long it would be before we moved onto first-name terms. For the present, however, we were still fencing, and the formal titles best suited our relationship.

'Well, Doctor, the little pantomime you laid on does seem to have achieved some success. She eventually went to sleep, still mumbling about nuclear fall-out zones. Perhaps you'd better pop in and see her.'

We visited her together. She was lying curled up in foetal position, soundly asleep, her silver conical hat lying beside her bed on the deck where it had fallen. I took her hand to check on her pulse, but my action disturbed her and she changed position slightly. Then she opened one eye, like a wary chicken, and seemed to recognize me. She mumbled;

'I didn't really think they were anti-nuclear pills.'

Then her eyelids closed and she fell back to sleep.

There wasn't anything else I could do for her now. Sleep would do more for her than any amount of talking, so I left her in Sally's capable hands and took my leave.

'Have a nice evening, Doctor.'

She seemed to mean it.

'I'll do my best, Sister. Good night.'

I hadn't yet decided whether to look for Susie, but perhaps my subconscious had, because I found myself walking to the nightclub. There was no particular reason to suppose she would be there, but it was something new for me to do in any case.

The lighting in the room was low enough for any uniform to blend in without attracting attention, so I could enjoy feeling anonymous for a short time. I ordered a Scotch from the bar and stood for a while taking in the atmosphere. The three-piece band had just changed from a fast disco piece and was moving into a slower tempo, a more romantic dance number. The couples, exhausted by their disco contortions, were moving off the floor, some of them mopping the sweat, caused by their unaccustomed activity after a heavy meal, from their foreheads. One particularly large, middle-aged man looked as if he might not survive the display he'd just put on for his much younger partner, and I hoped my medical skills were not about to be called upon. Wiser couples, who had anticipated the change in tempo, were taking their places on the small mirror-tiled dance floor. The roving multicoloured lights above their heads were providing alternating privacy and limelight, which most of them were unaware of as they snuggled against each other, their feet making minimal movements as a gesture to the music. I noticed a couple of officers' uniforms amongst the tuxedos and saw that John, in particular, had entered into the mood with the young lady from his second-class dining table.

My eyes had by now grown accustomed to the low lighting and, looking around the room, I realized that my subconscious instinct had been correct. Susie was here, sitting in the far corner with a group of passengers, no doubt doing her duty as social hostess. I walked across to speak to her. Because her back was towards me I managed, by way of a change, to surprise her. She was slightly startled by my hand on her shoulder.

'Oh, Doctor Michael, you surprised me.'

Then, after a short, calculating pause; 'I'm afraid I'm rather busy at the moment.'

I turned to walk away and leave her to her duties, but she grasped my arm; 'Not that busy, Doctor. Why don't you join us?'

I pulled up a nearby spare chair and moved into the gap the small group had made for me by shuffling around. We were now quite tightly packed so that my left leg was obliged to brush against Susie's thigh. I could have contracted a little, to lessen the contact, but my muscles weren't working that way; neither, it appeared, were hers. Her perfume was again the one that Alice used to wear and I had to fight the pulling effect it was having on my senses.

Susie introduced me to the rest of the group. There were two middle-aged couples and a well-built young man in his early twenties who appeared to be travelling alone. I suspected that he had designs on Susie, because there was a hint of hostility beneath his greeting smile and the bone-crushing nature of his hand-shake was not, I felt, intended to convey a gesture of sincerity. In a cave-man situation, I thought, he would have won without too much trouble. But Susie's regard for him appeared to be more to do with her duty to keep passengers happy than any deep affection. As if sensing his simmering antagonism she invited him to dance, leaving me to continue the conversation with the two couples. They were pleasant people; lifelong friends, who had done a lot of travelling together and we talked about my favourite topic, the Far East. My appetite for travel was building up as they described the exotic sights of India, Malaysia and the Philippines. Alice and I had planned to take a long holiday, visiting these places, so my enthusiasm was mixed with sadness for what could never now happen.

Paradoxically, also spoiling my enjoyment of the conversation were my occasional glimpses of Susie being clutched by the young American on the dance floor. There was not much footwork going on, but his hands appeared to be busy enough. Had they been dancing to one of the fast disco numbers, gyrating out of contact with each other it wouldn't have bothered me, but this was a particularly slow, romantic piece and happened to be one of my favourites. I wouldn't have put it past her to be steaming me up on purpose.

Jealousy is an ugly emotion and I had, in any case, no cause to feel it. There was no 'understanding' between Susie and myself, just a few teasing encounters. I tried to put it out of my mind and returned to the conversation, purposefully shifting my chair so that the dance floor was not in my line of vision.

I was amazed at how much the couples had travelled. Neither gave the impression of great affluence and from the men's hands I deduced that they were both manual workers. It transpired that they ran a plumbing business together and by working long hours they had managed to educate their children and travel the globe. I couldn't recall any British plumbers, nor doctors for that matter, with such wide experience.

We had discussed another two continents before the slow music ended and Susie and the young American returned. As she sat down she touched my arm lightly, presumably as a gesture of compensation. It felt good having her next to me again and the conversation flowed more freely with her present. Later, our glasses were looking empty so I offered to get the next round in. But Susie had other ideas; 'No, leave that for the moment, Doctor. I feel like a dance.'

She took my hand and led me to the dance floor. I thought she might have taken this action to pre-empt the young American who had looked as if he were plucking up courage to ask her for another dance, but she proved me wrong.

'Does a girl have to do all the asking? I've been waiting for you to invite me up to dance for the past ten minutes.'

'I was waiting for a slow number, Susie.'

'No thanks! I've had enough of that close encounters stuff for one evening!'

This remark did very little for my ego. She'd managed to cope with the American's close contact, so what was wrong with mine? There was no opportunity to discuss the matter as we were now on the dance floor trying to match our gyrations to the disco rhythm, each in our own separate orbits. If we touched it was by accident. This was not my idea of a romantic time, doing our own independent little jungle dances.

I looked around me and hoped that I didn't look as daft as some of the others on the floor. I found myself wondering what we would have looked like to someone totally deaf, unable to hear the music. I thought of the medical condition of the brain, known as St Vitus's Dance, which produces similar uncoordinated jerking movements. What I saw around me was a fair imitation of it.

However, there was, I began to realize, a compensation for the lack of intimacy in this type of dancing, and that was the view it allowed. Susie appeared to be making a reasonably artistic performance of the dance and watching her limbs and body in movement made me more aware of her attractiveness. As she moved in and out of the roving light, the shape of her body became more or less apparent as a silhouette through her far less than opaque dress. Whether or not she was aware of this I could only guess, but she was making some fairly provocative body movements, even though her face retained an angelic composure.

The dance eventually finished and before the band could break into another number she gripped my arm.

'You're not much good at this stuff, are you? You're supposed to move a bit yourself, not just goggle.'

'No, I'm not too good at it; ballroom or jiving is my scene, but I was enjoying the view.'

'Yes. I noticed! Let's leave the dancing for another time. A breath of fresh air is needed. I'll just say good-night to my guests and then I'll meet you on deck.'

I waited for her on the deck just aft of the nightclub. Apart from one couple deep in conversation, I was alone. The air was warmer than I'd expected and a calmness had descended on the Atlantic. It was one of those evenings at sea I'd seen in the movies; warm air, stars and moon reflected in a flat, silver sea. I leant on the rail watching the foaming white bow-wave lit up by the ship's lights. All I needed was a blonde and a Tchaikovsky overture to make the scene complete. The blonde arrived:

'Alone at last, Doctor Michael.'

'You could drop the "Doctor" now, Susie. We have been introduced.'

'I still think of you as a doctor.'

'Is that all?'

'You know it's not all.'

She was right. I knew she wanted more of me than my medical knowledge, even though that part of me seemed important to her. Probably that had been important to her with John. I'd learnt that some women are very attracted to the 'mystique' of doctors, but that was not a good foundation for a relationship.

She was close to me now, and her bare arm was touching my jacket sleeve. Even keeping my gaze on the bow wave, far below, I could tell she was looking at me intently, but I wanted to hear her words without being distracted by her face. It could have been the moment to kiss her, but I sensed that that was not what she wanted: not yet anyway.

'But the doctor is very important to you, Susie?'

'I can't deny that, but I wouldn't jump into bed with you for that reason.'

'Do you want to jump into bed with me?'

She didn't answer, just moved closer.

'Why are you staring into the sea, Michael?'

'Trying to find the meaning of life. Have a look.'

'OK, I'm looking.'

128

'What do you see?'

'Lots of frothy bubbles; pretty and sparkling.'

'And underneath?'

'God, you're morbid! You're thinking of miles of hidden depths – shipwrecks and sea monsters, aren't you?'

'Yes, but I'm trying to see only the froth.'

'Are you trying to tell me something? Do you think that I'm all froth and bubbles, with a monster underneath?'

I had made another blunder. I should have realized that she'd take it personally.

'Sorry, Susie, that wasn't what I was getting at. I was just thinking about the different ways people can look at the same picture.'

It was a lame explanation of my thought pattern and I guessed I'd ruined the evening: any second now she would storm off again. Instead, she put her hand on top of mine;

'Looking at the sea is bad for you, Doctor. Let's go back to your cabin.'

We did just that.

It felt unnatural not holding hands *en route*, but we were both aware of the 'goldfish bowl' we lived in and were not prepared to advertise our feelings.

In the cosy security of my cabin, however, things were different. I'd not finished closing the door before she planted a kiss on my cheek.

'Well, Doctor, now let's see how you can entertain a lady.'

There was no anticipating this girl. I'd been planning the route to seduction: the offering of a drink, the choice of music, the first tentative move towards intimacy. That had been the fashion when I'd seduced Alice, and she'd played along with it, not giving in too easily: obeying the rules of the game. Perhaps the rules had changed, or maybe this was just Susie's way. I felt that I had to take control;

'Susie, I want you to sit down and listen to Brahms' violin concerto with me.'

'No way, Doctor. You're not driving me to tears with that piece. It's Frank Sinatra or nothing.'

She'd found the cassette already and slotted it into the player. *Strangers in the Night* was pervading the atmosphere before I realized I'd been defeated.

'Now you can offer me a drink. I see you have the champagne prepared. You are a crafty one!'

To my amazement I saw that she was right. There was a bottle of champagne sitting in an ice bucket on the coffee table. I thought quickly; 'Of course, Susie, Boy Scout's motto "Always be prepared".'

I collected two glasses and lifted the champagne from the ice. There was a small label around the neck, it said;

> Thought you might enjoy this Doc.
> Gwilym.

This was not the moment to wonder about the depths of Gwilym's mind and I slipped the card into my pocket. I loosened the cork, allowing it to hit the deck-head with full force, and filled the glasses with assumed nonchalance. I handed her a glass, then clinked mine to it.

'Here's to whatever we both want, Susie.'

'I'll second that, Doctor. You are so sophisticated.'

Her tone of voice was mocking me as she said this, but her eyes, at least her left eye, was saying something different.

We both drank some of the champagne, but it had not left our mouths before we were kissing. More exactly, we were exchanging mouthfuls of the fizzy liquid, much of which was escaping down our chins. We drank some more and did the same thing, but she inhaled some and started to choke. I slapped her back, but it made her laugh more, and we both collapsed to the deck in a fit of coughing and laughing. Yet more champagne, which splashed over our clothes: then more; more coughing and laughing, both of us frothing like the sparkling bow wave, spraying champagne from our mouths, trying to kiss, but laughing too much.

Susie was now very wet and her dress was sticking to her. I could not resist touching her, feeling her laughing stomach muscles, moving my hand over her, searching for her bra-clip. I was on the crest of a wave. Laughter had broken through everything. The smell of Alice's perfume on her neck I could forget: her fling with John I could forget. This was the time to forget and to enjoy ourselves.

130

I had almost found her bra, was already anticipating removing it and feeling the softness of her breasts, the hard erectness of her nipples, when her hand grasped my wrist. I looked into her face: the laughter had gone and she was slowly shaking her head. The bubbly, frothy bow-wave had vanished and suddenly I was looking beneath it.

'No, Michael.'

She said this with a firmness that could not be ignored; but there was a sadness in her voice that stopped my anger.

'I want to talk to you first.'

The magic had been broken. Frank Sinatra was still crooning in the background about 'Lovers at first sight'. Two seconds before, his singing had sounded wonderful, now I wished he would shut up. I asked myself if I'd done anything wrong. Perhaps I'd pushed things too far?

'That's all right, Susie, perhaps we don't know each other well enough yet,' I forced out of myself.

'In a way you are right. You don't know enough about me. I have a deformity, Michael.'

'I can see that! You're covered with champagne for a start.'

Her response to my joke was a very weak smile.

'This isn't a joke. I'm serious.'

Frank Sinatra had got back to *Strangers in the Night* and I was feeling very much like a stranger. What could I have missed about Susie? She had a limb on each corner; her body moved well on the dance floor. The only problem I'd noticed was her eyes. Perhaps she was over-concerned about them; perhaps it wasn't just a squint, maybe she had a glass eye? But I should have noticed that.

'I can't imagine anything seriously wrong with you, Susie. You've got a squint which I find oddly attractive; otherwise you look perfect.'

She sat up, huddling herself with her arms. Frank Sinatra was now singing *Hey, Mrs Robinson*. There was half the bottle of champagne left and I filled her glass.

She asked; 'What's the worst thing you can imagine about a woman?'

She was testing me and I knew that my reply was of the utmost importance to her. She'd covered herself, protecting herself against the world, and had changed from a confident flirt to a vulnerable infant. I thought about all the women I'd met. The worst had been a patient of

131

mine; a humourless tyrant who had hounded her husband to death, pushing him to a goal he wasn't capable of.

'Well, the worst thing I can imagine is someone without feeling or humour. Anything else is trivial by comparison, Susie.'

'Is that your honest opinion, Doctor?'

'Yes. The best thing that has happened to me in months has been laughing with you just now; it made me realize just how important laughter really is.'

She sat silent for a while, appearing to be deep in thought. I was thinking about stopping Frank Sinatra and trying Brahms instead when, with a sudden movement, she stood up.

'Stay here, I'll tell you when I'm ready.'

With that she vanished into my bedroom, pulling the curtain behind her.

I could do nothing but sip champagne and wonder what she was up to. After two minutes' thought, I knew she was going to remove her glass eye, shock me with an empty socket, and I prepared my mind for it. For the shock of seeing her right eyelid sucked into the empty cavity, her face looking like half of a skeleton's skull.

'You can come in now.'

I took my drink with me, for companionship, trying to appear composed as I entered my bedroom. The main light was off, only the small reading lamp lit up her naked shape sitting on my bunk. I looked straight into her eyes, prepared for the cavity, but she looked the same as always, slightly squinted of course, but I knew by now to concentrate on her left eye, the good one.

The relief must have shown on my face.

'Well, what do you think?'

'I suspect you are trying to seduce me!'

'Is that all you can say?'

It would have been, had not my baser instincts led my eyes down her body. Her right breast was beautiful, enough to make the heart pump with lust. The left was missing; in its place a scar running diagonally across her chest, her ribs showing clearly through the stretched skin.

My professional mind was wondering who could have done that to her, instead of leaving her with a transplant. My emotions were frantically working out how to respond. The shock must have been showing on my face by now;

'Susie, there's a bit missing, but the rest is beautiful.'

I must have found the right answer; her arms were around my neck. It took an age to undress, even with her help.

I can't remember entering her, but I remember her shudders as I kissed the scar on her chest. There were lots of tears, and some laughter, and the explosion came quickly.

Afterwards she picked up the photo of Alice and asked me about it. The dawn light was piercing through the cabin porthole before I had finished talking.

'I guessed it was something like that.'

She murmured as she turned over to sleep.

Sleep did not come as easily to me. There was too much to think about. A lot about Susie was now explained; her need for love, but her dread of rejection, because of her disfigurement. Probably she thought that a doctor was less likely to be repelled, but it was not the doctor in me that found her attractive, in spite of the missing breast. I suspected that most men would have felt the same, after the initial shock. I wondered how far John had gone with her and whether he knew. Perhaps she had backed off at the last moment, which would explain the rancour between them.

I watched her sleeping, noticing how white her half-covered body looked in the grey morning light. No sign of a suntan: she wouldn't have risked sunbathing, nor could she follow the growing fashion for 'burning her bra'. I could see her bra, with its left-sided padding, poking out from under the pillow where she had hidden it. Maybe she had even avoided close dancing with me earlier, in case I could tell her secret, holding her against me.

She was breathing slowly and regularly, making quiet mumbling noises, as if dreaming. I felt lucky to be lying alongside her and wanted to touch her again but was afraid of disturbing her sleep. Instead I put the photograph back onto my desk. Alice was now in a different part of my mind.

Gwilym woke me up.

'Sleeping late this morning, Doc? There's some fresh tea on the table. Didn't want to disturb you too early.'

Instinctively I grabbed the sheet and pulled it up to cover Susie, but she'd gone. I looked at my watch - eight o'clock! My head didn't feel too good; must have swallowed more of the champagne than I realized. I better had drink some of Gwilym's tea and have a cold shower.

The cold water sobered me up quickly and I began to recall the previous night's events. The thought of Susie warmed me up as I towelled myself dry. As I started shaving I remembered Gwilym's present;

'Oh, Gwilym, thank you for the champagne.'

'Think nothing of it; I see most of it ended up on the carpet though.'

'Well, it was very much appreciated; but you shouldn't be spending your money on presents for me.'

'That's all right, Doc; charged it to your account.'

CHAPTER 10

I arrived at the hospital just in time to be five minutes late for the start of Sally's report, but she didn't comment, just stopped talking and raised her eyebrows while I settled myself onto the examination couch with the others. Then she resumed;

'Doctor Vaughan, in particular, will be pleased to hear that Mrs Franik slept soundly through the night and is now sitting up eating a hearty breakfast. She is still a little drowsy from the tablets, but seems quite sane and has made no mention of nuclear fallout.

'Sir Giles is comfortable and has very little pain, and his wound is clean. Millie is watching over him like a guardian angel and doesn't seem at all anxious to return to her cabin.

'Angus is doing well and is probably fit enough to leave the hospital. He seems keen to meet up with his mates in "The Pig". 'I'm off to bed.'

No one seemed too anxious to jump into action when she left. It seemed that everybody had had a late night. John's eyes were distinctly bleary and Janet looked slightly dishevelled with some wisps of hair falling from her neat bun. She prodded me in the ribs;

'Time to move, Doctor. You look as if you're dreaming.'

She wasn't far wrong. I was trying to pull my mind back into focus. Something about being at sea seemed to distort life. So much had happened in a short space of time that yesterday's activities felt as if they had happened two days ago. I had been three days at sea and it felt like a lifetime. It had felt natural sleeping with Susie, as if I had known her for months; yet in reality it had been a whirlwind romance. It was as if life itself was being compressed, or as if I had entered a time warp. I was beginning to understand how Mrs Franik's mind had become disturbed.

'No, Janet, I wasn't dreaming. I just think that the pace of life is getting to me.'

'Don't worry, Michael, it happens to everyone. Just wait until you've done three crossings in a row. You won't be able to tell your elbow from Good Friday: Remember, you're also losing an hour every night.'

I had forgotten that; we'd been putting the clock forward an hour each evening to allow us to catch up with British time before arrival in Southampton. That explained why everyone looked sleepy. I was relieved it wasn't just me. Janet brought me back to earth;

'Perhaps you'd better start with a ward round, Doctor; Angus wants to know if he can leave.'

'I think you're right, Janet.'

Yesterday's medical dramas flooded back to mind.

'I'll start with Angus. Let's take his dressings off and have a look at his face.'

The skin beneath the dressings was healthy and pink-looking. It would only be a short time before it was back to normal.

'How am I doing, Doctor?'

'You're face looks perfect. You can leave the hospital now. You'll have to keep your dressings on for a few days, just to keep the dirt out, but you'll be able to take them off when you get home.'

'Why do I have to go home?'

'Because your arm needs to be rested. It's still very bruised from your accident.'

'Och, I can lift it up well enough now, Doctor!'

He demonstrated, raising his arm half-way, enough to lift his drink I was sure, but I doubted he would be able to comb his hair.

'Now rub your head, Angus.'

He tried but the wince showed in his face.

'You see what I mean? You'll need a month's physiotherapy before you get back to work.'

He looked disappointed. Many a man would have jumped at the chance of an extra month at home, but of course Angus would not be keen to meet his brother, nor his ex-girlfriend.

'Do you have any friends you could stay with, instead of going home, Angus?'

'You remember my dilemma then, Doctor?'

'Of course.'

'Ah well, I'll maybe think of something.'

136

I left him to ponder a solution and moved on to Millie.

She was not in her bed, but sitting in a chair next to Sir Giles, who was sound asleep. There was a calmness about her as she quietly read her book. Sir Giles's head was turned towards her, as if he were aware of her presence, even in his sleep. I motioned to her to come with me to her room, to avoid disturbing him.

'You seem to have a full-time job there, Millie.'

'That's a work of love, Doctor,' she smiled at me in reply.

'Are you acting as his guardian angel, then?'

'That's a nice way of putting it. He seems to need me at the moment. He woke up once, early this morning, and started asking about his leg. I told him you were making him a new one. He smiled and went back to sleep.'

She looked happy, almost serene, as if she had found something she'd been seeking for many years. There was something very attractive about her, sitting on the edge of her bed, legs crossed, her slim little figure covered only by a frilly lace dressing-gown. Her hair was sparkling white and set into pretty curls.

'You've had your hair done, Millie.'

'Fancy you noticing a little thing like that, Doctor!'

Again, her coquettish look; 'That nice girl, Barbara, came down to the hospital to do it for me. She wouldn't take any payment.'

It seemed a reasonable assumption that Millie had taken Barbara under her wing, probably acting as a mother figure, listening to her problems.

'Well, she did a very good job, but I really came to check on your heart, not your hair.'

'Of course you did. Please carry on.'

She undid the bow at the top of her dressing gown, and parted the fabric, offering me a few square inches of chest. She was not really as shy as that, I felt, but was making a show of her modesty.

'I can't really examine you properly like that, Millie. You could be a little bit more generous. You can trust me, you know, I'm a doctor!'

'I suppose I'll have to.'

I pulled the curtains around her bed whilst she slipped out of her gown and slid under the sheets. As I folded the sheet back to enable me to examine her, she lay still, arms by her sides and eyes raised to heaven.

I listened carefully to her heart; still irregular, but the rate had slowed to 86 per minute.

'Millie, you've done very well. Your conducting has been excellent. Your heart is still a bit jazzy, but it's slowed right down.'

'It's probably partly due to your tablets as well though, Doctor.'

She pulled the sheet back over her, holding it in place as she sat up.

'By the way, I've solved the foxglove mystery.'

'What mystery?'

I remembered then our conversation: the way she had been more interested in the history of the flower than how the Digoxin was going to help to cure her.

'All right, Millie, tell me the answer.'

'Well, I think it was discovered by a stone-age man looking for something to poison his wife with, because she had been so irritable and crotchety. He crushed the leaves up and put them into her food. Then, instead of dying, her heart got better and she stopped being irritable and turned into a loving wife again. And they all lived happily ever after.'

'You've got a fairy-tale mind, Millie.'

'Well, they won't come true unless you believe in them.'

Perhaps she was believing her fairy-tale would come true. She certainly looked happy enough. I wondered how she was going to react to being told she could leave the hospital.

'If I can change the subject, Millie, I want to talk to you about leaving the hospital, now that you're so much better.'

Her face showed her disappointment, 'Do I have to? I'm really quite comfortable here.'

There was no real harm in her staying, but I was afraid that she would start making a nuisance of herself, now that she was well. Besides which she had paid for a cruise.

'Well, there is no medical reason for you to stay, and it does seem a shame for you to miss all the fun of the cruise you paid for.'

'I'm enjoying my cruise, right here.'

'I think it would be better if you returned to your cabin, but you can come down to visit the hospital any time.'

Her eyes brightened at this suggestion: 'Oh, well, that's all right then. I'll get dressed straight away, but you haven't seen the last of me.'

'I hope not, Millie.'

'You won't forget our dance?'

'No, I won't forget.'

I left her to do her dressing and packing. Somehow I didn't expect to see much less of her in the hospital, even when she was no longer officially in residence.

My next call was to Mrs Franik, and I was very curious to find out how much of her hallucination was still present. She was awake, but only just, huddled up on her side with her blanket up to her neck. She appeared to recognize me, but only dimly.

'Do you remember me, Mrs Franik?'

'Yes, we had a party together, didn't we?'

'That's right. Do you remember who else was there?'

'I remember the Captain; very nice man, intelligent.'

'Yes, he is. Do you feel well this morning?'

'I feel very sleepy.'

'You will do for another day or two. You've had a very trying time. Nurse will be giving you some tablets later.'

She nodded in agreement, then closed her eyes.

She looked peaceful and I hoped that she would stay that way until I could hand her over to a psychiatrist in Southampton. She needed good care if she was going to use her clever brain again in a useful way.

Sir Giles had been sedated, so there was no point in visiting him until later. I wondered how he was going to adjust to having one leg. I was sure he would put on a brave face, whatever his feelings. At least he would be able to attack his vintage port, with or without his leg. Perhaps Millie would be helping him?

It was now time for crew surgery. The small waiting area that led out to the busy working alleyway was packed full. I thought it must have been designed for quieter times, as the wooden bench provided seating for less than half of the motley crowd awaiting me. There was very little conversation going on, each of them being immersed in their own thoughts. A practised glance told me that at least one of them was really ill. He had, luckily, acquired a place on the bench and was leaning forward, his head supported by his hands, with his elbows resting on his knees; his face was as white as his waiter's jacket, and he was breathing faster than the others.

Terry was waiting for me in my office: 'Plenty to keep you occupied this morning, Sir.'

He placed a mound of files on my desk.

'Yes, I noticed, Terry. I was hoping for a quieter time; my head's none too strong today.'

'Aye, well that'll be lack of sleep from the clock changing, Sir.'

Then, with a neutral expression, too neutral, he added; 'And I expect you've a bit of entertaining to do, as well.'

There would be no finding out from Terry how much he knew of my 'entertaining'. If asked he would adopt an innocent ignorance of anything he'd heard from the grapevine. Better to forget his comment.

'I think we'd better start with the sick waiter, Terry. He looks in need of urgent attention.'

'He does that, Sir; says his ulcer's been playing him up for days and got much worse last night. I'll bring him in.'

We laid him on the examination couch, as he looked as if he couldn't stand up much longer. Without too much surprise I recognized him as the wine waiter who had served me my scotch so quickly at the cocktail party. Pete had told me his ulcer had been playing up – he'd been right, as usual!

He was a thin, anxious looking man in his mid-thirties. He seemed to be as worried about missing work as he did about his pain, confirming my experience that it was often such conscientious people that developed stomach ulcers. His description of his symptoms, and my examination of his abdomen, left little doubt that he had an ulcer, and that it was bleeding. His pulse was rapid and his breathing fast, suggesting that he'd lost a fair amount of blood. I took Terry into the next room:

'He needs a blood transfusion.'

'Aye, I thought as much; I've already done his blood group, just in case. Would you like to check it with me?'

As usual, Terry was on top of the situation. He must have noticed the waiter's sickly whiteness as soon as he'd arrived, and quickly calculated what was happening to him. In the Royal Navy he could well have been the only medical opinion aboard on some of the smaller vessels, which would have made him very self-reliant. He led me into his small laboratory and showed me the test cards. He'd repeated the test to make

140

sure.

'Group O, Rhesus negative, is what I make it, Sir.'

I checked the cards.

'I agree. Do we have any O negative blood on board?'

'Well, not in a blood bank, if that's what you're thinking ...'

'That's what I had been thinking; I'd assumed we carried an emergency supply.'

'... We carry it "on the hoof", so to speak.'

He then opened a drawer and pulled out a notebook. Inside was a list of maybe a hundred names of crew members, with their blood groups alongside.

'There you are, Sir. Take your pick. Mind you, they're not all on board at the moment.'

Group O, negative, is not a rare group, but neither is it common, and there were only five amongst this list of volunteer donors. We checked their names against the crew manifest. Only two of the five were on board. Terry crossed out one of these two.

'Can't use him,' he said.

'Why not?'

'Treated him for gonorrhoea last voyage; might still be carrying something. The other one's fine; good clean lad, only just joined the ship. He doesn't know what sex is about, yet.'

Terry's pragmatic approach to the problem was invaluable. He had a fine blend of medical knowledge and common sense.

'Right, could you get him down to the hospital, Terry? I'll go and talk to the patient.'

The wine waiter was still looking very anxious, and I explained to him what was going on. I told him that once I'd given him some blood and stopped his ulcer bleeding, he'd be as right as ninepence. Luckily the latest drugs for ulcers were almost miraculous and I calculated that, given intravenously, they would probably stop the bleeding. I didn't like to contemplate them failing to do so, which would leave one life-saving alternative - partial gastrectomy. Amputating a leg was enough excitement for one voyage. Opening an abdomen and removing part of a stomach was not on my list of favourite pastimes.

I pushed the thought from my mind and arranged with Janet for him to be admitted to the hospital and settled comfortably in bed.

Then I tackled some of the remaining crew surgery whilst Terry found the hapless donor. There were a myriad of small problems to resolve; coughs and colds that hadn't cleared up, back pains that were persisting, rashes that never appeared in textbooks. We were now only two days from Southampton so there were the homesick few, trying to be signed off sick so that they could go home instead of sailing on another voyage. There were some who wanted to stay, but had to be signed off sick. And there was Barbara Box, who wanted to stay, but had been told to go, not because she was sick, but because she had spoiled too many hairdos.

'They're picking on me, Doctor,' she said defiantly, as she entered my office. 'Other girls make mistakes and have got away with it. They just don't like me.'

'You'd better explain what's happened, Barbara.'

'I've been given the sack, told my work's not good enough!'

'Well, how can I help you with that problem? That's not really medical.'

'Couldn't you tell them I made the mistakes because I was ill? Perhaps they'd let me stay then, and prove how good I am really.'

I didn't think I could help her with this problem. Trying to solve the reason for her reputation was one thing; her poor work record was another. Yet she'd certainly made a good job of Millie's hair.

'I've noticed you're very good at your job sometimes, Barbara, but I expect you're having difficulty concentrating?'

'That's right, I am! I'm feeling very mixed up, what with people talking about me, and worrying about Angus.'

'There's no need to worry about Angus; he's doing fine.'

'I know, but if I have to leave the ship I might never see him again.'

'It's not inevitable, Barbara. Why don't you talk to him about it?'

'I can't yet. He's very kind to me, but he must be worried about my reputation. He's very religious you know, Doctor.'

I thought I could see her dilemma. She wanted to prove herself, somehow make herself worthy of him, which would take time. That Angus was probably too intelligent for that to be necessary didn't enter her calculation.

'Perhaps you'd better talk to him anyway. Take a chance. Nothing ventured, nothing gained.'

'I'll think about it.'

She left, looking less defiant, but sadder. I noticed that her skirt was slightly longer.

Terry had found the 'donor', a young-looking lad, still dressed in cook's apparel.

'I've been a blood donor before,' he said, after our introduction.

As if keen to prove his worthiness, he produced his donor card with the blood group stated clearly on it - Group O, Rhesus negative. That would save us the task of doing a group test ourselves.

Now all that was needed was a cross-match test to check that the two bloods were compatible in fact, as well as in theory. Terry organized this, taking a sample of blood from each, separating the serum from the cells, then mixing the cells of one with the serum of the other. We then observed the mixture under the microscope. If the cook's blood had contained any unusual antibodies, the waiter's red cells would have disintegrated. It was a relief to see that this did not happen. If they behaved well together in the laboratory, they should behave well in the waiter's body.

I returned to the cook; 'Your blood is a perfect match,' I told him, 'but I'm afraid I'll need to take two pints, rather than the one pint you usually donate.'

Then, to reassure him; 'But, as you're young and healthy, you'll soon make it up afterwards. I'll tell the chef to feed you extra steak for a few days.'

He didn't look at all dismayed.

'Oh, I don't mind, Doctor, if it's going to save someone's life.'

'It definitely will. The patient could well die without it. I can't thank you enough.'

He settled back on the bed and let me put a wide bore needle into his vein. His blood flowed freely into the plastic collecting bags and afterwards he didn't look too bad, considering he'd lost a fifth of his blood volume. Janet compensated him with a cup of tea and a chocolate biscuit, which I thought was rather a poor reward for his noble donation. I made a mental note to arrange for him to be put off duty, then rushed off with his blood to the deathly white waiter in the next room. I felt easier once I could see it flowing slowly into him. He'd probably lost a good deal more than two pints but that much should control the situation. I also injected the ulcer-curing drugs, then left him in peace, with Janet and God to take care of him.

With my tasks in the hospital done, a less serious problem came to mind; little Pepe. Setting off on the long climb to the kennels, I hoped that the poisonous amount of Digoxin had departed from his little body. I couldn't work out how long it should take as he'd been given enough for an animal four times his size.

It was a touching scene that greeted me in the kennels. Sitting on a stool, amidst the cages full of animals, was Miss Myers. Pepe, still too weak to resist, was being showered with kisses.

'Oh, my darling little boy, my little honey. You've eaten almost half of your food and you haven't thrown up once!'

Pepe seemed to be accepting her affection with a nonchalance borne from long experience. He still looked as if he might throw up, which wouldn't do Miss Myers' fur wrap much good. She eventually registered my presence, and raised her face from Pepe's neck.

'Oh, Doctor, how can I thank you? Whatever you've given to Pepe, he's getting better already!'

Then she resumed the kissing.

I didn't want to tell her that it was not what I'd given him, but what I hadn't given him that was making him better. Pepe was looking up at me, craning his neck away from his mistress's tight embrace. I wasn't sure whether he was looking for an ally, or wondering which bit of me to bite. Animals had always been a mystery to me. I decided to give him the benefit of the doubt, and took out my stethoscope. Remembering my bitten knuckles from our first encounter, I arranged for the kennel maid to hold him. This turned out to be an unnecessary precaution as he was much better-tempered and seemed quite happy to have my instrument placed on his chest. The sounds I heard were very encouraging. His heart rate had increased from 30 to 66 beats per minute, not yet normal, but an improvement. It struck me as strange that I was almost as anxious for Pepe's heart rate to increase as I had been for Millie's to decrease. I now felt able to pronounce partial success, so I retrieved my stethoscope before Pepe's good temper had time to change, and turned to Miss Myers.

'I'm pleased to say that he is beginning to recover.'

'Oh, thank you, Doctor. How long before he is completely well?'

144

I paused before replying, allowing my profoundest and wisest expression to develop; 'Well, Miss Myers, he is a very difficult case, but I will attend to him very carefully and I expect him to recover fully within two days.'

Her face lit up with relief. It seemed that Pepe was very important to her, perhaps as much as a child would be.

'I'm so grateful to you, Doctor. What can I do to repay you?'

That's exactly what I'd hoped she would say.

'Well, I'm not really in a position to give you a bill for veterinary services, but there is something you could help me with.'

She looked quizzically at me, no doubt considering what sort of favour I could expect her to provide. For a brief moment, she appeared to be visualizing something of an intimate nature, so I hastened to be more specific;

'One of the waiters, Julian James, has been to see me, worried sick because he's accused of intentionally burning you with a crêpe Suzette. I wondered if there had been a misunderstanding that you might help sort out?'

She blushed crimson; 'Oh, I'd almost forgotten that. Is he in bad trouble?'

'Well, he could lose his job.'

'I didn't think it would be that serious, but my friend swears he did it on purpose; I couldn't understand it because we'd been getting on so well together.'

'Well, perhaps you could talk to Julian himself. He could explain what happened. I think he's very hurt about it; he seemed to like you a lot.'

Her crimson blush deepened.

'Do you really think he likes me?'

'I'm certain of it, Miss Myers.'

'All right, Doctor. I'll talk to him as soon as possible.'

'It would help if you could manage it today.'

I was feeling hopeful. With luck they'd sort it out before Julian appeared on the bridge, perhaps even avoid him appearing on the bridge.

'I'll do just that,' she said.

She gave Pepe one last kiss, adjusted her dress, and set off purposefully.

145

With Miss Myers out of the way, I asked the kennel maid what she thought of Pepe's progress and was relieved to find that she thought he was getting better too.

'Mind you,' she said, 'I wish his mistress wouldn't keep trying to feed him. She keeps popping in with titbits from the dining-room. I told her that Pepe probably wouldn't like caviar, but she insisted; said it was very top quality and I was to try feeding it to him.'

'Did he eat any of it?'

'No; but I did!' she replied with a giggle.

I thought Pepe was in safe hands.

The kennels were situated temptingly near the promenade deck and I thought I wouldn't be missed for a few minutes. Outside I was reminded that it was summer. Gone were any signs of wind. The Atlantic could have been a pond and the bright sun was dazzling. There was no tang of salt in the air; it had been replaced by the far less subtle smell of suntan oil. Deck-chairs and sun-beds lined the deck. Acres of white flesh were beginning to fry. Smartly clad deck stewards were serving trays full of drinks at speed. Only two days before I'd had the same deck to myself, admittedly in a cold wind. Now it was difficult to find a walkway between the bodies, but find it I did and made my way aft, to the sun-decks proper.

From the aft end it was possible to look over the recreation areas which descended stepwise, like tiers of a wedding cake. They were even more densely packed with bodies than the area I'd left, and the fragrance of suntan oil was here mixed with that of hamburgers being prepared for those too hungry to wait until lunch. The deck immediately below me contained a swimming pool which was full of thrashing forms of all shapes and sizes. There seemed to be a game in progress as the area was surrounded by laughing onlookers.

I looked more closely. The object of the game seemed to be to acquire as many of the oranges floating in the pool as possible. The acquired oranges were being stored in the swim-wear of the contestants and the resulting deformities were the apparent cause of mirth.

Organizing the game from the sidelines was Susie. Dressed in a short white tennis skirt and short-sleeved polo shirt, she looked just as appealing as she had the night before. Her gym shoes and short white socks gave her the little-girl look, and leaning far forward to shout encouragement to the contestants in the pool caused her skirt to rise up tantalizingly near to the panty level. Standing on the deck above, my view could have been nowhere near as good as that of the young American who was sprawled on the deck near the pool. His attention was far less on the water sports than on Susie's thighs. I could have kicked sand in his face; but there was no sand and he was no seven-stone weakling.

'You're taking your inspection duties a bit seriously, Doc.'

I'd been too intent on watching Susie to notice Pete's arrival. He was leaning on the ship's rail next to me. We were in the same uniform, except that he was wearing his hat and carrying a clipboard.

'Not as seriously as you, by the look of your clipboard!'

'Just checking the condition of the decks, Mike. I'm looking for signs of wear and tear.'

'Found any?'

'Not yet; too many bodies in the way. I suppose you're checking for signs of sunburn amongst the passengers?'

'Part of the job, Pete.'

We continued leaning on the rail for a while, in silence; both of us intent on our jobs. The water game below had come to its conclusion and Susie was presenting a bottle of champagne to the winner, a well-upholstered lady who'd managed to increase her volume with a dozen or so oranges. Her husband was photographing the occasion with enthusiastic pride. I was struck by how happy they looked, but couldn't help wondering how Susie felt watching the woman disgorge those oranges from her bikini top. Again I wondered if I was the only person on board who knew her secret. Pete was reading my thoughts;

'She looks great doesn't she?'

I nodded in agreement.

'How'd you get on with her after your dance last night?'

Again I felt the goldfish bowl sensation; but I was no longer surprised that he should know about our dancing together.

'You don't expect an answer to that, do you, Pete?'

'Course not, Doc. Not from a cagey quack like you!'

But I doubted that he needed an answer. There would have been plenty of midnight eyes around the ship to witness Susie and me heading for my cabin. Not that I really cared what anyone knew, or guessed at, except that I didn't really know myself how we had got on together. It had been an emotionally wracking night, and we'd made love, but she'd vanished before I woke up; and, looking at her now in the bright sunlight, I could hardly believe it had happened. Last night she'd looked seductive and womanly in her thin evening dress; now she looked schoolgirlish in her sports kit. She was doing her job well, keeping a party atmosphere going, and I could see that it wasn't only the young American who was entranced by her. A few older men had decided to join in the fun and games. One of them looked as if he hadn't stirred his bones in years, but he managed a manly type dive into the pool, in spite of his arthritic hips, and I could see his wife giving him a very old-fashioned look from her deck-chair.

No doubt, I thought, she has the power of attraction, and I should feel lucky I'd spent a night with her. But where do we go from here?

Pete prevented me pondering any further on the matter;

'What's happening about that waiter, Mike? I've got to log him tomorrow.'

I had to pull my mind back; 'You mean young Julian? Well my 24 hours isn't up yet, Pete, but I think his problem will be solved by tomorrow.'

'Better be! See you around, Doc.'

He disappeared to inspect some more decking, and I thought about going down to speak to Susie.

The water sports were over and she was talking to the young American, who was now standing. I could understand now how he'd managed to crush my knuckles during our handshake in the nightclub. There was a lot of him, and it was all muscle; he was making the most of it, standing erect on his sturdy tree-trunk legs, chest well forward, one hand incidentally on his hip, to allow his biceps to stand out, and the other gripping a pair of tennis rackets. His stomach would have been flat, even if he hadn't contracted his muscles to make it so. I couldn't stop my hand feeling my own stomach, which was just beginning to paunch from too much sedentary life and a good appetite. His swimming trunks were brief and tight, so tight that even Terry's mythical man on

148

a galloping horse couldn't have helped being impressed by his manhood.

In spite of this fine display, I decided to join their conversation and so descended the stairway to the pool deck, feeling a bit like Daniel entering the lion's den.

As I walked towards them, Susie's head turned slightly my way so that she must have seen me. I smiled, but her head turned back quickly and she grasped the young American's arm;

'Right,' she said, 'let's go and start the deck tennis.'

They walked off quickly to the other stairway before I had chance to talk to her.

Perhaps, I thought, *she didn't see me. Her vision's none too good.*

But it had been the left side of her face which had turned towards me; the side with the good eye. She had seen me.

I would not be exaggerating to say that I felt, at that moment, like a balloon that had landed on a hedgehog. I was mature enough to know that one night of passion does not a romance make, but being avoided like a leper was not only difficult to understand; it was bloody difficult to bear. I could have rushed after them and challenged her, faced her out and made a scene; but in front of the young American I'd have made a fool of myself. Perhaps she'd fallen for the young man after all. He was handsome enough. But I didn't believe she could be as fickle as that. I just couldn't believe that after our intimacy she could behave as she had. She'd revealed her disfigurement to me: bared her soul. Perhaps I hadn't responded to her 'secret' in the right way. Perhaps I had deeply offended her; patronized her maybe. I didn't own her just because she had shared her problem, but I'd have been happy to go on helping her with it. I'd felt a depth of passion with her that almost matched what I'd felt for Alice - almost.

I couldn't think about it any more. Luckily I had work to do. I swallowed the pain and returned to the hospital to check the waiter.

Already the blood transfusion had started to reach his cheeks and a faint glow of colour was developing; enough at least to enable me to distinguish him from the white pillowslip. His pulse and breathing had slowed a little and he looked less anxious.

'You're on the mend already,' I reassured him.

'What's going to happen to me, Doctor?'

'Not a lot. Your ulcer will heal up and stop bleeding; then you'll start to feel better.'

'When will I get back to work?'

That was another problem. It would be risky for him to stay at sea, in case his ulcer bled again. We couldn't keep on bleeding the cook to save his life every voyage. It would be a decision for a specialist ashore. I didn't want to worry him with this aspect of his illness.

'You'll have to spend some time at home and see a specialist before you return to work. I can't tell you how long that will be.'

'I've been at sea for twenty years now, Doctor. Can't think what else I'd do.'

'I wouldn't worry about that now. Modern drugs work miracles with ulcers.'

I didn't know if they were miraculous enough to enable him to return to sea life, but it would give him some hope for the time being. He looked a bit reassured.

Treating him had made me realize how vulnerable a seafarer's life is. On a cargo ship, without a doctor on board, he would probably have died. It also occurred to me that I was the person who'd saved his life, as I had Sir Giles's. As a doctor on land I must have saved many lives, but only indirectly, by sending them to hospital specialists. Yet, within a few days at sea, with my own hands and brain, I'd directly saved two lives, three if I counted Pepe; Millie might have lived without my help anyway, knowing her.

I allowed a feeling of pride to start washing away my depression over Susie. Perhaps I'd been right about her in the beginning. She'd probably just been using me; found someone who could accept her 'warts and all' just to boost her ego. Now she didn't need me any more. She wasn't worth worrying about. I had more important things to do. I decided to visit Sir Giles.

He did look better. He had his smoking jacket on, kerchief in place, and his hair was well groomed. A magnum of champagne stood in an ice bucket on his locker.

'Doctor Vaughan, how nice to see you! Come and join me in a glass of champagne.'

His glass was already half empty, so I topped it up and poured myself a glass.

'Your good health, Sir Giles,' I toasted, 'but I didn't expect you to be drinking so soon!'

'Well, Doctor Crawley brought it for me. He said I couldn't smoke, but a drop of champagne would probably help my circulation. One can't disobey a doctor's orders, can one?'

I suspected that he had persuaded John into letting him either smoke or drink. I thought John had made a wise choice.

'You're looking better than I expected. It's only 24 hours since your operation.'

'Can't keep a good man down, Doctor. Mustn't let a little operation stop the flow of life.'

Nor the flow of champagne, I thought, as I looked around the room. There were several bouquets of flowers waiting for vases and a large 'get well soon' card, but something was missing.

'I'm surprised that Millie isn't here, Sir Giles.'

'She left an hour ago - went to do some shopping. She has been a great help to me, you know; hardly left my side. A rather exceptional lady, don't you think, Doctor?'

I had to agree with him. I'd never met anyone quite like her and, although I could imagine her becoming exasperating after a time, she was a very endearing woman. I wondered if he had visions of taking her back to his stately home with him. I thought I'd test the water;

'I couldn't agree more with you. It isn't often that I meet a patient like her. You seem to be getting along well together?'

'Hmm, well, we have had some interesting conversations.'

He seemed a little embarrassed as he reached for his cigarettes, which had been removed from his locker by Sally.

'You don't happen to have any cigarettes on you, Doctor?'

'Sorry, Sir Giles, I don't; and you'd better forget the habit if you want to keep your other leg. Stick to the champagne.'

'Yes, of course, you're right, I know; but I've got so used to them over the years.'

Then he added with a resigned smile; 'I don't think Millie approves of smoking either.'

I decided to change the subject; 'When we arrive in Southampton, I'll have to arrange for you to be admitted to hospital. Your leg will need checking up by a specialist and a prosthesis made for you.'

'Of course, a peg leg. Pity you can't fit one on board. Millie's keen on dancing you know.'

'Yes, I do know,' I replied, remembering my promise to her.

'I'm sure you'll be able to dance eventually; not the light fantastic; but at least a slow waltz,' I reassured him.

'Never could do more than that anyway, Doctor Vaughan. Perhaps I could call you Michael now?'

'Yes, of course, but I'd rather stick to "Sir Giles" for you.'

'Then I'll call you Doctor Michael.'

'Agreed.'

'Right then, Doctor Michael, another glass before you leave?'

'A small one, please.'

It wasn't my favourite drink, but it tasted better in good company. He filled my glass; I don't think he understood 'small'.

'Now, a question for you, Doctor Michael,' he said, lifting his glass to me. 'Was this your first amputation?'

He had me there. Somehow I couldn't lie to a man like him; 'I must confess; it was.'

'Then congratulations, Sir!'

He swallowed his glass full as if it were a tot of brandy. I tried my best with mine, then took my leave. I could hear Millie's footsteps approaching.

Talking to Sir Giles had cheered me up a little. I admired his spirit and strength of character. In spite of his weakness for cigarettes and alcohol, he had a firm hold on the joy of life. He'd decided that life would still be fun, even without his leg. Perhaps Millie was part of his inspiration. I could sense a love developing between them and felt envious of it. I'd lost my love and was in danger of giving my heart to a lost cause.

I tried to persuade myself that Susie wasn't worth my efforts; that I'd been grabbed only by a superficial attraction to her. I could do better than that. She didn't want me like Millie wanted Sir Giles. She was attractive enough to find herself an Adonis, like the young American. But she had slept with me; there must have been an attraction. Somehow I must have switched her off. Perhaps it was something simple; I cupped my hand over my mouth and tried sniffing my breath – smelled all right to me.

'Telephone for you, Sir.'

Patrick tried to ignore my sniffing act as he called me into the office; 'It's the Captain.'

I took the phone from him: 'Hello, Doctor Vaughan here.'

'Ah, Doctor. I'm just calling to see how Mrs Franik is today.'

'She seems a lot better, Captain. Drowsy from the "antinuclear pills" but quite calm. I'll be transferring her to a psychiatrist in Southampton.'

'Excellent idea, Doctor. Now, about he other matter we discussed, whilst you were sorting out my little problem - young Barbara Box.'

'Yes, Sir. Is she going to stay on board?'

'Afraid not, Doctor. Outside my hands. Hairdressing manager is dismissing her. It appears that she had not entirely satisfied some of her customers. That's outside my sphere of judgement; don't know too much about hair-styling. Do you?'

'Not much, Captain.'

'I didn't think you would. However, I have made a few enquiries and I'm quite satisfied about her moral character; not that that makes much difference to the situation now, I suppose.'

I thought how disappointed Barbara would be at leaving the ship, but I was curious about the cause of her bad reputation;

'No, Captain, it won't make much difference. She'll be very unhappy about leaving, but thank you for trying.'

'It's my duty, Doctor; to try to avoid injustice on board my vessel. Perhaps you could reassure her that her character has been cleared, by way of consolation.'

'I'd like to do that, Sir.'

'Well. Suffice it to say that her bad name has arisen from an incident with one of the officers on board. Evidently he tried to "get his leg over", if you'll pardon the expression, Doctor.'

I'd not heard the expression before, but the meaning seemed clear enough; 'Yes, I understand your meaning, Captain.'

'Well, I understand that the young lady was not prepared to oblige and he took her refusal rather badly; then spread rumours about her. I don't think he'll behave like that again.'

There was a pause, then he added; 'Before you ask, I doubt whether you've met the officer concerned.'

'Thank you for the trouble you've taken, Captain.'

'No trouble at all, Doctor.'

He rang off.

He had gone to a lot of trouble to investigate Barbara's problem, and I was sure that, in his own way, he'd sorted the matter out. He had told me enough. I didn't need to know any more. What I knew wouldn't help Barbara, but it might be useful to Angus. Perhaps I'd get a chance to talk to him sometime. I thought I understood a bit of Barbara's tantrum now; why she felt everyone was against her, particularly officers. Probably she'd been too afraid to mention the incident the Captain had told me about. I could imagine her being flattered by the attentions of an officer before she fully realized what she was letting herself in for. But she was old enough to know what she was doing.

I couldn't fathom it out and it was not really my problem. She was leaving the ship for reasons outside my control.

Besides, my own emotional disappointment over Susie was pushing out my concern for what happened between her and Angus. I found my mind wandering back to the cause of my failure with Susie. Sitting alone in my little consulting room, surrounded by textbooks on everything from Psychiatry to Tropical Medicine, I didn't have the means to answer my own problem. Nobody had written a book on 'What turns off a woman with blonde hair, long legs, a squint, and other minor problems'. I grabbed a large medical tome and looked up 'Halitosis' - the condition of having bad breath, was all it said - very useful! If I hadn't known that I couldn't have looked it up in the first place. I tried another book - *Common Complaints and their Causes.* Under halitosis it listed 26 causes, including alcohol, cancer of the stomach and eating too fast. I could have had any of the conditions, except cancer of the stomach - I was putting on weight, not losing it.

I tried sniffing my breath again, this time using both hands cupped over my mouth and nose, trying to keep my fingers together.

'Are you busy at the moment, Doctor?'

I'd been too preoccupied trying to make an airtight cup with my hands to notice Janet's arrival.

'God! Is there no privacy in this place!' I yelled at her.

'Sorry, Doctor. I didn't mean to disturb you!'

She was trying, unsuccessfully, to look apologetic. Then she added with a suppressed grin; 'Is anything bothering you?'

'No, there isn't anything bothering me. I was just doing some reading.'

She glanced across at the open textbooks, long enough to read the headings; 'Of course, Doctor, you have to keep up to date.'

'All right, Janet, there is something bothering me. Could you tell me if my breath smells?'

'Certainly, Doctor.'

She leant across, with her eyes closed and her nose within sniffing distance of my mouth. After a suitable pause, she gave her verdict;

'I've smelled worse, Doctor; a touch of Dom Perignon perhaps, but good enough for the head chef, who's waiting outside to see you. I don't think he'll notice.'

She was right. I don't think the head chef would have noticed my breath, even had it been stinking of garlic. He was pacing up and down in a very agitated state. Without his tall chef's hat he'd have been considerably shorter than me, but his stocky frame, the firm set of his shoulders and the aggressive look on his face made him look a formidable opponent.

'Would you like to come in?' I asked in an appeasing tone, anticipating trouble.

'Yes, I certainly would. What I have to say can't be said in the doorway!'

I showed him into the consulting room and offered him a seat, which he declined, preferring instead, to place his fists on his hips and glower at me from a standing position. In the tiny office there was no way of escape. I couldn't think of anything I'd done to offend him. I hadn't even met him before.

'Can I help you?' I tried.

'What the bloody hell have you done to my cook?'

'Which cook?' I asked, playing for time as I searched my memory.

'The one you've been bleeding all voyage, of course!'

'You must mean the young lad who volunteered as a blood donor for the emergency this morning.'

I'd forgotten his name.

'That's right, and the rest!'

I didn't know what he was getting at, what 'rest'?

'What exactly is the problem? Is he a bit tired after his donation?'

I remembered then that I'd forgotten to put him off duty for the day.

'Is he a bit tired!' he replied with sarcasm. 'He's falling asleep in't bloody soup. E's got as much life in 'im as a pound of soggy tripe; an 'e don't look much different either!'

His Yorkshire accent was now coming out, as he became more excited. I'd have to retrieve the situation, try to find out what had happened. The two pints of blood I'd taken would have made him tired, but it sounded worse than that.

'What do you mean by "bleeding all voyage", Chef?'

"E was down earlier in't voyage to have blood taken. That's what I mean.'

'I don't think so,' I said.

'I bloody know so!' he replied.

Some mistake must have been made and I'd have to find out what it was. Perhaps John might be able to help.

'Look, Chef, could you wait outside for a moment, while I make some enquiries?'

He didn't look too happy about the idea, but he agreed, reluctantly.

'Right, I will; but don't take too much bloody time. I'm a busy man, you know. Got to finish me bloody boeuf bourguignon!'

With him out of the way, I did some rapid telephoning and eventually found John in the bar with the rubber-tree plant.

'Doctor Crawley speaking.'

'Hi, John, it's Mike. I've got a problem down here. Do you know anything about a cook having blood taken earlier in the voyage?'

He didn't have to think too long; 'Yes, nice young lad from the main galley. Group O negative. Took a pint from him before Sir Giles's operation, just in case he haemorrhaged. Luckily, we didn't need it.'

'Oh God, I've just taken another two pints from him. I didn't know you'd already bled him. He didn't mention it himself and Terry didn't know about it.'

'Well, Terry was busy at the time, so I just got on with it myself. Are you in trouble then?'

'Too damn right, I am; Head Chef's hopping mad with me because his best cook is falling asleep in the soup.'

'Ah well, Mike, I'm sure you'll sort it out. I've every confidence in you.'

'Thanks!' I replied, as I pictured him returning to the rubber-tree

156

plant and his pretty guest from the second-class restaurant.

I called the Chef back into the office; 'It looks like you're right. A mistake has been made. Doctor Crawley had already taken some blood from him for the operation we did yesterday. Could you send the cook down to the hospital so that we can look after him?'

'Too damn right I will. 'E's no bloody good to me as 'e is!'

'I'm very sorry about all this, Chef.' I tried to appease him.

'So you bloody well should be. Th'art nought but a bloody vampire!' He stormed off to his 'bloody boeuf bourguignon'.

Ah well, I thought, *at least I've got a pint of blood in the fridge to give back to the cook, or the waiter, whoever seems most in need of it.*

CHAPTER 11

'STARLIGHT, STARLIGHT - ATLANTA RESTAURANT, ATLANTA RESTAURANT - STARLIGHT, STARLIGHT.'

It took me two seconds to realize that the piercing tannoy announcement was not an advertisement for a new delicacy about to be served in the first-class restaurant.

I grabbed my medical bag and started running, mentally calculating the quickest route up the staggered stairway system. Waiting for elevators was out of the question. If it was a cardiac arrest we'd been called to then seconds counted, as the patient's brain tissue would be dying within three minutes of his heart stopping.

Always assume the worst, and hope for the best, I thought, hoping that my own heart wouldn't stop before I reached my destination: running uphill carrying an emergency bag was beginning to tell on my own untrained physique. My brain should have been calculating what drugs I had in my bag; but I found myself, instead, wondering who had dreamed up 'Starlight' as the call sign for medical emergencies. It has such romantic connotations. What I was about to face was likely to be as far removed from romance as a rotting kipper was from a bouquet of roses.

I stopped running at the entrance to the restaurant, partly because I had been taught always to instil an atmosphere of calm; but mostly because I was extremely out of breath! The Maître D' met me and guided me with sophisticated speed to the scene of the drama.

'One of the passengers appears to have fainted,' he explained in subdued tones, as we weaved between the tables, avoiding waiters busy serving bowls of soup.

He was doing his best to both expedite medical attention to his customer, and avoid disturbing the sophisticated, calm atmosphere of

158

his restaurant. His efforts at discretion were spoiled by the booming voice of Mr Howard Sinclair Jr.;

'Hey, Doctor, over here, Pa's collapsed!'

Now everybody knew; he was more effective than the tannoy announcement. There was no longer any point in trying to appear calm; I rushed to his table and did indeed find 'Pa' collapsed.

His head was slumped forward onto his chest and his arms were hanging limply. His face was very pale and there was no sign of breathing. I was the first of the medical team to arrive on the scene, but the medical student from my table had beaten me to it. He'd loosened Pa's collar and was feeling for his pulse.

'I sure am pleased you've arrived, Doctor. I can't find his pulse. What do you think?'

'Forget his pulse! Let's get him on the deck,' I ordered.

With the help of his strong arms I soon had the patient laid out flat. If his heart was still beating, the blood would now have a chance to reach his brain. I searched for the carotid pulse in his neck - nothing. No blood going anywhere. His heart had stopped.

'Quick, let's get his coat off and tear the shirt open,' I yelled at the medical student.

Passengers were beginning to gather around us. Food had temporarily been forgotten.

Sinclair Junior was kneeling by my side: 'How is Pa, Doctor?' he asked in an unusually quiet voice.

'Don't know yet, Howard,' I replied, 'but if you want to help, get rid of the onlookers.'

He stood upright and used his booming voice to full effect: 'Right, all you folks, get back to your tables, and your eating. Doctor and Pa cain't breath properly with you all crowding them out!'

They all obeyed him.

Pa wasn't breathing at all.

'What do you do now?' asked the worried looking medical student.

'Mouth to mouth, and cardiac massage. We'll start with the mouth to mouth.'

He instantly put his mouth over Pa's and started blowing.

'No good like that,' I said, pushing him out of the way, 'we've got to get his teeth out first and then stretch his neck back.'

I dug out his false teeth and then tilted his head backwards so that his neck stretched out in a straight line to take any kinks out of his airway.

'Watch me carefully,' I instructed my helper.

I pinched Pa's nose, placed my mouth over his, then blew, watching to see if his chest rose up. It did. Now another two breaths to get more oxygen into his lungs. I then handed the head end over to the student; 'Do the same as I did, when I tell you.'

Now to the chest. Place the heel of my hand over the lower part of his breast bone, then press. Chest very brittle from old age. Must press harder to squeeze blood out of his heart. A bit harder - crack! Damn, his ribs have broken! Never mind, ribs will heal later. Keep heart pumping. Count, one and two - press, three and four - press ... Five presses done.

'OK, now blow. Keep his neck stretched, make sure his chest rises.'

He was a good student. The chest rose well. There were no gurgling noises from the stomach, which told me that all the air was going down the correct tube. Now, continue the heart massage. Five more presses, then another mouth to mouth. Setting a rhythm now.

'Feel for his carotid pulse while I'm pressing.'

The student's fingers searched for the carotid pulse in exactly the right spot in the neck. He must have been reading his textbooks already. His face lit up; 'I can feel it!' he shouted excitedly.

'OK, get on with the mouth to mouth.'

I thought we might be getting somewhere, the heart massage was getting his blood flowing towards his brain, but I was becoming exhausted with the non-stop procedure. With relief I saw Terry and Sally arrive, carrying the ECG monitor and defibrillator.

'Sally, take over from me.'

She moved into my place, taking up the regular heart massage. The medical student now had his routine well practised and matched his actions to her rhythm, as he had to mine. I set up the ECG and prepared the defibrillator, with Terry.

'Stop massage, let's see if anything's happening.'

I watched the ECG monitor - nothing. His heart hadn't started beating on its own yet.

'Carry on, I'll put up a drip.'

I found a vein in Pa's arm, but it was a long time before enough blood came around his circulation to fill it up. After an age it filled enough to enable me to puncture it and set up a drip line. Terry read my thoughts and handed me a bag of bicarbonate solution to feed into Pa's body. This would correct the chemical imbalance that would have developed whilst his circulation had been stopped.

I looked around me. Most of the diners were now engrossed in their meals again, only a few giving occasional glances to the drama. Sinclair Junior and his mother, Mary Lou, were kneeling nearby, helpless, and clearly desperate to see signs of life develop in Sinclair Senior. I could sense Mary Lou's fear that she might have lost her lifelong feuding partner. Sally's small body was rocking rhythmically from her knees, as she regularly transferred her weight down through her straightened arms, onto Pa's chest. Her determined look was willing life back into the patient, almost commanding it.

'His chest feels rather "crunchy", Doctor,' she said, looking at me.

'Couldn't be helped, Sister, his ribs were too brittle.'

The medical student was emptying his lungs into the patient, with enthusiasm. I knew from the zeal showing on his face that his heart was rejoicing at being able to help save a life, for the first time – I had felt the same on the first occasion it had happened to me.

I was thinking how slender were the chances of resuscitating such an old man, with his worn-out heart. I'd been down this path before, desperately trying to save the unsaveable. Yet, somehow I felt different this time. There was so much will-power surrounding him, like a tangible force, willing life into him. Sinclair Jr. now had his hands together in prayer, asking for help in his quieter voice. In the distance I could hear the hum of normal lunchtime chatter resuming, even the occasional burst of laughter from the far corner of the room. It felt like we were a little island of sadness in a sea of festivity.

I filled two syringes, one with lignocaine, the other with adrenaline, and placed them down in readiness; 'Right, stop massaging, Sally. Let's look again.'

We watched the heart monitor. A straight white line was all that showed on the little screen. I was about to tell Sally to restart massaging, when a blip appeared, then another, the beautiful little double spiked blip of the normal heart beat. They were coming faster now, 30 per

161

minute, 60 per minute,- 90, 130 - too damn fast! Then they stopped and were replaced by a series of large, ugly, jagged spikes. Ugly and deadly; 'He's fibrillating!'

Ventricular fibrillation; the heart wasn't beating now; it was a quivering lump of twitching muscle fibres, none or them working together;

'Terry, the defibrillator, quick!'

He already had the little machine in readiness, fully charged up. He handed me the two paddles, each consisting of a flat circular metal plate mounted on plastic handles, insulated to prevent the large voltage passing into the operator, as well as the patient. I placed one over the front of Pa's chest, the other over the left side.

'Everybody stand clear - don't touch him.'

I was particularly concerned that the medical student, not familiar with the routine, might find himself flung across the room.

Now, press the two buttons simultaneously. Seventy joules of electricity entered Pa's chest. His body arched, then relaxed. I watched the monitor - damn, still fibrillating.

'Turn it up to 100, Terry.'

He already had.

'Right, everybody stand aside.'

Press the buttons again; 100 joules entered his body and he arched up, more violently this time, then slumped. Now remove the paddles and watch.

Everyone's eyes were now on the monitor, like waiting for a TV programme to start. The jagged lines were gone, just one straight line - back to nothing again! Wait a bit longer; give it time. It started; one beautiful, normal blip, then another, two in a row, then a pause, another two in a row, then they came regularly, evenly spaced. After a full minute the beats were still regular. The electricity had worked; had bullied the heart muscle fibres into working together, in harmony. I took a deep breath, we all did. Everybody had been holding their breath, waiting. We'd succeeded; so far at least!

I injected the lignocaine into the drip line, this would calm the heart muscle; stop it fibrillating again - I hoped.

Mary Lou and Sinclair Jr. were still glued to the monitor, watching it as if it were the last episode of *Dallas*.

162

'Is Pa all right now, Doctor?' asked Sinclair Jr.

'Not out of the woods yet, Howard, but his heart's beating again. It's a start.'

He put his hands together again, and turned his attention away from the monitor, towards heaven; 'Thank you, dear Jesus,' he said.

Mary Lou was more down to earth. She kissed Pa on the lips, then whispered in his ear: 'Howard Sinclair, you old fool! You almost spoiled a good meal.'

The tears ran down her cheeks.

* * * * * * * * * * * * * * *

We transferred Sinclair Senior to the hospital on a stretcher. He would have to be kept under close observation with the cardiac monitor attached to his chest for the rest of the voyage. There was no telling if he would survive, but every hour that passed made the possibility more likely. The medical student came with us to help.

'Do you think he'll survive, Doctor?' he asked.

'He's got a chance, not a big one, but he'd have had no chance at all if you hadn't been on the scene to help me.'

'Do you really think so?'

He was blushing a little. I liked the way his feelings showed so easily. He was still too young to have learned to camouflage them.

'Certain of it,' I said, 'I couldn't have done both jobs myself.'

That was not strictly true. I could have alternated between massaging the heart and doing the mouth to mouth. But it would have been very exhausting and I doubted if it would have been as successful as our joint operation.

'But I didn't know anything!' he protested.

'You do now, you learnt damn fast.'

He was now smiling and blushing at the same time. I thought I'd test him out; 'I'm now going to ask you the same question you asked me, at dinner yesterday.'

'What was that?' he asked, clearly puzzled.

'Have you any doubts about wanting to be a doctor?'

'None at all,' he responded instantly, 'not now! None at all.'

'Good,' I replied.

When I'd finished checking over Sinclair Senior and discussed with Sally how we'd deal with any setback in his condition, I made my way to the bridge. I wanted to collect a walkie-talkie hand-set, so that I could be contacted instantly if anything went wrong with my new patient. I'd rather avoid any unnecessary 'Starlight' announcements. Besides, I wondered if the tannoy system was totally effective, and whether it reached all corners of the ship. John, I'd noticed, had not arrived at the dining-room emergency. Yet, I had no doubt that he would have been there if he had heard it.

Perhaps 'rubber-tree plants' are an effective sound barrier, I thought, wryly.

Thinking of 'Starlight' reminded me of the previous evening on deck, when I'd met Susie, It had been a lovely sky. Perhaps I should have studied the stars whilst waiting for her, instead of the depths of the ocean. Pondering on the unknown horrors of the dark depths beneath the ship had depressed me, made me think of death and its dreadful finality and, of course, Alice.

'I will lift up mine eyes unto the hills, from whence cometh my help,' the psalmist had said.

Perhaps he should have said, 'I will lift up mine eyes unto the stars ...' I thought, it would have been more appropriate. But maybe the Israelites were too short-sighted to see the stars?

Now, it occurred to me, *I'm beginning to think like Millie!*

But my mind had drifted onto religion, and I recalled my early student days; sitting talking into the night over a few beers, with my friends. In those days we were split fifty:fifty between those who believed in God, and those who were downright atheists or agnostics.

'Where's the evidence for a God?' one of my friends had said. 'You're born, with luck you have a bit of fun, then you die. Dead bodies look pretty lifeless to me.'

I'd had a firm grounding in religion and I believed in God at that time, but I couldn't answer him. As our medical student and early doctoring years went by, the percentage of agnostics and atheists amongst us grew. Facing the hard realities of death and disease had eventually pulled me into that percentage of doubters.

'It's all down to science and technique,' I'd eventually decided. 'Give the right drugs to the right patients and they'll live; otherwise their "mortal coils" will perish.'

Well, nothing had happened since those days to change my view. Like most people I could pay lip-service to a 'god', a useful concept; part of the social cement for civilization. But as for miracles? I'd not seen any.

However, I'd had an uneasy feeling during the drama in the restaurant. Whilst I'd been busy pounding on Pa's chest, injecting drugs, trying to save the unsaveable; Howard Junior, that huge, but straightforward farmer from Texas, had been on his knees with his hands together in prayer, totally unafraid and unabashed in that sophisticated restaurant.

Well, Sinclair Senior had survived, so far; against the odds. It didn't prove anything, but it had been a disturbing experience, nonetheless.

My thoughts had occupied me for the entire time it took to reach the bridge. Pete was alone there, drawing lines on charts, tapping his foot, and singing to himself.

'She was only sixteen, only sixteen,
With eyes that could glow-ow-ow.
She was too young, to fall in love,
And I was too young to know.'

His gravelly voice would not have got him very far in show-business, but it seemed to entertain him.

I coughed; 'Anyone in?' I tried.

He looked up; 'Sorry, Doc, didn't see you there, I was absorbed in my charts.'

'And a sixteen-year-old girl?' I asked.

He looked puzzled; 'What girl?'

He obviously hadn't heard himself singing, which was just as well!

'Never mind, it's not important. I've come to borrow a walkie-talkie.'

He looked askance at me.

'Don't know about that, Doc. Precious things, walkie-talkies; we've only got one spare.'

'Well, I'd look after it, Pete.'

'I'm not so sure about that,' he replied. 'Careless buggers, doctors are. Couple of voyages back I lent one to John. He left it in a bar in San

Juan! The "Spics" are probably still listening in to us.'

'Shouldn't do much harm, Pete ... as long as you don't sing over it!'

His puzzled look returned. Clearly he was totally oblivious to his pastime. He shrugged; 'Anyway, why do you need a walkie-talkie? What's wrong with the tannoy system?'

'I've got a serious case in the hospital, so I need to be instantly available. I'm not too happy with the tannoy, John didn't hear the "Starlight" announcement.'

'That's funny,' he said, 'I was just thinking about John.'

I hazarded a guess; 'And his young girlfriend?'

He looked at me; 'How'd you know that?'

'Pure intuition, Pete. Pure intuition.'

He shrugged again; 'OK, I'll lend you the walkie-talkie, as you're a friend, but if you lose it, I'll log you!'

He handed one to me.

'I'll guard it like the crown jewels,' I reassured him.

'You better had! I'll have it back from you when I've sorted out the tannoy system. I can't understand why John didn't hear the announcement. Where was he?'

'I don't know, haven't seen him yet.'

'Well, he should have heard it. Crew announcements go through all the working areas and public rooms. Only area we don't send them through is passenger cabins.'

We both realized the significance of his last statement at the same instant. We looked at each other.

'Passenger cabins ...' he repeated slowly.

'I don't think so,' I said in reply to his unspoken conclusion. 'John wouldn't dare, she's too young.'

'Don't you believe it,' he said. 'Pure illusion, Doc. It's the way she dresses. I've studied her closely, and she's nearer to 23 than 20.'

'That surprises me. You don't think she's sixteen then?'

'Never said I did! Did I?' he replied, puzzled again.

'No, I don't suppose you did, come to think about it. Anyway, see you around, Pete. Thanks for the walkie-talkie.'

I left, humming to myself.

* * * * * * * * * * * * *

166

I returned to the hospital to make another check on Sinclair Senior. *En route* I thought about John's little escapade. His private life was his own affair, but I'd make sure he knew about the vagaries of the tannoy system; in a subtle way, of course.

In the hospital Mr Sinclair didn't look too bad at all. He was breathing normally, colour had returned to his face, and he was conscious; 'What am I doing in this place, young man?' he demanded.

Perhaps he didn't know what had happened to him yet.

'Well, Mr Sinclair, your heart stopped beating while you were having lunch. I had to start it up again. You were very ill for a time.'

'I know all that already, Mary-Lou told me. That ain't no reason to be lying down here now, missing the cruise!'

Mary Lou was sitting alongside him, holding his hand, trying to calm him; 'Now, Howard, you behave yourself. Doctor knows what's best for you.'

She was behaving more gently towards him now. She hadn't called him 'old fool'.

'Well, if he knows so much, ask him why my ribs is aching so.'

'You can ask him yourself. You've got a tongue in your head,' she replied tersely.

I didn't need the question repeated. I explained to him what had happened. 'I had to massage your heart, Mr Sinclair, by pressing on your chest. I think one of your ribs cracked.'

That was an understatement. I reckoned I'd cracked four or five.

'Well, that was damn careless, young man, ain't you got no respect for elderly folk?'

I was less amazed by his aggressive words than I was by his ability to talk at all. At best, I'd expected him to be flat out and barely conscious of his surroundings. I decided to try to win him over; 'I really am sorry about your ribs, Mr Sinclair, but I couldn't help it. If I hadn't pressed so hard on your chest, your heart wouldn't have started beating again.'

He thought about this for a few moments before replying; 'Well, maybe you're right, and maybe you ain't. I cain't hardly argue with you, not having your kinda learning. Anyway, why've you got me all trussed up like this, with all these wires and contraptions?'

Mary Lou was beginning to lose patience with him: 'Howard Sinclair!

You ain't got no cause to be talkin' to the doctor like that. I saw him with my own eyes, working mighty hard on you, and you came to life, jus' when I'd given you up for dead. Like a rooster you were; ready for the pot. Now just you listen to the doctor, an' do exactly what he says!'

She gave me a nod; her permission to give instructions to her petulant husband. He looked slightly subdued. He'd lost this round on points, if not a knockout. I followed through, taking advantage of his temporary defeat; 'Your wife's right. You are lucky to be alive. I want you to stay in hospital until I am sure you've recovered. You have had a sort of heart attack, and the wires and contraptions are there for your own good. They'll help your heart to recover.'

'I suppose I don't have much choice,' he replied grudgingly.

Then, as if in order to avoid complete defeat, he added; 'But no monkey business. Don't you go experimentin' on me with any fancy new English drugs!'

I reassured him that I wouldn't experiment on him, then left, whilst the going was good.

After arranging with Sally to give him a sedative and a pain-killer, I tried to decide what to do. It was time to eat, but the episode in the restaurant had removed my appetite. Besides which, my stomach was still screwed up over Susie. Enough excitement had occurred to push her from my mind, but she wouldn't go away - damn her!

You're no better than a lovesick youth, I thought. *Get a grip on yourself.*

It was no good. I could no more banish her from my mind, than I could eat a six-course meal, in my present state. I would have to tackle the problem; face her out; ask her what she thought she was up to, ignoring me after our night of passion. I'd show her she couldn't treat me like that. Just let her try ignoring me again.

I worked myself up into a fine state of righteous indignation. I'd find her somewhere. She must have finished lunch by now; was probably organizing a passenger bridge tournament, or somesuch; if she'd finished playing deck tennis with the young American - the Adonis - that narcissistic heap of muscle! Well, muscle wasn't everything, I'd show them; I'd go into battle.

'Stiffen up the sinews, summon up the blood. Assume the aspect of a tiger.'

That's how Shakespeare had advised on going into battle. If it was

168

good enough for Shakespeare, it was good enough for me.

With that thought I assumed the aspect of a tiger and set off, with determined stride. Up the stairways, heading for a full frontal assault on the public rooms. That's where I'd find her.

I found her all right. More specifically I ran into her as I made a sharp left turn at the top of 'C' stairway.

'Oh, hello Michael. Fancy meeting you here! What are you up to?'

'Well, er... As it happens I was looking for... well, nothing in particular; just taking a walk. Felt I needed the exercise.'

'That will be good for your health. Don't let me keep you.'

She started to walk away.

'Susie, hang on a second.'

She stopped and turned to me. 'Yes, Michael?'

'Could I meet you, after dinner, tonight?'

'Sorry Michael, I've got a lot to do this evening.'

She walked away, leaving me standing at the top of 'C' stairway, wondering which way to walk now; and also wondering what had happened to the 'aspect of the tiger'.

I made two quick decisions; one, to find a drink, as soon as possible; and two, to stop reading Shakespeare.

At least she didn't call me 'Doctor Michael', I thought, as I headed back to the hospital to collect my walkie-talkie, which I'd forgotten to pick up in my state of agitation.

I found it quickly, clipped it to my trouser belt and set off on my urgent quest for a drink. I'd not reached the top of the first flight of stairs before a voice, and a hand grasping my arm, stopped my rapid progress.

'Och, Doctor, you're in a dreadful hurry!'

I turned around, angry at this interruption to my urgent journey. It was Angus.

'What do you want, Angus. I'm very busy,' I barked.

'Well, I can see that, Doctor Vaughan! I've been running to catch up with you. I wanted to invite you for a drink with me, in the Pig, like I promised. But I can see you're in none too good a humour!'

I felt instantly sorry that I'd snapped at him. I was angry with Susie, not him; 'I'm sorry, Angus. I didn't mean to be abrupt. It's just that something important is on my mind, something I'd rather not put off.'

I noticed that he had removed the dressings from his burns, and his skin now looked quite healthy and normal, apart from the vivid pink areas where the skin was still regenerating on the left side of his face. Disappointment was showing on both sides of his face.

'Aye, of course, Doctor,' he replied. 'I understand if you've important business to attend to; but it is rather a special occasion for me and I really wanted you to be there.'

I could feel myself weakening. My 'important business' was, after all, only to down a glass of ale, and he was inviting me to just such an opportunity. I'd rather drink alone in my present mood and I wasn't sure if my company would be an asset to his special occasion, but I could try; 'All right Angus, just a quick one then.'

'Thank you, Doctor. You can have as many quick ones as you wish.'

I did an about-turn, and together we headed for the Pig.

It was not an elegant route we followed. In contrast to the opulent decor of the passenger areas of the ship, the grimy working alleyway, with lengths of steel pipe to step over, and oil patches to avoid, did not foster a feeling of festivity. The banging and drilling noises echoing off the steel bulkheads could not compete with the soft music that pervaded the public rooms. Nor did the oil and dust fumes have the same sensual effect as the perfume fragrance that drifted off the elegant ladies upstairs. This was 'below deck'; the area where almost as many souls toiled to maintain the upstairs opulence, as there were passengers to enjoy that opulence. It was not, however, a depressing atmosphere, in this 'bowels' section of the ship. For the most part, the grimy faces that we passed were cheerful, and it was possible, even during the short journey, to detect an atmosphere of companionship.

At the end of the working alleyway we passed through a steel door into the crew living quarters. Here we weaved our way through narrow alleyways, past closely-packed crew cabins. The linoleum floor-covering was pattered with oily bootprints. These prints varied only in size, the patterns being identical from the standard issue safety-footwear. I soon became completely disorientated by the frequent changes of direction needed to negotiate our way through this honeycomb. I was certain that I'd not be able to find my way back alone.

'Here we are then, Doctor. We've arrived,' said Angus.

He pulled open a door, indicating with his head, as his injured arm was still in a sling, that I should enter first.

In contrast to the spartan atmosphere of the cabin area, the room I was about to enter revealed no signs of austerity. Fully carpeted, with thickly upholstered chairs and couches, indirect lighting, neat little table lamps, and velvet curtains framing the small portholes, it could be criticized as being a bit 'over the top' in its plushness. But it was clearly the pride and joy of its inhabitants; their haven, their escape from their barren work-place. I noticed that the dozen or so crew already drinking there were smartly dressed, with no sign of a boiler suit amongst them.

As the room was situated near to the engine compartment, there was a background noise of machinery and the room juddered at regular intervals, each time the after end of the ship, and its propellers, rose above the waves, that I'd noticed had been building up again. Those waves could be seen passing the portholes, which were almost at sea-level.

The machinery noises might have been irritating, had not Rod Stewart been doing his best to cover them up, singing 'We are sailing, We are sailing...' The stereo system was going full blast, so I had difficulty in hearing Angus.

'Don't just stand there, Doctor. Come in and have a drink.'

We walked across to the bar which had obviously had the same amount of devotion given to it as the rest of the room. I couldn't stop myself fingering the fine veneer of the thick mahogany bar counter, as I had a passion for wood; 'Nice, ain't it, Doc?' shouted the bartender, clearly used to raising his voice above Rod Stewart's.

'No doubt about that,' I replied, 'it must have cost a packet.'

'Rescued from one of our older ships, before it was scrapped. There's a fair bit of history in this piece of timber. It used to be in one of the first-class bars. A lot of aristocratic elbows have leant on that! Anyhow, Sir, what do you fancy? This drink's on the house, seeing as it's your first visit.'

'I think the doctor would like a wee dram, Fred.' Angus interjected, '... but none of your sassenach rubbish! A pure malt is what he needs.'

The barman offered me a wide choice of malts from his extremely well-stocked spirits shelves. I chose a Glenfiddich, which I was familiar with.

171

'Not a bad choice, Doctor Vaughan, for a sassenach that is. There's better, mind you, for those in the know.'

Angus gave me a brief wink, before adding; 'I'll have the same, Fred, to keep the doctor company.'

When our 'wee drams' were placed in front of us, I realized that 'wee' could not strictly be interpreted as meaning 'small'. We both added a touch of water to the sacred golden liquid, and Angus raised his glass;

'To your exceedingly good health, Sir.'

'And to yours, Angus, and whatever your special occasion is.'

The malt whisky had a penetrating effect as we confirmed our toast. I was beginning to feel pleased that I'd accepted Angus's invitation after all. I felt surrounded by a warm and cosy atmosphere, and even Rod Stewart's rendition sounded in keeping, particularly as the ship was beginning to move about a little, making his words seem even more appropriate.

'You'll no doubt be anxious to know what my special occasion is, Doctor?'

'Yes, of course I am, Angus.'

I had been rather negligent of my host, letting my thoughts drift off. I should have asked him already; 'You're looking very cheerful,' I added, 'is it your birthday by any chance?'

'No, you're way off the mark. It's more in the way of an engagement.'

'Good Heavens, Angus! That's a surprise. Is it the girl back home? Has she had second thoughts and left your brother?'

'Och, no, Doctor! I wouldn'ae take her back now, if she went on her knees to me.'

He was breaking back into his dialect as he became excited.

'Then tell me, for God's sake, Angus! No, let me guess. It's Barbara Box, isn't it?'

'Well guessed! We're not exactly engaged, mind you, but we could be moving that way. She's got to leave the ship, as you probably know, and you've put me on long sick leave, so I'm going to move in with her and her parents; for the time being at least. See where it goes from there, eh?'

He gave me another brief wink.

'I'm very pleased for you both, Angus. Let's toast the occasion.'

He took another swift swig of his malt.

'But isn't there something missing; where's Barbara?'

172

'Och, she'll be along directly. She's no doubt putting the finishing touches to a platinum blonde. I wanted to have a wee chat with you first, before she arrives.'

'My pleasure, Angus.'

'Right, let's take a seat, behind the pillar. It's quieter there, and more private.'

We prepared to move off to the corner bench seat, but not before Angus had ordered another two malts; 'The last round was on the house,' he said, 'this one's on me.'

Rod Stewart was now singing a quieter number, and it felt more relaxed sitting in the corner, leaning against the padded bulkhead. We were rocking gently now, and I could almost feel the sea as it rushed past, only a few inches away from my back. Angus opened the conversation: 'I understand that Barbara's been to see you, Doctor?'

'That's rather confidential, Angus.'

'Aye, I know that, but she told me about her consultation with you.'

I wondered if she had told him everything; whether she'd mentioned how she'd stormed out after our first meeting.

'What I'm really worried about,' he added, 'is this reputation she's stuck with.'

'Ah, well, I can reassure you about that Angus ...'

He interrupted; 'It's not reassurance I'm seeking, Doctor. I don't believe the rumours about her. I've been at sea long enough to know how these things start.'

He took a sip of his malt, then added; 'In any case, it wouldn'a make any difference if she had been playing around. She's a fine lass at heart.'

I was a bit surprised at his last remark, as he'd been so upset about his girlfriend's philandering back in Scotland. My surprise must have shown on my face.

'You don't believe me, Doctor? Well, consider Mary Magdalene; she was a wee bit generous with her favours, but she turned out a good'un in the end; at least that's what the Bible would have us believe.'

Now he was surprising me. That had not been his response to his Scottish girlfriend. I recalled him calling her 'a whore', or some such.

'You didn't feel that way about your girl back home, Angus.'

He took another sip or his drink whilst thinking; 'That was different: that was downright betrayal, going off with my brother like that. You'd

173

no be forgiving Judas, would you?'

He had a point, though I was a bit bemused by his moral code. Whatever, it clearly suited him to think this way.

'I see what you're getting at, but if that's the way you feel about Barbara, why are you so concerned about her reputation?'

'It's no my concern, Doctor, it's hers. She's convinced I'm only being nice to her when I tell her I don't believe any of the scandal being spread about. She seems to think that because I'm religious, she'd no be good enough for me.'

'Well, you are going to live with her Angus. Time should sort that little problem out.'

'We'll no be "living together" in that sense. I'll be a lodger, so to speak; at first, anyway.'

I thought about the information that the Captain had entrusted to me, about the cause for the rumours.

'Look, Angus, if it's any use, I happen to know how the rumours started; they were completely unjustified.'

He looked at me; 'Are you sure about that?'

'Certain of it! I got the information from the highest authority.'

Thinking about the implications of the incident told to me by the Captain, I decided not to disclose the details; 'I'm not in a position to tell you any more though, Angus.'

He nodded; 'I understand that, Doctor, but it would help if you could let Barbara know that she's in the clear. I think she has a high regard for you.'

Remembering her little tantrum in my consulting room, I didn't feel that her regard for me could be that high, so I doubted if my words would have much influence on her.

'All right, Angus, I'll try.'

His face lit up, until I added; 'But I really don't think it will make much difference.'

His face dropped again; 'Och, Doctor, you're a real Job's comfort!'

Yet another biblical reference; I couldn't let it pass; 'You do seem to have a religious turn of phrase, Angus?'

'So I should have,' he replied, 'I studied theology for two years in Edinburgh before my Dad died. Had to give it up then, to look after my mother. Maybe I'll take it up again someday.'

174

Now I understood how the grimy little mechanic I'd first met in my consulting room could be so eloquent about his despair. I looked at him more closely. His hands were rough and cracked from constant manual work; even after two days away from work the oil had not completely left the cracks in his skin, nor the edges of his cuticles. But his face had a directness about it and a firm, almost aggressive, sincerity showed in his eyes. I could just imagine him, cleaned up a bit, standing in a pulpit, giving stick to his congregation.

'I think you should go back to it, Angus. I reckon you could put the fear of God into a few backsliders!'

'Perhaps I'll do that, eventually.'

'Then let's drink to it, Angus.'

The malt slipped easily down our throats, and I was now well aware of its warming glow inside. Angus's attention was diverted; I noticed then that Barbara had entered the Pig.

He stood up; 'Come over and meet her, Doctor,' he said as he nudged my ribs. Then whispered, 'Don't forget your promise, will you?'

Barbara had changed a little. She still looked bouncy and provocative, but far less of her thighs were visible, and the signs of make-up on her face were very discreet.

Perhaps Millie has been talking to her, I thought.

The bar had filled up a bit now, and I noticed that it was not only Angus who was interested in her. A number of men were giving only half their attention to their beer mugs. The rumours about her did not appear to have disturbed their baser instincts too much.

Angus introduced us; 'You've met Barbara before of course, Doctor; in a different setting.'

'Yes, but it's nicer meeting in a social way,' I replied.

Barbara was blushing a little, no doubt remembering the details of our previous encounters. She managed, eventually, to respond: 'You look less, sort of, official, with a drink in your hand.'

'Well, only part of me is a doctor, Barbara, and I'm not here officially, but to celebrate your special occasion.'

She moved closer to Angus, putting an arm around his waist; 'Yes,' she replied, 'Angus and me are getting together, not officially; but he's coming to live with me and me Mum, during his sick leave anyway.'

She turned to Angus, having said enough to me; 'Hey, what about

175

my drink, Angus? You've got a head start on me.'

'Gin and tonic for the lady, Fred,' Angus yelled over the counter.

We settled into a mundane conversation about the weather outside and the music inside. Barbara gradually relaxed over her gin and tonic and, after five minutes or so, seemed more comfortable in my company. Angus nudged me in the ribs, surreptitiously, then addressed Barbara; 'There's a pal of mine over in the corner, I need to talk to. You don't mind if I leave you in the doctor's company for a few minutes, do you?'

'All right, Angus,' she agreed nervously, 'but don't leave me too long. I know what you're like when you get talking.'

'I promise I won't be long, Barbara. You don't mind looking after Barbara for a few minutes do you, Doctor?'

He nudged me in the ribs again; 'Not at all. That's fine Angus.'

My ribs were beginning to hurt. I'd got his message. He was giving me the opportunity to talk to Barbara alone.

'Well, Barbara,' I said after he'd left, 'can I get you another drink?'

'No thank you. I get giggly with more than one.'

'You and Angus seem to be getting on very well together,' I mentioned as an opener.

'Oh yes, we are,' she replied, then, with a slightly sad look, added; 'but I don't know how far it will go.'

'What do you mean?'

'Well, I can't see us getting married, or anything, not with him wanting to be a church minister, and me with my reputation.'

This was my opportunity. 'I don't think you need to worry about that. That's all been cleared up now.'

'You're just trying to cheer me up, Doctor. Nothing's changed.'

'Oh yes it has,' I replied firmly, 'I have it on the highest authority that your name has been cleared.'

'What "highest authority"?'

'The Captain's.'

'Oh!' she exclaimed, putting her hand to her mouth. 'You haven't spoken to him, have you?'

'I certainly have. After our last little talk I made it my business to enquire into what was happening. The Captain then made a full investigation, and told me, in complete confidence, of course, about a certain incident with an officer, which led to these nasty rumours about you.'

'Oh no!' she exclaimed again. 'He didn't go into all the details, did he?'

'No,' I reassured her, 'just enough to convince me that you'd been unjustly maligned.'

She looked a bit relieved now, as she dropped her hand from her face. Then she frowned a little; 'That's all very well, but Angus doesn't know this.'

'Yes he does, I've told him.'

'Not all the details!'

'No, just enough to convince him.'

She was smiling now; 'Tell me, how did he react?'

'He was over the moon,' I said, 'over the moon.'

'Oh, I'm so happy, Doctor, so happy!'

She flung her arms around me and kissed me, full on the lips.

It was quite a long kiss, and I could feel her breasts pressing against my chest. The relaxing effect of the malt whisky was allowing me to appreciate exactly how bouncy her breasts were.

A thought occurred to me, just a fleeting thought; *I wonder what did happen between her and that officer the Captain told me about?*

Then my thoughts really shamed me; *Perhaps she is, after all, a Mary Magdalene? I'll never know. Anyway, what the hell does it matter? As long as they're happy.*

I eased her body away from me. From the corner of my eye, I could see Angus returning.

CHAPTER 12

My session with Angus and Barbara in The Pig had cheered me up considerably. I felt really pleased for them. In an odd way, they had the makings of a good partnership; a mutual dependency. His rather serious and solid nature would be well balanced by her bounciness. I wondered what sort of theologian's wife she would make, as I felt certain that Angus would eventually return to his studies. In a way I also felt envious.

Thou shalt not covet thy neighbour's wife, I thought, catching onto Angus's biblical habit; but it wasn't her that I coveted, just their new-found happiness. I wondered if Susie and I could ever achieve such happiness? Then I dismissed the thought as being utterly ridiculous. I had known her for such a short time and what I had learned of her nature completely baffled me. It would be better for me, I decided, to seek happiness in my work, for the time being at least, and to forget any notions of a permanent relationship with that infuriating female.

I had eventually found my way back from The Pig, through the maze of the crew cabin area, mainly by following the oily footprints. Opening the door onto the working alleyway, the din that greeted me disturbed my meditative mood. I checked my watch, still an hour left to myself before evening passenger surgery; time enough to find some solace in the sun, if there was any left. Next I checked my trouser belt; the 'precious' walkie-talkie was still securely fastened there. *Lose that, and I've lost a friend!* I thought.

There was still some sun left on the open decks, though it was partly occluded by a patch of thin cloud. The ship was not rolling, but very gently pitching from end to end. Not enough to have sent too many of the sunbathers indoors, but enough to cause the water in the swimming pool to slop around a lot.

I could not feel the wind that was causing the sea waves and

178

calculated that the ship must be moving in the same direction, at the same speed as the wind, which would cancel it out. *Pure nautical mathematics; I'll soon be a proper sailor!* I thought, feeling rather proud of myself.

I found a spare deck-chair and settled down to enjoy the warmth, and amuse myself watching the swimmers being thrown around in the pool. It looked rather fun, if you didn't mind being smashed against the edge occasionally.

I noticed a large lady hauling herself out of the pool, taking advantage of the tidal flow to assist her exit. The assistance proved to be greater than she expected, so that she landed belly-down on the surrounding deck, like a stranded whale. However, it did not take her too long to recover her poise and stand upright and I could now recognize her as Miss Myers. A small part of her anatomy had been coaxed into a brief bikini which, in its present soggy state, appeared to be reluctant to provide even a modicum of modesty. But she seemed happy enough and there was definitely a voluptuousness about her large proportions. As she pushed her dripping hair back from her eyes, she spotted me; 'Hi, Doctor! Mind if I join you?'

She didn't wait for my reply, but walked over and pulled up a spare deck-chair.

'It's fantastic fun in that pool,' she said as she shook the water from her hair.

I didn't mind too much getting wet, as I was planning to change my shirt in any case. I guessed that she might have picked up the shaking technique for drying from little Pepe.

'Be my guest,' I said, encouraging her to join me.

'I haven't had such fun in years!' she enthused. 'Why aren't you in the pool, Doctor?'

I didn't like to tell her that I'd just discovered an easier way to get wet.

'I haven't plucked up courage yet; perhaps I'll try it tomorrow.'

'Could be too rough tomorrow,' she pointed out, 'it's bad enough in there today.'

We both looked at the pool, watching the waves swish the swimmers from end to end.

'Tell me,' she asked, 'what kind of water is it in the pool?'

179

'Just sea water,' I replied, 'sucked up by a pipe, I think.'

'Ah, well, that explains it!'

'Explains what?'

'That explains why the pool is so full of waves, of course.'

I had to think for a moment; about what she meant;

'You're absolutely right!' I said.

Then, to give her the full benefit of my nautical expertise, I added; 'Especially the Atlantic water, the Atlantic is so rough.'

She looked at me with an expression of respect; 'Gee, you must get to learn an awful lot, working on a ship all the time?'

'Oh, yes, I do,' I assured her, then quickly changed the subject before her questions became too searching.

'Tell me, Miss Myers, how is little Pepe coming along? I haven't had a chance to visit him since this morning.'

'Oh, he's fine, Doctor; thanks to you. He's eating absolutely everything now, and hasn't thrown up at all.'

'I'm very pleased,' I replied, 'it sounds like he's completely cured, but get him checked out by the vet when you get home, just in case; in the meantime go easy on his heart tablets - only one per day. He might have been sensitive to them.'

'I'll do that, Doctor, but I'll have to find a vet in England, because I'm staying over for a time.'

'That shouldn't be a problem,' I assured her, 'but Pepe will have to go into quarantine during your stay. It's the law.'

'I know that,' she said, 'and I'm going to miss him a lot, but I'll have Julian to keep me company. He'll be on leave and he's promised to show me around the country.'

That was a turn-up for the books. She'd clearly worked pretty fast on Julian. I assumed his problem with the Chief Officer would now be resolved; 'Well, I hope you have a lovely holiday together, Miss Myers. Can I assume that you have sorted out the problem over the accident in the restaurant?'

'You certainly can, Doctor. After talking to Julian I went straight to the Captain on the bridge and told him that it had all be a mistake; that Julian hadn't burnt my fanny on purpose.'

I could just imagine the Captain's face as he received this information. 'What did he say?' I asked.

'Well, I'm not sure he knew anything about it, but he said something like; "He was extremely pleased to hear my information, that it had considerably brightened his day, and that he would pass it onto his Chief Officer at his earliest opportunity." He also said that he hoped the area concerned would heal up as rapidly as possible.

'He was really formal, and a bit strict-looking, but very nice. I could have fallen for him if I hadn't already met Julian.'

That's the Captain, I thought. *I wonder if I dare tell him about his latest fan.*

Then I remembered her travelling companion, the 'friend' who had caused all the trouble; 'What's going to happen to your friend,' I asked, 'while you're touring England with Julian?'

'Oh, I sorted her out!' she replied, emphatically.

'I'm very curious to know,' I mentioned.

'Well, I bought a packet of drawing pins, and put one of them on her chair at lunch-time. You should have seen her jump. Spilled her soup everywhere! She was furious; said she didn't think much of me as a friend. I said "Please yourself" and she got up and left. Suits me fine.'

All's fair in love and war, I thought.

* *

After Miss Myers had dripped off to her cabin, I realized that there was insufficient time left to take a nap in the sun, so I looked around for any other source of entertainment.

On the other side of the deck, in the shade, I spotted an unexpected small group of people. Sir Giles, sitting in a wheelchair with his shortened leg resting on a frame support, was accompanied by Millie, sitting next to him, holding his hand, and Patrick, standing to one side, with one hand on the wheelchair and the other holding a glass of liquid. Most of his attention was on the ice bucket, containing the magnum of champagne, as it appeared to be sliding on the table surface with the pitching of the ship. I walked over to speak to them.

'Ah, Doctor Michael; would you care to join the party? Pull up a seat and join us in a glass of champagne.'

I pulled up a chair, but declined the drink; Angus's malt whisky was still floating around my circulation;

'Thank you, Sir Giles, but I'll pass on the drink; I have to keep my head clear for evening surgery.'

'I understand, old chap,' he replied. 'Can't have a drunken doctor killing off passengers. Bad for the image!'

'This is an unexpected gathering,' I commented. 'A bit adventurous, you coming out on deck so early after your operation!'

'Life's too short to waste a sunny day, Doctor. I had to work hard on Doctor John though. He eventually agreed to let me out, provided Patrick stayed with me to guard the wheelchair and make sure I didn't get up to any mischief. He's doing a pretty good job too; aren't you, Patrick?'

'Ah well, Sir Giles, I always take my job seriously,' Patrick replied, as he seriously topped up his glass, after filling the others.

'Millie thought the sun would do me good, didn't you Dear?'

'Of course I did, Honey. I couldn't leave you lying around in that stuffy hospital forever!'

I could tell that their relationship had progressed somewhat, but their terms of endearment seemed oddly mixed, and I wondered how 'honey' would sound in his stately home.

'Do you have any plans for when we arrive in England?' I ventured. 'After the leg has been fixed up, of course.'

I felt I knew them well enough now to ask this question, but had forgotten Patrick standing behind us.

Sir Giles turned to him; 'Patrick, be a good chap and fetch another bottle of champagne. Doctor Michael can hang on to the wheelchair while you're gone.'

With Patrick out of the way, he leant over towards me in a confidential manner, taking hold of Millie's hand; 'Confidentially, between you and me, old chap, Millie and I have decided to take things a bit seriously.'

Millie smiled at me to confirm his words. He continued; 'Now I know we've only just met, and you might think me an old fool ...'

'Not at all,' I protested.

'Never mind being polite, Doctor; my son, Rodney, thinks I'm a fool; and we all know, "there's no fool like an old fool". However, Millie is something special, and when one gets to my age, one doesn't know now much longer one has got! We haven't got time to "umm and aar" and think about things too much. Decisions, Doctor Michael,

182

decisions! That's what built the Empire! What think you, Millie?'

'Oh Sweetie, who could disagree with a man like you?'

Well, that seemed to have been decided. I was surrounded by romance: Angus and Barbara; Julian and Miss Myers; and now Sir Giles and Millie.

What's wrong with me? I thought. Then, remembering the occasion, said; 'I will accept a small glass, Sir Giles.'

He poured some champagne and I raised my glass to them; 'To you both - many congratulations,' I toasted.

'And to you, for getting us together,' added Millie.

This was the most unusual conclusion to a gangrenous leg and a case of atrial fibrillation that I had ever come across!

CHAPTER 13

'You're not your usual, diligent self this afternoon, Doctor Vaughan.'

Janet was sitting on the edge of my desk as she said this, perusing the notes I had just completed on the first half-dozen patients I'd seen. She was probably right about me not being very enthusiastic. I would rather have been making little snoring noises in my cabin than talking to the rather tedious set of patients that had so far turned up to afternoon surgery. Janet had sensed this and we'd decided to have a short break before the next patient.

'Sorry, Janet, just feeling a bit sleepy. I'll try to show more enthusiasm for the rest.'

'You're managing all right with the patients, Doctor; it's your notes that worry me.'

'What's wrong with them?'

'Well, they're a bit brief, aren't they?'

I took some of them from her and glanced at them. They looked all right to me. I could recall easily from the few scribbled lines on each what had happened with the patient referred to.

'They might be brief, Janet, but they tell me all I need to know,' I commented.

'They might be good enough for your practice in England, Doctor, but they really aren't good enough when you're at sea. Most of these patients are Americans; they occasionally have a nasty habit of suing doctors when things go wrong; even when it's not your fault sometimes, unless you can prove otherwise.'

'You're getting very stuffy with me today, Janet.'

'Just warning you, for your own good. Imagine that you are in a court of law in Houston, Texas.'

She jumped down from her perched position on my desk and started pacing the small consulting room. Putting her hands behind her back, holding her head up in an arrogant manner, and thrusting her well-endowed chest forward, she said;

'I am the prosecuting attorney. Now tell me, Doctor Vaughan, exactly what did you find wrong with my client, your patient that is, on the afternoon in question?'

'Stop mucking about, Janet, there's work to be done.'

'Doctor Vaughan! That is no way to conduct yourself in a court of law,' she admonished me sternly.

She was a good actress, I had to admit.

'All right, Janet, if it makes you happy, carry on. Which patient are you talking about?'

'This patient,' she said, picking up one of the sets of notes from the pile, '... perhaps your notes will help you to refresh your memory.'

I looked at the set she had chosen; the third patient I had seen. A cough, she'd had. She'd been in every day of the voyage so far, with something or the other; always trivial complaints.

'Could you explain to the jury what was wrong with the patient?' Janet proceeded.

'Tickly cough,' I replied.

'Ah yes, Doctor, a potentially serious problem I think you would agree?'

'Not really, Janet. You know damn well that she's neurotic. You mention a symptom and she's got it!'

'This is a court of law, Doctor Vaughan!' she admonished me again.

My God, I thought, *this girl's missed her vocation. She should be on the stage somewhere, rather than pestering me.*

She continued;

'Now, kindly explain to me what you've written on the next line, here. This O/E - what does that mean?'

'On examination, of course!' I was getting exasperated with her now.

'And alongside it, Doctor? B.A. - what does B.A. mean in medical terms?'

'You know damn well what it means!'

'Please explain it to the court,' she insisted with a sweeping gesture.

'It means "Bugger All", you know that.'

'I see, "Bugger All" - some typically English medical expression I take it?'

'It means, Janet,' I replied, getting more exasperated, '... that on clinical examination I could find no significant abnormality.'

'I see. I'm sure that the jury will understand that. Now, on the next line, this little triangular sign. Explain to the court what that stands for.'

'That stands for diagnosis.'

'And alongside it? Those letters - G.O.K. - can you please tell us what that stands for?'

'Come off it, Janet, you must know what that means.'

'No. Please explain it to the jury.'

'It means "God Only Knows".'

She paused dramatically to absorb this information;

'Then may I summarize, Doctor. You examined the patient; found "Bugger All", and diagnosed "God Only Knows", for which condition you treated her with antiseptic lozenges?'

'That is correct,' I agreed, willing now to agree to anything to get her little performance over with.

She stood upright and turned to her imaginary jury;

'I put it to you,' she said, her hands tucked in imaginary waistcoat pockets, 'that this doctor is not only lazy and incompetent, but grossly negligent. My patient is dying, only 5 years after this examination, of cancer of the lung. He should be found guilty.'

She paused and then added;

'But if you cannot find him guilty on this charge, then you must surely find him guilty on an even more serious charge.'

'OK, what's that then, Janet?'

'His breath smells!'

'Janet, I'll kill you.'

She neatly ducked away and left the room to find the next patient before I could throttle her. I sat down to start correcting my notes.

* * * * * * * * * * * * * * *

The next patient could not in any way be considered as trivial. I wouldn't have dared. Indeed she did not, at first, present herself as a patient, but as the Senior Nursing Sister, calling in to discuss an important professional matter.

'Could you wait outside for a few minutes, Janet?' Sally said as she entered the office. 'I have something to discuss with Doctor Vaughan.'

Janet demurred to her senior, without question, and left us alone. I had a sneaky suspicion that Sally had turned up to give me another of her caustic lectures. Probably she'd discovered the same brevity in my notes that Janet had so dramatically brought to my attention.

'If you're concerned about my notes, Sister, Janet has already mentioned them, and I am at this very moment in the process of putting the matter to rights.'

'No, Doctor Vaughan, that is not the reason for my visit; but as you mention it, I had planned to discuss them with you sometime. I've come about a more personal matter, though.'

'Really, Sister?' I raised my eyebrows.

'Yes, I want your opinion, as a doctor.'

This was surprising. It is easy to forget that even colleagues can be patients sometimes. It was also a relief that I was not in for a session of criticism.

'Then fire away, Sister.'

She evidently didn't like the tone of my voice;

'I hope you're going to be sympathetic,' she said.

'Of course,' I replied, trying to adopt the same attitude I would apply to an 'ordinary' patient.

'Well, Doctor, I have some chest pain.'

Her sharp little features looked anxious. Across her forehead, which at her age should still have been smooth, were thin, but definite worry lines. Her eyes were not sparkling as they usually were, even in moments of aggression. Her right hand was placed across the left side of her chest, indicating exactly the area of the pain.

'Are you thinking you're having a heart attack, Sister?'

'I don't know, that's why I've come to see you!' she replied tersely.

She seemed to hate having to admit to a degree of failure; failure at not having more insight into her own condition. She was rightly proud of herself. She had a degree of competence and knowledge that would have shown up many doctors. I remembered from my own periods of hypochondria how terrifying medical insight can be, when applied to one's own symptoms. I decided to try to be a little kinder;

'Sorry, Sally, it's taking me time to get used to you as a patient. You must be worried, I'd better examine you.'

She stood up, walked to the examination couch and sat on the very edge of it.

'You've never called me Sally before, Dr Vaughan.'

She was right, I hadn't: but I noticed that she still called me 'Doctor Vaughan'.

'Well, you're a patient now, Sister. Perhaps you had better take something off, if I'm going to examine you.'

She quickly unbuttoned her uniform dress, slid it off and placed it very neatly over the end of the couch; then she resumed her sitting position, looking slightly embarrassed in just her waist slip and bra.

'I think we'll need your bra off as well, Sister.'

'Is that absolutely necessary, Doctor Vaughan?' she replied, knowing, of course, that it was.

'I wouldn't want you accusing me of being any less than thorough in my examination, Sister.'

She got the point. We were still fencing.

'Exactly, Doctor!' she admitted as she unclipped the article, removed it rapidly and threw it on top of her dress.

Because she was a respected colleague, and a patient, I did not of course notice how attractive her breasts looked on her slender rib cage; but confined myself to professional observations. She was sitting very straight, her spine was firm and my fingers could detect a rigidity in the slender but firm neck muscles that held her head erect. Using my stethoscope I could find no abnormality of her heart, except that it was beating a little too hard and fast, probably because she was anxious. Next I pressed my fingers between her ribs.

'Ouch!' was all she said.

'That's all right, Sister, you can get dressed again now. There's no problem.'

'What about an ECG, Doctor?'

'Can do, if you really want one,' I replied, 'but it's not necessary. The diagnosis is obvious.'

'And what might that be, Doctor?' she responded, clipping her bra back in place.

'Muscle spasm. Pure muscle spasm between your ribs. Very common condition, you know, and I haven't known anyone die of it, yet!'

'And do you have any learned insight into what is causing this so-called muscle spasm?'

I didn't think she believed me completely; scepticism was evident in both her eyes and her voice.

'Tension, Sister; maybe you are a little anxious about something?'

She had buttoned up her dress now, and had sat herself back down in the patient's chair.

'Are you suggesting that I'm a "nut-case", Doctor?' she replied indignantly.

'Not at all,' I hastened to reassure her, 'but you are a bit "All work and no play" at the moment. Not much relaxation in your life, is there?'

I was hoping that this comment would give her the opportunity to open up a bit about the personal problem that John had mentioned, and Millie had enlarged upon;

'That's none of your business, Doctor!' she replied, as if she had been reading my thoughts.

'Of course it isn't, Sister.'

'Right, I'll go. You're sure I'll live, are you?'

'Certain of it, Sister.'

'Fine. I'll see you tomorrow then; at the hospital meeting.'

She stood up and walked out of the office, pausing at the door only to say;

'Prompt, of course.'

CHAPTER 14

Back in the hospital, I was pleased to find that Mr Sinclair Sr. was in a stable condition. The cardiac monitor showed that his heart was beating in a normal sinus rhythm. The regular double-peaked waves on the little 'television screen' were now providing boring viewing, with not a flicker of deviation from the normal. *Sometimes*, I thought, *boredom is very reassuring.*

From the chart clipped to his bed, I found that his blood pressure was remaining within the standard range for a man of his age, and his respiration rate was only a little faster than could be expected. With cracked ribs, I reasoned, he's bound to breathe more shallowly because of the pain, so he'll need to breathe faster to keep up his oxygen supply. It was a strange feeling, that I'd had to break the poor old man's ribs to keep him alive, and I hoped that one day he'd appreciate that I hadn't done it through carelessness. I recalled Janet's lecture and made a mental note to enter all the details in the file, just in case he decided to sue me; in Houston, Texas.

Because of the pain from his cracked ribs, he'd been sedated quite heavily, was sleeping soundly, and was in no position to ask questions of me. Not so his son, Howard Sinclair Jr., who had taken over from Mary Lou as ever-vigilant bedside companion.

'What do you think of Pa now, Doctor?' he asked as he stood up to greet me.

'I'm feeling more optimistic now, Howard,' I replied, keeping my hands firmly in my pockets, to avoid any temptation to shake his hand, 'but he's by no means out of the woods yet. At his age, and with his past history, he could have another heart attack at any time.'

'Oh, I really hope not, Doctor. Don't know what I'd do without him. Apart from loving the old varmint, I wouldn't know how to run the farm if he wasn't there.'

'You can only pray for him, Howard.'

'I'll do just that,' he replied, '... it always helps.'

'Yes, I know what you mean,' I responded, remembering my feeling of an uncanny force during the restaurant drama.

'I'd like to thank you for what you did for Pa, Doctor. I was mighty impressed by how you brought him back to life. You've got a very good team as well. I noticed how efficient that pretty little nurse was. She didn't let up once, pumping his chest, 'spite of her tiny frame. Fair sweatin' she was, but she didn't let up!'

'You must mean Sister Sally Scott,' I informed him.

His face dropped a little; 'Did you say "Sister" Sally, Doctor?'

'Yes, that's what I said, Howard.'

'Does that mean she's some kinda nun?'

I realized that I must have stumbled into some sort of language problem; 'Don't you call Senior Nurses "Sister" back home, Howard?'

He thought for a moment before replying; 'Only if they're nuns, or very closely related, Doctor!'

I felt it was my duty to explain the situation in England; 'All Senior Nurses are called "Sister" in England. It dates from way back, when nurses were mostly from religious orders. It hasn't been that way for many years though.'

He looked happier after absorbing that information; 'I'm mighty relieved to hear that, Doctor. Truth is I've been looking for a wife, and that pretty little gal looks just right for me. Bit small for farming, mind you, but Ma ain't too big and she's managed all right. That Sister Scott looks like she's got a lot of spunk - suit me just fine. She ain't married is she?'

I was a bit taken aback at this forthright declaration. He'd come to a very rapid conclusion about Sally's suitability as a wife. He clearly prided himself on his ability to make quick decisions about such matters, probably almost as much as his ability to choose a worthy head of cattle at market! I also felt unexpectedly protective towards Sally. I didn't like to think of her tiny frame being "bear-hugged" by this massive Texan.

'No, Howard,' I replied, 'she isn't married, but I'm not really sure if she's in a position to consider an offer at the present time. There could well be a man in her life already.'

'Don't look like it to me, Doctor,' he replied. 'Too many worry lines on that pretty little face. I bet you, as much as you like, there ain't no man making her happy at present!'

'I can't really confirm one way or the other, Howard. We have a purely professional relationship.'

'I understand, Doctor. Can't expect you to know everything; but maybe you could arrange an appointment for me to meet the young lady?'

I could just imagine Sally's reaction to that suggestion, but I didn't want to offend him; 'I can't promise anything, Howard, but I'll see what I can do.'

'Gee, thank you, Doctor. Let's shake on it.'

Too late I remembered my vow to avoid his handshake. I was now doubly in trouble; my knuckles were bruised and I'd agreed to a task I had neither the inclination, nor the bravery, to undertake.

* * * * * * * * * * * * * * * *

I met John in the treatment room.

'How's the heart attack you admitted, Mike?' he asked. 'I didn't hear anything about it until just now.'

Not surprising, I thought to myself, wondering whether to mention the vagaries of the tannoy system to him yet.

'He's not too bad, considering,' I replied. 'It's a bit of a miracle he survived really.'

'Yes, Terry was telling me about it. It was lucky you got to him so quickly. I'm just admitting another heart case myself; not as bad as yours, but she'll need close observation, so I'm putting her in the same ward as your Mr Sinclair. They can both be observed together then.'

'We'll soon have an intensive-care ward set up,' I replied. 'It's beginning to feel more like working in a general hospital than a general practice.'

'Don't say I didn't warn you, Mike. I told you that it wasn't all beer and skittles at sea!'

He was beginning to resume his arrogant attitude again. His comment was innocent enough, but his tone of voice was meant to impress his seniority on me. It was unnecessary; I respected him anyway, for his experience and skills.

'Yes, John, I'm beginning to appreciate what you said now: but I've noticed that there is time for "beer and skittles" occasionally.'

I must have been smiling as I spoke because his slightly quizzical expression suggested that he thought my remark could be more than a passing comment; but he only seemed to half-suspect that I might be getting at him. He shook off his quizzical expression, with a sniff; 'Tell you what, Mike, let's have a drink together sometime; get to know each other better. We haven't had much opportunity so far.'

'I'd like that,' I replied, honestly, 'see you around later then?'

I left him to get on with his work, but not before adding; 'Almost forgot to tell you, John, I discovered something important today.'

'What's that?'

'Well, when you didn't turn up to the "Starlight" call in the Atlanta, I checked on the tannoy system. Did you know that Starlight calls didn't go through the passenger cabins?'

'Oh,' he replied, allowing himself half a smile, 'I'd better look into that! Thanks for the information.'

'My pleasure, John.'

* * * * * * * * * * * * * *

After leaving John, I bumped into Sally - literally. She was walking as quickly as myself when our paths met at the cross-alleyway junction.

'Doctor Vaughan,' she scolded me, 'do be careful of my chest!'

'Sorry, Sister, I wasn't looking where I was going.'

Suddenly I remembered my message for her, and thought I might as well strike while the iron was hot; 'Actually, it's lucky I bumped into you: I've a message for you. Howard Sinclair Jr. would like to meet you.'

I walked quickly away, leaving her standing there.

'Is that all?' she shouted after me. 'No details?'

'Sorry, Sister, can't stop to chat now. I'm in a hurry.'

I headed rapidly for my cabin. I'd kept my promise; delivered my message from Howard Sinclair Junior, Texan farmer, looking for a wife.

* * * * * * * * * * * * * *

193

Back in the security of my cabin, I drew a long bath and added the remaining bubble-bath mixture. I wanted to relax, to let the day's events percolate through my brain. Whilst undressing, I checked that the walkie-talkie was still clipped to my belt. The responsibility for this 'precious' item was beginning to nag at me.

Lying in the bath I promised myself to buy another bottle of the bubble mixture. I was becoming addicted to its perfume and the caressing sensation of the bubbles. It was not, however, producing the same sensual affect on my body as it had on the previous occasion. Thinking of Susie was now having a negative effect that the bubbles were unable to counteract. I wondered why I'd become so obsessed with her. It was really too early for me to be looking for a replacement for Alice. On many occasions I'd advised patients in their bereaved state to be patient with themselves, to allow time for their emotions to recover an even keel.

'You might make a bad mistake if you jump into a new relationship too quickly,' I'd advised them.

Where was all my wisdom now? Blown away, with the first breeze of romance!

Yet romance was all around me, blossoming rapidly, like plants in a greenhouse. I decided that perhaps there was some 'passion catalyst' in a cruise ship. Perhaps it was the drinking water, or maybe the champagne. Even Millie and Sir Giles, with all their years of accumulated wisdom, had fallen very quickly in love.

Well, I'm not going to fall into the same trap, I thought to myself. *I'll fight this 'passion catalyst', whatever it is. Susie is a pipe dream. I'll concentrate on doctoring; there's enough excitement there for the time being.*

With that firm resolution I stood up, stepped out of the bath, and started drying myself.

'Heard you had an exciting day, Doc?' Gwilym shouted above the vacuum cleaner.

'Can't hear you properly above that racket, Gwilym! Either switch it off, or wait till you've finished.'

He switched it off. I suspected that his heart wasn't really in the job.

'Maître D' told me about your drama in the restaurant. He said he was very impressed!'

'I just hope it doesn't happen too often, Gwilym. I'm not sure I can cope with too much excitement like that.'

'Oh, that sort of thing happens a lot at sea, Doc. You'll need to keep fit; not too many late nights,' he added, granting me the wisdom acquired from his many years of looking after doctors.

'Thanks for the advice, Gwilym! Could you fix me a scotch and water when you've finished vacuuming?'

I preferred to keep him busy, rather than listening to any more of his advice.

'Not too much to drink either, Doc!' He was not to be defeated easily.

I'd now become used to his regular visits, but wondered why he always arrived at just the time I'd planned to spend in a few moments peaceful solitude, before starting the evening's activities. I wondered what he did during the rest of the day.

'Been rushed off my feet today, Doc!' he said, reading my thoughts.

'Really?' I asked, summoning up an interest.

'Yes. Had to help prepare the Captain's private cocktail party. He has one in his cabin every voyage for his favourite passengers; and some of the senior officers, of course.'

That didn't surprise me: keeping regular travellers happy would be an important part of the Captain's job. There wasn't much to comment upon.

'That's interesting, Gwilym. Have you fixed my drink yet?'

He brought it over. 'I expect you'll be invited along; after you've been at sea a few more years.'

There was no reply to that either. He replaced the vacuum cleaner into its cubby-hole.

'Oh, almost forgot. Doc. Got a message for you.'

'From whom, Gwilym? Not the social hostess was it?' I asked hopefully, in spite of my newly-made resolution.

'No, not her; passenger it was. Miss Montrose. She asked if you could meet her in the Midship's Bar for a drink, about seven o'clock.'

'What time is it now?'

He looked at his watch, 'Five past seven, Doc.'

CHAPTER 15

Millie did not appear to be upset by my late arrival. She was absorbed in the large jigsaw puzzle that lay on a table just outside the Midship's Bar. Many of the passengers whiled away a few idle moments, trying to fit it together, but it had, so far, been only half completed.

'Hello, Millie. Sorry I'm late.'

She looked up from the puzzle; 'Nice to see you, Doctor. I hadn't really expected you to be early; I know how busy you are. It was good of you to spare me a few minutes.'

'It's my pleasure to meet you any time,' I replied with not insincere flattery. 'Have you figured out any of the jigsaw yet?'

'Not yet. There are so many pieces. I'm trying to find a piece of England.'

I looked at the puzzle. It consisted of a map, with an area of the Atlantic Ocean and a large chunk of Europe and Britain. The clues to the ocean included mermaids and sea serpents, and to the land, major roads, rivers and cities. She was holding a piece that could have belonged to a part of Britain.

'Are you trying to find the bit where Sir Giles lives?' I asked with a flash of inspiration.

She smiled up at me; 'You're so clever, Doctor! Let's take a seat.'

She took my arm and led me to the table she'd reserved in the bar. 'I've ordered your drink already, Scotch and water isn't it?'

She'd done her homework, she must have asked the stewards what my favourite tipple was. With her kind of mind for detail, she'd make an excellent hostess.

'Yes it is, Millie. I won't ask you how you knew.'

'Not much point, Doctor. I wouldn't tell you. Trade secrets are precious!'

'You'd make a brilliant hostess, Millie.'

196

She looked quite lovely sitting, relaxed but poised, in her chair. Her neat, curly, grey hair and blue eyes were set off well by her tasteful peacock-blue cocktail dress. Her diamond earrings, necklace and brooch looked expensive, but small enough to avoid flamboyance. There was a touch of honeysuckle in the fragrance that drifted from her. Neat and attractive; I thought that she would fit in anywhere. Her sparkle dimmed slightly though as she considered my last comment.

'I've been thinking about that, Doctor. About being a hostess I mean.' She took a sip of her white wine.

'You're probably wondering how you'll fit into Sir Giles's social circle, aren't you?'

'There you go again, being a clever doctor; but you're right. That is exactly what I was wondering. I thought that perhaps I could talk to you about it as you know Sir Giles and myself as well as anyone on board.'

I hadn't expected to become Millie's confidant. She had always seemed on top of everything; always ready with an answer; but I was willing to do my best to help.

'Any specific worries, Millie?'

'Well, my accent, for a start. It sounds so brash against your cultured English voices.'

There was no denying that there was a difference; but I'd been enjoying the novelty of her long drawn-out vowels, and the heavy emphasis on the first syllable of her words, compared to the duller English stressing of the second.

'There are brash examples of any accent, Millie, and yours isn't one of them. You have a lovely Southern voice.'

'Not like them "damn Yankees", you mean, Doc?' she said, doing a parody of the 'movies' American accent.

'You know what I mean.'

'Ah certainly do, Doctor,' she replied, parodying her own accent now.

I couldn't help laughing at her impish sense of humour; 'Seriously, Millie, I don't think it'll be a problem. The Brits can be a bit stiff and starchy to start with, but once they've caught onto a novelty, they become addicted. You'll bowl 'em over, once they've got used to you.'

I hoped I was right, that I wasn't being a bit too generous to my compatriots.

'You surely don't think I'm a "novelty", do you?' she said with mock anger.

'Sorry, perhaps I chose the wrong word. I meant to imply that you are very charming, in a different way, a way they're not used to.'

'Now you're just being diplomatic.'

I wasn't sure whether she was beginning to tease me again; 'It's not diplomacy, Millie, it's the truth.'

'All right, I'll believe you, but there are still all the other things; odd customs and a different way of eating, for a start.'

She had a point there. I'd noticed in the restaurant how my American guests cut their food up first, before discarding the knife and proceeding with the fork alone, in the right hand. Using the British technique of first balancing a little of everything on the slippery side of my fork, before transporting the precarious load to my mouth, made me much slower. Consequently the rest of the table were ready for rapid conversation, whilst I was still eating. Not a major problem, but I could imagine she'd feel as out of place as I did, in the reverse situation.

'Well, you could either brazen it out, Millie, or learn the British technique. It's not that difficult!'

'I know; it's not really the technicalities that bother me. I just don't want to embarrass him, particularly as I don't think that his son, Rodney, approves of me. He's hardly been to visit his father since we've been friendly. I think he might be jealous.'

I could well imagine that Rodney would be jealous; I'd heard no mention of Rodney's wife, so he probably lived with his father. Come to think of it, I'd not met him at all – he was probably busy enjoying himself around the ship. However, living together back in Sir Giles's home would be different; encounters and frictions would be unavoidable. It was likely to be an uphill struggle for Millie, if not for Sir Giles himself, although I suspected that he had the strength of character to overcome most problems and he did not strike me as a snob.

'I think Sir Giles is a law unto himself. He's old enough to know what really matters,' I said.

'I think you're right, Michael. I'll either have to call it off, or take a chance.'

I gathered from the look in her eyes that she'd decided to take the chance.

Millie had not finished her drink; she sipped it very slowly. Mine was almost empty and she had noticed: 'Would you like another drink, Doctor?'

I thought about the ensuing evening ahead, and the lunchtime session I'd already had with Angus, not to mention the champagne up on deck. 'No thank you, Millie, I'll make this one last. Anyway I don't need more alcohol to talk to you.'

'We've talked enough about me; how are you getting on?'

'Pretty well, Millie. Busy, of course.'

'I gather this is your first voyage?'

'Can't deny that, but I had hoped it didn't show.'

'Not at all, you look very professional, except for your bow-tie.' She leant across and straightened it. 'You must have dressed in a mighty hurry! Rushing to meet me, I expect.'

'Of course.'

'Are you meeting any other young ladies tonight? she enquired mischievously.

'I don't think so.'

'That's a shame. What happened to that nice young lady, Susie?'

There was no end to her mine of information; but I wasn't keen to continue with this line of conversation, light-hearted though Millie was making it.

'There isn't much between us, Millie, just a bit of flirtation.'

'Really!' she said, not bothering to hide her disbelief. 'Pity, she seems such a charming young lady.'

You're right off the track there, I thought, *Susie's about as charming as a witch on a broken broomstick, to me at any rate.* Aloud I said, 'She's got her good points, but I'm a bit fussy. I don't think she's quite right for me.'

She raised her eyebrows, and looked straight at me; 'She's turned you down, hasn't she?'

She'd got me. I couldn't easily lie to her; besides, if I had to confide in anybody, I'd rather it were Millie.

'That's not exactly right, Millie. We started off fine, but she's turned awkward. Well, to be precise, she's actually ignoring me. There must be something wrong with me, but I haven't worked it out yet.'

'It's no good feeling sorry for yourself, young man!' she exclaimed.

'Get up and go for it. Talk to her, tackle her right up front.'

'I've tried that, Millie,' I replied, remembering the 'aspect of a tiger' and its downright failure.

She thought for a few moments before responding; 'Then maybe you're looking in the wrong direction. You're thinking about yourself too much; maybe it's more to do with her.'

'Thanks, Millie,' I replied, not quite sure how to take what she'd said, nor how to act upon it.

She stood up; 'Time to visit Giles before dinner. See you tomorrow, Doctor.'

'Yes, good night, Millie.'

* * * * * * * * * * * * * * * * *

Shortly after Millie left the bar I stood up to go, but the bar steward called me over; Telephone for you, Sir. It's Doctor Crawley.'

I took the receiver from him; 'Hi, John, what can I do for you?'

'I just wondered if you could do me a favour?'

'Sure, what is it?'

'Captain's expecting me at his private cocktail party, but I've got something else to do. I wondered if you could stand in for me. He always likes one of the doctors to be present. It should be starting soon.'

'OK, I've nothing else in particular to do.'

'Thanks.'

I paid a brief visit to the 'gents', mainly to make sure that Millie had made a good job of straightening my bow-tie, then set off on the climb to the Captain's cabin. *I must remember to tell Gwilym tomorrow how much I enjoyed the Captain's private function,* I thought as I ascended 'A' stairway.

When I arrived I wondered just how much I was going to enjoy it. Susie was there; no doubt in her official role of hostess. She had not yet started her duties as I had arrived early, and the only passenger who had so far turned up was in deep conversation with the Captain. I'd have to speak to her as she was the only other person in the whole room; I couldn't ignore her.

'Hello, Susie.'

'Michael, I didn't expect to see you here.' She had a neutral, social

200

hostess smile on her face; not a hint of intimacy.

I decided to try to penetrate her refrigerated aura: 'You've been ignoring me today.'

'You haven't got a drink yet, Michael.'

'You're doing it again.'

'What do you want?' she hissed at me, 'a kiss, in front of the Captain?'

'I'd settle for something less passionate; maybe a word of explanation?'

There was a hint of anger showing in her eyes now; 'There's nothing to explain. You don't own me, just because we slept together!'

'Is that all it was, just a one night stand?'

'Keep your voice down, do you want the whole bloody room to hear?'

I looked around; the 'whole room' consisted of the Captain, engrossed in conversation with a middle-aged lady, and an elderly couple who'd just arrived, and were still occupied with ordering their drinks. I didn't have much longer before our social duties would break up our conversation. I turned back to her;

'I just want to know what went wrong; is there something wrong with me? Does my breath smell or something?'

She laughed into her drink; 'Typical bloody male,' she said when she had recovered, 'always thinking of their bodies, their vanity! Do you think I give a damn what your breath smells like, or about your pot belly?'

That, I thought, was hitting below the belt - well, almost; 'Well, you seem to like that young American's body!'

She laughed again; 'If I fancied someone like him, do you really think I'd have slept with you?'

That hurt. I pulled in my stomach and went in for the attack; 'Right,' I snarled, 'what is the matter then?'

'You don't remember, do you?'

'Remember what?'

'Our conversation that night, of course.'

'Yes, I remember, you asked me about Alice, and I answered your question.'

'Answered my question! You spent the whole damn night talking about her. It was dawn before you finished telling me how perfect she was. What a saint she was. Even her name is bloody holy!'

I was taken aback, I hadn't expected such venom; 'That's no way to talk about the dead!'

'Exactly,' she snapped, 'she's dead. You seem to have immortalized her.'

I was angry now, and really felt like giving her a piece of my mind, but the Captain's hand landed on my shoulder;

'Excuse me, Doctor, if you've finished your conversation, I would like you to meet one of my guests.'

'Of course, Captain,' I replied, 'my pleasure.'

I walked away with him, giving only a swift backwards glance. Susie's drink was vanishing rapidly down her throat. *Hope it chokes her,* I thought.

The Captain guided me across his large cabin: 'You'll find this lady extremely interesting, Doctor. Her husband was a naval surgeon and she is very keen to meet you.'

He introduced me to a middle-aged lady who was quite buxom in a sturdy sort of way, rather severely dressed, and authoritative in manner. After fifteen minutes of listening to the life history of her husband, I realized why the Captain had been so anxious to pass her on to me. I tried to show some enthusiasm; 'You and your husband must have had a hard life during the War?'

'Good Heavens, young man, I'm not that old!'

I made a quick mental calculation; 'Of course not, how stupid of me. I must have miscalculated the dates. You can't possibly remember the war, you can't be older than fifty.'

That produced a smile, as she preened herself a little; 'Well you're not far out, Doctor.'

Only ten years or so, I thought.

'Mind you,' she added, 'we haven't had an easy life.' Then she whispered into my ear; 'I had a breast removed, ten years ago; they only gave me three years to live, but I've beaten them.'

Back to medicine, I thought, *this always happens at parties.* Then I remembered Susie's similar problem. I wondered how many years they'd given her, whether she was worried about the growth recurring in her other breast, or somewhere else. Of course she would be worried. I'd been a complete idiot, totally forgetting this aspect of her; worrying too much about what my own inadequacies might be. All I'd done that night was talk about Alice. Fat lot of use I was to someone with worries of her own.

'Excuse me, Doctor, have I said something to upset you? You look rather dismayed.'

My distracted thoughts must have shown. The Naval Surgeon's wife seemed genuinely concerned that she might have upset me.

'Of course not,' I hastened to reassure her, 'it was just that you reminded me of another problem I have to deal with. It's been so nice talking to you, but I'm afraid I must leave now.'

I found Susie in the corner of the room, doing her duties; as usual the life and soul of the group she was talking to. If she is worried, I thought, she's doing an excellent job of covering it up.

I put my hand on her shoulder to gain her attention; 'Excuse me a moment, Susie, can I interrupt for a second?'

'What do you want, Michael?' she spoke in a softer voice.

'Just a chance to talk to you quietly, later.'

She paused before replying; 'I'd rather think things over, Michael, if you don't mind.'

Enough said, there was no point in pushing it; 'OK, Susie, see you around.'

I left her and delved into the nearest group of passengers to talk, talk about anything, to keep my mind occupied.

* * * * * * * * * * * * * * * * *

During dinner that evening I was not feeling pleased with myself, and my appetite could not do justice to the fine meal. Luckily the medical student, and his father, kept me occupied in conversation.

'My son was delighted to be able to help you with the emergency today, Doctor.'

'It was lucky he was there,' I replied, 'he was a great help, and very efficient. I think he'll make a good doctor if he keeps on like that.'

'Don't praise him too much, Doctor; his head's big enough already!'

This was the first time that his sister had spoken, apart from a few syllables of greeting. She was glowering at him as she spoke.

'Well, at least I'm doing something, not just sitting around reading romantic trash!' he retorted.

'There's no romance in you! You're just an egghead. Anyway, you only want to be a doctor 'cause the money's good.'

'That's not true! It's a vocation, isn't that right, Doctor?'

I didn't feel in the mood for arbitrating a family dispute, but I was obliged to say something. I compromised; 'You're right, it is a vocation, but at the same time it helps to know that it's well paid.'

'There you are; I told you it was about money. Dad keeps saying how much you're going to be able to earn.'

Her mother could clearly see a big row looming up; 'Be quiet, Honey,' she admonished, 'you're embarrassing the doctor.'

I thought that she was embarrassing her father more than me; his face was flushed, but I felt none too comfortable either.

The scene reminded me too much of my own childhood, when my parents doted on my decision to become a doctor. My sister had been similarly jealous, and even after twenty years my mind still cringed at the memories of those old arguments. It was during a lesson on family psychology at medical school that I had first realized what had been happening in my own childhood, and I'd first started feeling guilty about the way she'd been made to feel inferior by comparison.

Luckily the argument was brought to a halt by the waiter's arrival. He asked for our dessert orders and, without hesitation, the daughter spoke up; 'Can we have a special for all of us please?'

'Certainly, what would you like?'

'Spotted Dick.'

There was no discussion. He took the order and it duly arrived, a heavy suet pudding studded with raisins. She seemed to be much happier during the pudding course, probably because she knew her brother hated it. He grimaced at every mouthful.

'Are you enjoying your spotted dick, Brother?' she asked him, seeming to revel in the crudity of the name.

'Of course, Sister,' he replied with grudging grace.

'I'm so pleased!'

Revenge is sweet; sickly sweet, I thought, as I ploughed through my portion with hardly more enthusiasm than the medical student.

CHAPTER 16

The spotted dick did not sit too easily in my stomach, so I returned to my cabin after dinner for a brandy to help it along. A light sorbet would have been sufficient and it wouldn't have contributed to my pot belly to the same extent.

I had been worrying about this increasing pot above my waistline, but at least I knew that it hadn't been that that had turned off Susie's passion. She'd made it quite plain that it was something more serious. Millie had been correct in saying that I'd been looking in the wrong direction; I'd been quite blind about her. It struck me then that what I could see quite clearly in a patient would completely bypass my brain when it involved someone I felt strongly about. It had been the same with Alice. If a patient had complained of the same symptoms she'd had, I'd have been alerted to the diagnosis immediately. It was an enigma that I hoped one day to resolve. As for the present, I needed some music.

I selected the Brahms' Violin concerto that Susie had declined during our night of passion. It was soothing to start with, but after a time I found myself drifting into a mood of self-pity, as the sickly sweet violin passages descended into deep sadness. I remembered what a sad life Brahms had led, so gifted yet unable to achieve any satisfying human passion in his own life. The brandy, the picture of Alice staring at me from the desk, and Brahms, were too much. I switched it off and headed out to find some company.

The music in the Princess Room was a far cry from Brahms, and the girls dancing to its light hearted and sexy rhythm were a pleasant antidote to my gloomy mood. I selected a seat near the back of the room and watched the show.

There was plenty to feast the eye upon. The girls bedecked with sequined costumes, multicoloured plumed head-dresses and provocative feathered tails meandered around the dance floor. They were all of the same height and it was difficult to choose who had the best pair of legs. I'd almost decided, when they reached their finale by forming a sensual corridor leading to the stage, preparing the entrance for the celebrity singer.

He looked like a younger version of Tom Jones, complete with medallion on bronzed, hairy chest. His singing soon settled everyone into a romantic mood and I noticed with envy couples edging closer together. The drinks were being discretely topped up or replaced by wine stewards, and the air of contented relaxation was almost tangible. Sitting back and idly watching a show was something I hadn't indulged in for a long time and if only there were someone sitting beside me, Susie perhaps, my feeling of contentment would have been complete. I had a sneaky feeling of guilt at being cossetted in such luxurious surroundings, but I didn't let it bother me too much.

On the singer's departure the lights brightened and the mood was broken by the arrival of the comedian. 'Aha! Caught you at it, have I? I've never seen so much blatant sexual behaviour going on in all my life. Well, you can all move back to your wives and husbands now. We've got to the serious part of the show!'

For twenty minutes his soft Irish voice bantered and teased the audience, and I rediscovered the meaning of belly laughter. Being entertained by an artist in the flesh, rather than on television, was a refreshing experience and I could happily have listened to him for twice as long. However, when he left the stage the mood changed once again.

The stage spotlights vanished and the overhead lighting dimmed into a subtle mixture of pinks, reds and a hint of blue, bathing the room in a soft, warming glow. From theatre, the room had changed into a nightclub. Covered by the background hum of quiet conversation, the band moved surreptitiously on stage. A chord of music was struck and, after an expectant pause, the maestro himself made a well-timed entrance.

Within seconds Joe Loss had commanded complete attention. Short in stature, slim of build, yet his presence was impossible to ignore. Perhaps it was his silver hair and magnetic features that captured everyone's attention. With a few soft words he set the atmosphere:

'Ladies and Gentlemen, it is my honour and privilege to be with you tonight on this magnificent ship. I know that you are going to enjoy yourselves; indeed I insist upon it. I want you all, and I mean everyone, to get up with your partner and make this one of the most memorable evenings of your life.'

With that, he half turned to his band; after a swift, whispered instruction and a nod of encouragement he turned back to the audience. Right hand raised, with just the two outer fingers lifted, he struck up the rhythm. *In the Mood* started.

Unlike any dance I had ever been to the floor was instantly flooded with obedient couples. With a unique magic the rhythm moved into the oldest bones, arthritic hips swayed, gouty feet pranced, and ungainly young couples moved into harmony.

I suddenly remembered Millie and my promise to dance with her, and wondered if I'd now get the opportunity.

'Well, Michael, what are you doing sitting at the back of the room, all by yourself?'

Susie had done it again. When I least expected to see her she turned up. Not just turned up, but sat herself next to me. Within a split second my earlier resolve to forget about her vanished. Her eyes and teasing voice had captured me again. *Why can't you leave me alone to forget about you!* the voice in the back of my head shouted. My voice said; 'I didn't expect to see you so soon.'

'That's because you're a dumb male.'

I wanted to take her hand and kiss her lightly on the lips, but my body wouldn't obey me. Somehow she managed to paralyse me, like a small mammal frozen into inactivity by a snake.

She broke the spell; 'Well, are you just going to sit there by yourself, or are you coming to join the party?'

'What party, Susie?'

'Millie and Sir Giles's engagement party. They decided to have a little get-together to celebrate and they want you to join them.'

She took my hand and we made our way around the edge of the room. I would have liked to pull her onto the dance floor. It was just the right number being played, but she seemed set on joining the party.

We found them in the corner of the room; Sir Giles in a wheelchair with Millie next to him, holding his hand affectionately as ever. They were not alone. I was not surprised to find John and his mystery girlfriend but I was surprised to find Sally, especially as she was sitting very cosily next to her partner - Howard Sinclair Junior, Texan farmer looking for a wife. I stifled my surprise and paid my respects to Millie, kissing her on the proffered cheek.

'So pleased you could join us, Doctor. Now the party's complete.'

'Never mind this kissing business,' said Sir Giles. 'Give the man a drink!'

John did the honours by passing me a glass of champagne and then introduced his girlfriend. Sinclair Junior removed his arm from around Sally's shoulder and shook my hand again, though this time I gave him only three fingers to squeeze.

'Pleased to meet you again, Doctor. Thank you for arranging for me to meet Sally.'

He turned his head to smile at her, perhaps to ensure that she was still there. Sally gave me a noncommittal smile and I wasn't sure whether she was thanking me for the introduction, or secretly cursing me. That Sinclair Junior's arm was around her shoulder didn't prove anything; from her typically rigid position it was not possible to deduce whether his arm was welcome or not. There was, however, no doubt about the degree of affection between Sir Giles and Millie and John and his girlfriend; their body language told the whole story. I sat down next to Susie and secretly prayed that some of the atmosphere of budding romance would float our way.

It certainly felt romantic. Our little gathering seemed to be cocooned and isolated within the pool of soft light cast by the small table-lamp. The glasses of champagne were sparkling almost as much as Millie's eyes, and Susie's perfume was playing little tunes on my senses. Together with the tune from Joe Loss's gentle waltz it was causing me to feel an overwhelming urge to ask her to dance. This was not however to be. It was not Susie that I would be holding in my arms on the dance floor.

It was too soon after my arrival, of course, to leave the party for the dance floor. In any case, Millie was about to make an announcement. She tapped her glass to draw our attention;

'Now that we are altogether, Sir Giles and I want to thank you all for the way you have looked after us, particularly of course for saving our lives, and also to Susie for arranging this little party. You, and fate, have brought us together and even though you may think us to be old fools, we have decided to get "hitched up"! I'm sure that Giles only needs me for a walking stick, but I need him for his old-world charm, and his stock of champagne!'

No one commented on her joke, but Sir Giles made a little cough to cover his emotion, then, with just a hint of moisture in his eyes, responded; 'Yes, that just about sums it up. I hope you will all, one day, be as happy as we are. Now drink up.'

There was a small round of applause. Then the kissing started. Sir Giles seemed to enjoy the attention, even Sally's rather demure kiss on the cheek. Susie's was a full-blown kiss on the lips, which left me feeling rather jealous. Sinclair Junior almost shook his hand off, and Millie was hugged until she had to call it off. 'That's enough of that. I'm too fragile for all this hugging!'

It was a happy occasion, and felt almost like a family party, except that one person was missing; Sir Giles's son, Rodney. When I came to think about it, I hadn't seen him around at all. He'd made his one appearance at the hospital when he'd spoken to Sally, then vanished. Millie had mentioned that he was jealous, but he could have swallowed his pride and made a brief appearance at his father's big occasion. I decided not to mention it, as it didn't seem to bother Sir Giles at all.

Millie, as usual, was using her social talents well, and soon had John's girlfriend talking, sensing that she felt rather out of her depth. John had introduced her to me as 'Mercedes', an unusual choice of name I thought, particularly as she looked nothing like a solidly built German car. She was, in fact, very slim, with a slender neck. Her voice was upper teens, but her face showed her to be in her mid-twenties. She seemed to be doting on John, harking on every word he spoke.

Sinclair Junior appeared to be enjoying the occasion, although he said very little, most of his attention being centred on Sally, but it still wasn't possible to deduce whether she welcomed this attention, perhaps it was growing on her; her posture had become less rigid.

I had little opportunity to speak to Susie. In her social-hostess way she divided her attentions evenly amongst the gathering.

The conversation centred on how Millie was looking forward to living with Sir Giles and how she wanted to explore England with him. She seemed to have lost the doubts that she'd expressed to me earlier, and I decided that if anyone was capable of making a fairy tale come true, it was her. Sir Giles, however, was a little subdued and, although he supported her comments very heartily, he seemed somewhat preoccupied; probably, I thought, he was rather tired. Whatever his preoccupation, whenever he looked at Millie, his adoration was obvious.

I was beginning to lose my aversion to champagne, probably because Sir Giles ordered only the best. We had all developed a little alcoholic glow, and the combined effects of the alcohol, good company, and soft music were making the world feel a wonderful place, at least for the moment. The music had in fact become slightly more than background and I noticed that Millie's feet, in particular, were beating out the rhythm and a faraway look had developed in her eyes. Sir Giles picked it up; 'You'd like to dance, wouldn't you, dear?'

'Oh, no, just enjoying the music, Honey.'

'You can't fool me! I thought that you'd arranged to dance with Dr Vaughan? Now is your opportunity.'

I hadn't forgotten my promise to dance with Millie, but had decided that it was now inappropriate, giving due regard to Sir Giles's feelings, and his one leg.

However, he seemed to have anticipated my reservations;

'Dr Vaughan, I know that Millie is dying to dance, and as a medical man you must realize the difficulty I would have partnering her with only one leg. Would you please do me the honour of accompanying her. It would give me great pleasure to see her enjoying herself.'

In his typically aristocratic manner he had resolved the situation, and in a certain way had issued an order. There was now no alternative. I stood up; 'Millie, would you please do me the honour of dancing with me?'

Millie seemed to appreciate the formality of my words and smiled as she took my arm. 'I thought you'd never ask!'

The moment had been chosen well as a soft, slow waltz was being played. She was remarkably easy to dance with, as if she instinctively knew where my feet would be, so not once did I crush her toes. With amazing suppleness her body swayed and bent in perfect harmony to the music and we even avoided jostling into any of the other dancers now filling the dance floor. Sensing the mood of the crowd, Joe Loss kept the tempo of the music at exactly the right pace as, imperceptibly we were moved from slow to faster waltz, then into slow foxtrot.

This was a dance I had never mastered and yet we were gliding over the floor with not a foot movement out of place. The magic of the music enveloped everyone, with the feet of young and old alike moving with graceful easiness. The soft overhead lighting bathed us all in a warm, flattering glow – eyes sparkled, everyone looked beautiful.

'Heaven, I'm in heaven,
and the fears that mill around me through the week;
seem to vanish like a gambler's lucky streak;
when we're out together dancing cheek to cheek.'

The words of the well-known refrain floated over us. Millie's face was radiant, the years melted away from her with each bar of the music. She was eighteen again; the movement of her limbs proved it, the sparkle in her eyes proved it; her silver hair had become blond in the soft light. Her voice was soft and seductive as she whispered in my ear; 'What do you think of my jazzy heart now, Doctor?'

'I'd really rather not think about it, Millie!'

The tempo of the music changed.

'And now, ladies and gentlemen, for the nimble amongst us, and I'm sure that includes everyone, a favourite number from Fred Astaire – *Putting on the Ritz.*'

I'd watched this dance numerous times in the old movies, and had been very impressed by the athletic footwork, but had never even contemplated trying it at the school dancing lessons. To be honest entering those lessons had merely been an excuse to get a closer insight into the mysteries of the opposite sex. Although some dancing technique must have rubbed off on me, I was not at all happy to attempt this dance for the first time with an elderly lady suffering from atrial fibrillation.

'Perhaps this is the time to take a pause and have a drink, Millie?'

'I didn't think you would tire so easily, Doctor.'

'But this is a really fast one!'

'Are you nervous?'

Too late now anyway; we'd started. Her body bent and weaved with the fast rhythm. My legs followed hers in a complex sequence of footwork, alternating quick as lightning feather steps with slow, gliding movements, sudden halts and rapid changes of direction. A space had gradually cleared around us. I felt a distinct prickling sensation of nervousness coming on. I'd never danced like this! Yet still we performed on, not a false step, nor a break in rhythm, not a hint of breathlessness in Millie.

'That was wonderful,' she whispered as we reached the finale and a round of applause broke out from the other dancers who had stopped dancing to watch. 'I think we could join the others for our drink now, Doctor.'

As we made our way back to our chairs, she took my hand and said; 'You're a very good dancer. You lead beautifully.'

'I rather thought that it was the other way around, Millie!'

'Perhaps, but nobody else needs to know that, do they?'

As we reached our table the others rose; 'Hey, what a performance, you two should become professional!' said Mercedes.

'I'd rather think of it as my wonderful swan-song performance' replied Millie, settling into her chair with the slightest sigh.

'Don't you go talking like that, Dear,' said Sir Giles, 'You've plenty of dancing left in you.'

'Perhaps.'

We all chatted on for a little while before Millie announced that she was rather weary and wanted to retire to bed. I arranged for Patrick to collect Sir Giles and wheel him back to the hospital ward. John and Mercedes offered to walk Millie back to her cabin, overcoming her protestations that she was all right and could manage alone. So after a few more kisses the party broke up.

Millie wished me good night, and added 'Thank you so much for the dance, Doctor.'

'It was my pleasure,' I replied, with feeling.

Following their departure Sinclair Junior lost no time in pulling Sally onto the dance-floor and it was a wondrous sight. Her delicate form dwarfed by his mountainous frame so that her head barely reached his chest. She was having no difficulty matching his footwork; he appeared to be carrying her as he whirled his way, with surprising agility, around the perimeter of the floor. His pathway appeared to clear miraculously.

Susie and I sat and watched them in silence for a little while, before I plucked up the courage to ask her to dance.

'Perhaps we could join them on the dance-floor, Susie?'

212

She paused before replying; 'All right, Michael, but not quite so enthusiastically please.'

It was the nicest end to the evening I could have hoped for, holding her close to me again. The dance had changed into one of those slow smoochy numbers, so that I didn't even have to concentrate on the footwork; just the steering, to ensure that we didn't collide with the Texan farmer and Sally, who seemed to be everywhere. My body was as close to hers as could be managed, with dignity, and I was preparing myself to whisper something suave and romantic into her ear.

'Michael, I hope you don't mind me mentioning it, but there is something sticking into me.'

I was a little surprised, being fairly certain that my romantic mood hadn't progressed quite that far. I eased myself away a little.

'Try your belt!' she hissed, smiling.

I felt around my belt and sure enough, I found the walkie-talkie had moved around so that it was sticking into her abdomen. I eased it to a more comfortable position. 'Sorry about that, Susie, I must remember to return it to Pete. I don't really need it any more.'

'You feel much more comfortable without it,' she reassured me as she cuddled up closer in a very encouraging manner.

We must have danced like that for ten minutes or so, in silence, neither of us wishing to break the mood. I suspect that we both realized that moments like this were too rare to be shattered. It was not until the fast music started that we left the floor, 'I don't feel up to that Fred Astaire stuff,' she said, 'let's sit down.'

We found our seats and tackled the remaining champagne.

'It's time to talk, Susie,' I ventured.

'I know,' she replied. 'It's not very easy, after the harsh things I said to you earlier this evening.'

'Well, perhaps I deserved it?' I wasn't convinced that I did deserve the bluntness of her words, but I was prepared to compromise.

'Well, you are carrying a ghost around with you, and I don't think that it is very good for you.'

'Not for you?'

'That's right. I like you a lot, have done since I met you in the bar, and before you ask I did enjoy the other evening with you. It was afterwards I had my doubts; I can't afford to make any more mistakes.'

She'd lost her harshness now and was again looking vulnerable. Her arms were crossed over her chest and she was huddled forwards.

'I suppose it's going to take time,' I ventured.

'Yes, it is. I'd like to see you again, but take things slowly.'

'I'd like that.'

'So would I,' she said as she kissed me very lightly before leaving.

CHAPTER 17

This was our finest performance.

Ginger and I were moving as weightless heavenly bodies, swirling around the stage, moving from dazzling light-footed quickstep, to graceful long-striding foxtrot, and on to the tango. Ginger's body bent back into a graceful dip before I raised her up to move into yet another dazzling array of turns, my black tails flying out behind me, her sequined skirt swirling and shimmering in the spotlights which followed us around the stage. Five thousand people watched with bated breath, afraid to break the magic of our spectacular display. The final triple turn culminated in our bodies separating out with one hand still firmly held, to take our final bow.

Loud applause and cheering; 'Encore! Encore!'

Bouquets of flowers landed at Ginger's feet.

Pete strode across the stage, smartly dressed in full 'blues' rig; 'Mike, come on, come on . . . you can't stay here any longer, the Captain's furious! Let's get back to the ship – we were due to sail half an hour ago and we can't leave because John's been taken sick. You're the only doctor, for God's sake! Let's go, we're costing the company millions of dollars for every minute we delay!'

'I can't leave now, Pete, the audience is yelling for more.'

'Mike, you'll lose your job if you don't come now!'

Gwilym joined him; 'Brought your uniform, Doc, so you can change in the taxi. Save time, see!'

Ginger, in tears, clutched hold of my arm; 'Please don't go; don't spoil our finest hour!'

'Sorry, Ginger, I must go now; "a man's got to do what a man's got to do"!'

As I strode across the stage, dragging her with me, I ordered Gwilym to find a taxi. Eventually, breaking free of Ginger, I escaped through the stage-door.

Outside the Carnegie Hall the taxi was waiting; 'Where you wanna go?'

I looked at the taxi driver, at his Latin American face with drooping moustachios.

'Oh no! I know you . . . go away, I'll get another taxi!'

'Why you no come with me, eh? I'll tell you more about my brother in England.'

Forget the taxi; start running. Only two miles to the ship. Oh God, I'm lost! High tenement buildings surround me; evil looking characters with knives approach, one grabs me by the arm and starts to shake me.

* * * * * * * * * * * * * * *

'Wake up! Wake up, Doc, hospital's trying to get you.'

'What's the matter, Gwilym; don't stop me now, I'm trying to get back to the ship!'

'Not dreaming is it, Doc? Been ringing you for five minutes the sister has. You must have been out cold!'

I jumped out of bed and grabbed some clothes; 'What did she say? What's the problem?'

'Cabin 3026. Says she needs you there, urgent!'

Pull on shirt and trousers, fix tie on the way. *Cabin 3026*, I thought, *that rings a bell.*

Sally looked up as I entered the cabin; 'You sleep soundly don't you!'

'Over-tired I think, Sister. What's happened?'

'It's too late now, I'm afraid. I tried external massage, and mouth-to-mouth respiration, but it was no good. It was probably a massive heart attack. She'd called the hospital to say that she had a chest pain. I got here within minutes, but she'd gone.'

I looked down at the pale, frail form lying in her nightdress, her slight, 5'1" body barely used up half the bunk. She looked 76 again.

'She was only eighteen the last time I saw her.'

'What *are* you talking about, Doctor!'

'Nothing, Sister,' I replied. 'I'm just going to freshen up, won't be a moment.'

Entering her tiny cabin bathroom I was hit by the lingering smell of the perfume that she had probably applied so carefully earlier this evening. I clutched the edge of the wash-basin, the cold surface echoing my feeling of bleakness. Silence; apart from the irritating hum of the extractor fan, drawing away the last of her fragrance. My knuckles were white from the fierceness of my grip. Looking up, the vanity mirror reflected my sense of guilt directly back into my soul, and the harsh fluorescent light did nothing to soften the blow.

Should I have danced with her? Should I have refused to dance the fast Fred Astaire number? Should I have checked her over when she said she was so tired? *You'll never know, Dr Vaughan. You'll never know.*

I angrily switched off the light, shutting off the harshness, and the tormenting noise of the fan.

In the dark silence I knew it was not just guilt I was feeling. I turned on the cold water and splashed my face.

CHAPTER 18

It took me a long time to get back to sleep. I lectured myself at length about the stupidity of feeling guilty about Millie's death. It was, after all, pure coincidence that she'd died after dancing with me. A woman of her age, with her history, could have died at any time. I hadn't wanted to do that last dance with her but she had been eager to do it. Strangely I hadn't even felt as if I were dancing with an older woman. I knew that I would not resolve the dilemma in my mind. The hard fact was that I knew, as her doctor, that she had a heart condition, and it was the same man that had partnered her in a dance that had made him, forty years younger, short of breath. Could the man be separated from the doctor? Could I just say, '*Non mea culpa* - I wasn't wearing my stethoscope at the time.'

It wasn't just guilt that bothered me. There was a strange sense of loss. The world would be poorer for the loss of her vivacity and charm. If not the world, then certainly Sir Giles would be the poorer. But that was a problem for the next day.

I doubt if I slept for more than two hours before Gwilym woke me; 'Getting late, Doc. I've brought your tea. Better drink it before it gets cold.'

As I struggled out of bed the previous night's events flooded back through my mind, like a kaleidoscope, fact mixing with dream.

However, the first sip of Gwilym's tea soon brought reality back into focus; 'Bloody Hell, Gwilym, what's that?' I managed, after spitting the first mouthful back into the cup. 'It tastes like disinfectant!'

'That's probably the extra chlorine in the water, Doc. Chief Engineer always tops it up as we're coming into port. On account of the Port Health Authority checking us for hygiene.'

'You could have warned me, Gwilym!'

'Well, most experienced officers stock up on bottled water for these occasions. Couldn't find any in your drinks cupboard.'

I deduced that Gwilym wasn't expecting too large a tip from me for this voyage, unless he reasoned that his information was golden. But he had reminded me of something important. We were arriving in Southampton that day. My first voyage was coming to an end. I now had ten days leave during which I had to decide whether to return to sea on a more permanent basis. Perhaps the decision wouldn't be mine. The Shipping Line had the equal right to decide they didn't want me. I didn't like to think of this. Besides there wasn't enough time. There were a lot of important tasks to be completed before I could leave the ship and the foremost on my mind was visiting Sir Giles.

Before I could face him, however, I had to clear my head, so I sacrificed breakfast for a stroll on deck.

The air was warm and the clear sky promised a fine summer's day over the England that I'd left just a short while ago. A short while; it felt more like a year. I'd been in a time warp that had distorted my previous life as if it belonged to someone else. The question in my mind was whether I welcomed this time warp.

Seagulls were beginning to appear with the proximity of the land and with them I imagined the old memories flew towards me. Which were most real? Those old memories or the more recent ones pressing on my mind. I could even detect the tang of seaweed on the air, bringing reminders of those seaside picnics. But as Susie had pointed out, dwelling on the past was bad for me; better to concentrate on the present, even though the immediate present was going to be very uncomfortable.

As I made my way to the hospital I tried the old trick of taking deep breaths and relaxing the muscles to achieve an appearance of calm professionalism. I was going to tell Sir Giles how sorry I was that Millie had died, and that I understood how devastated he must feel. That she could have died at any time, that her spirit would somehow live on, that she was going to live with Jesus in a far happier land that outshone the sun. I just wished that I could believe it.

'Good morning, Doctor. I am pleased you came to see me. You look dreadfully tired.'

He looked the same as ever in his smoking jacket, with a magazine held in his hand, except that it wasn't a magazine but a Bible, and there was no champagne on his locker.

'There's not much I can say, Sir Giles; except how sorry I am.'

'Of course, old chap; there's not much one can say really. Life's a bit like that, a few moments of bliss before the curtain comes down.'

'She was a very special person.'

'I know, I knew it from the moment I met her; there are very few like her.'

His cultured casual tone of voice could not disguise the depth of his feelings. It was not that he appeared to be near to tears, but his words were rather clipped.

'I notice you're reading the Bible.'

'Where else to seek solace; don't know of any other book; do you?'

'No, but I didn't think you were a religious man.'

'Never have been, but Terry brought it for me; he thought it might help.'

'You're going to feel rather lonely now. It must be a comfort to have your son with you.'

He didn't reply immediately. Then said; 'Ah yes, Rodney. As you say, he must be a comfort.' Then he looked at me; 'But there's something else on your mind, isn't there, Doctor Vaughan? I suspect that you feel responsible for her death.'

'Yes, to be honest. I think we overdid that last dance.'

'And do you think you could have stopped her dancing, either then or on another occasion?'

'Probably not.'

'Exactly, because that is the way she'd have chosen to die. You see I know quite a lot about her. She told me her life story. Many years ago she was one of the top-rated dancers and headed for stardom, had it not been for a motor-bike accident. Her fiancé was killed and both her legs were broken. It took her years to recover and she had lost her big opportunity, but the old sparkle never deserted her.'

'That would explain how she led me around the dance floor so well. I've never been that good, you know.'

'Yes, I guessed as much. No disrespect of course. Anyway, old chap, no point in feeling guilty, is there?'

'I think that you've been more help to me, than I have been to you, Sir Giles. I'd no idea that Millie had such a past, though I thought she could have been an actress.'

'She's been on stage most of her life, in small parts mainly. She told me she'd been in a few films. I expect I'll be spending a lot of time watching old movies, trying to find her. Anyway, it'll keep me out of mischief.'

The thought seemed to give him some consolation, and he looked a bit less depressed, though he'd developed a faraway look, as if he'd already decided that life would be purely fantasy and memory from now on. I decided it was time to become more practical.

'We're arranging for you to go into hospital in Southampton on arrival, unless you have another preference; a favourite surgeon perhaps?'

'No, I'll leave the choice to you and John. Never had much to do with doctors; a gloomy bunch of people by and large, present company excepted, of course.'

I shook his hand, told him that I would see him again before he left the ship and took my leave. He resumed his study of the Gideon's Bible that Terry had given him, although he did not look too convinced by it, and I wondered how much thought he'd ever given to religion, apart from weddings and funerals. Whatever his beliefs, I felt grateful to him for making me feel more comfortable.

It was time for the hospital meeting, and I was the first to arrive. Sally didn't bother to hide her surprise; 'Bright and early this morning, Doctor!'

'Yes, I skipped breakfast. I wanted to talk to Sir Giles. He's coping better than I expected.'

'And how are you taking it?'

'What do you mean by that, Sister?'

'Well, you didn't seem quite yourself after we'd dealt with Millie last night. Mustn't take these things to heart, you know.'

I knew what she meant. It was the old training; one of the first lessons; don't get personally involved with patients, it clouds the judgement and makes life too painful. Well, she didn't need to repeat the lecture. I'd learned the techniques, learned how to adopt the emotionally blast-proof veneer, learned that almost fixed expression of concern without anguish, could maintain it to cope with a failed cure for dandruff, or the loss of a precious life. But I wasn't fooled by it, either in myself or other doctors. Some patients did get close, and disguising the pain was of only temporary value. Guilt, of course, was always part of the problem – 'Could I have done something sooner, or something different?' I'd done what I could for Millie before I'd danced her into heart failure, and Sally had done her best when she'd collapsed in the night. There was no overwhelming reason for guilt and Sally was probably correct in her rebuke.

'Was it that obvious?'

'Yes, it was.'

'Well, I noticed that you were shaken as well. You're not as blast-proof as you make out.'

For the first time I noticed her back off a little, she lowered her eyes; 'Perhaps,' she said. 'She was rather special.'

* * * * * * * * * * * * * * *

After the others arrived at the meeting there was no further mention of Millie, except of course the clinical facts. Nobody seemed to want to elaborate, as if a pact of silence had been subconsciously agreed upon.

The main topic of discussion was our imminent arrival in Southampton. John enumerated the tasks to be carried out, making sure I knew that letters on all my patients had to be completed, voyage report prepared and transport for hospital patients organized on-shore. The process of tidying up had started. Life might be a continuous process, but voyages weren't. Within twelve hours of arrival the ship would be starting a new voyage and all the problems of this voyage would be tidied away, including Millie.

Before the letters could be started, however, the remaining sick needed to be seen and Terry had prepared them for me; 'Just a few for you to sort out this morning, Sir. Nothing too complicated.'

I looked at the small pile of notes he'd handed me; 'Nothing like my first day at sea then, Terry?'

'Aye, well, they've better things to think about when we're getting into port.'

He was right that there was nothing too complicated. I treated a couple of mild rashes and removed a splinter, then Julian came in to see me. I was a bit concerned that he was going to present another complicated problem, but all he wanted was my reassurance that he definitely didn't have any venereal disease, before he proceeded on leave with Miss Myers.

'Well, Julian,' I reassured him after I had examined the area thoroughly, 'in all my time at sea, I've never seen such a healthy-looking organ as yours!'

'Really, Doctor?' he replied looking quite proud.

'Really, Julian.'

He looked a bit suspicious; 'How long have you been at sea then Doctor?'

'Oh, about five days.'

He grinned at me as he left the office.

* * * * * * * * * * * * * * * * *

With crew surgery over I had no excuse to put off the letter-writing, which I had always found an irksome task back at my previous surgery. Converting medical events into cold, written facts was a difficult exercise. People and their problems stuck as pictures in the mind, and abbreviating them into a few sentences seemed inadequate.

How, for instance, could I describe Mrs Franik's drama briefly without labelling her illness as an acute schizophrenic episode? That's what it was, but how much more should I tell her future psychiatrist? that she was a brilliant woman with a mathematical brain? that I'd conned her into taking antinuclear pills? that I'd have failed if it hadn't been for Millie's timely intervention?

Ultimately I decided to tell the whole story so that her future doctors could make their own decision. I wouldn't however tell how strange she'd made me feel; nor how many had gathered in that little cabin to persuade her to swallow the pills. I didn't want them thinking that I was a complete amateur at psychiatry.

The letter to Angus's doctor provided no difficulty; he'd made good progress; his face was healed and his arm was moving well: physiotherapy was all he needed to make his recovery complete, that and the ministrations of Barbara Box. I wondered whether I'd ever meet him again, and whether he'd return to sea. Somehow I could visualize him wearing a dog-collar before too long, and perhaps Barbara would end up serving tea and scones to his parishioners.

223

Howard Sinclair Senior required a long letter describing how he'd been resuscitated after his heart attack and how, in spite of his age and complicated past history, he'd recovered well. I didn't write about how cantankerous he'd been, nor how he was still demanding to be let out of hospital to enjoy his cruise, nor how he still thought we were poisoning him with 'high falutin' English drugs. Mary Lou had kept that aspect of him under control and would, no doubt, continue to do so until they were back home. Neither did I describe how her son had prayed on his knees while Sally and I had almost despaired of bringing him back to life. Some things just didn't look right in a medical letter.

After completing the correspondence, the voyage report was relatively straightforward, requiring only the enumeration of the types of cases, and brief mention of cases of note. There had been 106 cases of seasickness, including myself; 8 injuries, including Angus; 32 respiratory illnesses; 24 rashes of various types; 2 heart attacks; 1 death; 1 amputation and 45 miscellaneous problems, including Miss Myers' Pepe, who was going to confuse the statistics somewhat as he couldn't really be classed as either passenger or crew member; but that was someone else's problem.

I checked the report through, making sure that I hadn't missed anything of importance and then signed it, with a flourish. My first voyage report completed; five days work encapsulated in two sheets of paper. I felt strangely proud of it, knowing that it would enter the files as a permanent record, a legal account of my five days at sea; but as I handed it to John, I began to worry about whether it would be my last report.

'Your first trip almost over then, Mike. How do you feel about it?' John asked.

'I'm almost convinced that I enjoyed it!'

'Have you decided whether you want to come back yet?'

'I'd like to think about it for a few days. That'll give the company time to decide about me as well.'

He read my report and countersigned it before making any comment; 'Shouldn't be any problems, Mike; I'll put in a good word for you. Anyway, time to go on deck. This is the best part of the voyage.'

* * * * * * * * * * * * * * * *

224

Almost everyone else seemed to think it was the best part of the voyage too. There was no leaning room left on the ship's rail. We were sailing past the Isle of Wight and the gleaming white needles seemed to have everyone mesmerized. An air of excitement grew as we moved on through the Solent, almost as if everyone was surprised that we had made it across the Atlantic. I could understand why the Americans on board would feel excited at seeing England for the first time, but I couldn't fathom out why I, and dozens of other crew members, should feel the same.

'I suppose we must have been getting homesick,' I commented to John.

'It's always the same, this last bit, Mike. It gives me a funny feeling in the stomach. Never feel it when I fly back from the States.'

I could feel a similar sensation in my own stomach; a mixture of homesickness and sense of achievement. I thought that flying could never give the same feeling, probably because it was a form of blasphemy; insulting the grandeur of the world, belittling the size of the oceans. America was, in truth, a long way from Britain and I felt I'd experienced a sizeable chunk of life during the crossing. In a plane I'd have read a magazine and dozed through a film, oblivious to the 3000 miles travelled; then I'd have wondered why I didn't feel quite right for the next seven days. At least now I had some idea of what the Pilgrim Fathers must have felt.

Somewhere deep inside I could feel an addiction growing. Perhaps it was merely an addiction to the sealaden breeze hitting my face, perhaps it was an addiction to the luxury of life on a great liner; the smart uniform; fine food; dancing under soft lights. But there was something more gut-crunching than luxury and romance working its way into my consciousness. It was the feeling of sheer fright; of not knowing what was going to happen next; what emergency I would meet; what decisions I would have to make; what inner resources I would have to find to cope. I had never been challenged as much as I had in the past five days, but in exchange for the fear was a feeling of being alive, dangerously alive. I tried to compare my practice ashore, which provided ample enough emergencies, but there was always the safety net, the local hospital with specialists to pull me out of trouble. What I was now contemplating was life without a safety net. Was that what I really wanted? Or would I rather settle for a life of waiting for my pension, perhaps living with the ghost of Alice until a suitable replacement turned up? I would have to decide soon, but for the moment I was content to savour the sensation of the breeze on my face.

Far below I could see the pilot's launch pull alongside and watching him climb up into the ship through the shell door reminded me of my own arrival, only five days previously. If I'd known then that it was such a focus of attention I'd have felt even more embarrassed. But that was in the past. The five intervening days had changed me from an embarrassed ignorant new arrival into a budding professional seaman.

You wouldn't have deduced my new 'professional seaman's' status from Gwilym's attitude as he helped me pack my cases;

'First trip over then, Doc; didn't think you'd make it at first, but you're beginning to learn the ropes.'

'Can I take that as a compliment, Gwilym?'

He concentrated on carefully folding some shirts before cramming them into a spare corner of the case; 'Can't say yet, Doc,' he eventually answered.

By the means of Gwilym's modified shovel technique the packing didn't take long, but I felt quite sad seeing the uniform tucked away inside the case and I didn't like the feel of my 'civilian' clothes which I had changed into. Gwilym had finished buckling up the case straps but didn't seem in a hurry to leave. Of course, I had to say my goodbye.

I was in the middle of thanking him for his help when I remembered probably the most important sea tradition of all. I asked him to wait a moment while I fished around for an appropriate number of dollar notes, then tucked them into an envelope before handing them to him.

'That's very kind of you, Doc,' he said, then added as he reached the door, 'Hope to see you back sometime.'

CHAPTER 19

We were now alongside in Southampton and the whole ship seemed to buzz with activity. It was hardly safe to enter the alleyways because of the turmoil of passing trolley-loads of suitcases heading for the shell doors.

The calm atmosphere of the past five days had been replaced by a state of agitation, with groups of passengers demanding explanations from long suffering stewards about when they could get off the ship and what was happening to their cases, as if they imagined that they were being tipped into the docks.

I managed to clamber over cases and weave along the alleyway and down the stairway to the relatively calm atmosphere of the hospital where I had to perform the last task of the voyage; convince the port health doctor that none of my patients were infectious.

He was a pleasant enough man but made it quite plain that nobody could leave the ship until he had studied my case histories and was happy that we weren't importing typhoid, smallpox, cholera, or any other of a list of nasties. Luckily neither Sir Giles, Howard Sinclair Senior, nor Mrs Franik appeared remotely infectious, so he gave me permission to transfer them to the waiting ambulances and passed the ship as free from infection.

There wasn't much time left to spend with the patients as the ambulance team were anxious to get on with their work. Mrs Franik seemed quite prepared to leave and looked at ease with the psychiatric nurse who had been sent to collect her.

'It's been nice meeting you Mrs Franik,' I said as I shook her hand. 'I hope you've been comfortable in the hospital?'

'Yes, thank you,' she replied. She looked an entirely different woman to the deranged and rather frightening spectacle I had first met a few days ago. I hoped that her illness was only temporary, perhaps a reaction to the stress and the strangeness of being at sea. She certainly gave the appearance of being normal at the moment.

She reached down to her holdall and took out a scroll of paper. Smiling, she handed it to me; 'Could you please give this to the Captain?'

I couldn't resist unrolling it, and my heart started to sink as I noticed the outline of a world map; but there were no lines of nuclear fall-out on it; just a beautifully hand-drawn map of the world with a sketch of the ship taking up half of the Atlantic Ocean. 'It's beautiful,' I exclaimed, 'he'll be really pleased with it!'

'I do hope so,' she replied.

* *

Sinclair Senior didn't seem to be too happy about the ambulance team preparing him for his trip to an English hospital but, with barely any movement of his lips, he managed to say; 'Thank you for looking after me, Doctor.'

I noticed that Mary Lou was glowering at him throughout the little speech, and wondered if she could be a ventriloquist.

They both shook my hand, and I wished them well. Somehow, I felt, they would be feuding for a while longer yet.

Sir Giles was in the stretcher, about to be wheeled out when I caught up with him. He already had a farewell party consisting of John, Sally and Janet, Patrick and Terry surrounding him. 'You seem to be very popular,' I exclaimed, pushing my way through to grasp his hand.

'We're just trying to get rid of him!' said Janet as she finished kissing him, leaving a full-blown lipstick mark on his cheek.

Sally was not, of course, quite as demonstrative, but I noticed that her voice quavered a little as she ordered everyone to; 'Get a move on because the ambulance is waiting'.

If Sir Giles was feeling despondent, he didn't show it;

'Thanks for all your help, old chap,' he said to me, 'and if you ever feel like helping an old man out with his vintage port, you know my address. That applies to all of you, of course!'

The ambulance men were about to wheel him out when Patrick came running into the room; 'Hang on! You can't leave without this. The ship's carpenter's been working on it for days.'

He placed a gift-wrapped parcel on the stretcher alongside where Sir Giles's leg would have been.

'What is it?' Sir Giles asked.

'You'll just have to open it if you want to find out,' answered Patrick. 'You see we wanted you to leave the ship, approximately the same way you joined it.'

Sir Giles unwrapped the parcel to reveal a finely carved peg-leg which could have been a replica of Long John Silver's. Attached to the socket end was an engraved metal plaque stating;

To Sir Giles Underwood.
Hoping this will keep you on an even keel.
From the Medical Department.

Sir Giles lifted it up, smoothed it, then cradled it against his chest. 'I just don't know what to say,' he managed.

At this point there was a tear forming in at least one of his eyes and Patrick, noticing this, came to the rescue; 'We tried to fix you up proper, but we're fresh out of parrots!'

'OK, let's get a move on,' said Sally. 'We can't keep the ambulance waiting all day.'

The ambulance-men took the hint and wheeled him out of the hospital. Sir Giles didn't look back, but he waved his peg-leg in a farewell salute.

CHAPTER 20

With all my duties despatched, there was now nothing stopping me from leaving and, although I had mixed feelings about going ashore, I was looking forward to the relative peace and calm of living in my own house and sleeping in a bed that could be guaranteed not to move.

As I didn't really want any more farewells, I decided to carry my cases myself, and made a swift exit via the passenger gangway. However, I chose the wrong gangway; Sally and Janet were there, bidding farewell to some friends.

'Leaving so quickly, Doctor? Are you not bothering to say goodbye?' remarked Sally.

'Well, I expect I'll see you again before too long?'

'You won't see me for some time. I'm off on a long leave.' She said this with a degree of emphasis so that it seemed impolite not to enquire further;

'Going anywhere interesting, Sally?'

'Just a farm in Texas, Doctor!'

This shouldn't have surprised me too much, after watching her dancing with Howard Sinclair Junior, but I felt a sneaky, irrational pang of jealousy. Of course, it was the fear of losing her as a professional colleague that bothered me; or was it?

'Has the "farmer found a wife" then, Sally?'

'Only time will tell that, Doctor.'

There was nothing else to say. We were on professional terms as always. Her face was as sharp as it had been when we first met, though I was getting better at detecting the occasional smile hidden beneath her mask.

Janet broke the ice; 'Don't worry, Michael, I'll be here to look after you if you do decide to come back.'

There was, as usual, a cheeky grin on her face and the pinch on the bottom she gave me could have been taken in a number of ways. 'By the way, Doctor, why are you still wearing your walkie-talkie?'

'Oh hell, I knew there was something I'd forgotten. Could you watch my cases for a couple of minutes, Janet? I'll have to return it to Pete.'

I set off along the promenade deck, towards the bridge to find Pete. In another thirty seconds I would have reached my goal, but there was a shout from behind; 'Doctor, stop!'

I looked around. Miss Myers was doing her very best to catch me up. 'Stop, Doctor,' she repeated. 'I've been looking for you everywhere.'

'What's the matter?' I asked, rather worried that something might have happened to Pepe.

'Gee, nothing's the matter,' she said, 'I just wanted to thank you for curing Pepe. He's completely back to normal now!'

It was nice to be thanked, but I wasn't quite prepared for her enthusiasm. She flung her arms around me and squeezed me in a very affectionate bear hug. I think she kissed me next, but my attention was on the walkie talkie that she'd managed to knock out of my grasp and which had fallen to the deck.

'Hang on a second, Miss Myers,' I gasped, 'I've dropped something!' But she was not to be deterred from her display of gratitude and in trying to move away from her I managed to kick the walkie talkie so that it continued its progress across the deck and under the ship's rail. I watched, as well as I could from my trapped position, as it splashed into the water in the narrow gap between the ship and the quayside, and slowly sank.

Miss Myers eventually released me. I wished her a happy time in England and reminded her to stick to the correct dosage for Pepe's pills.

I retrieved my suitcases, deciding that the best course of action would be to send a cheque for the lost walkie-talkie to the Southampton office.

'That was quick!' Janet exclaimed.

I didn't answer. Just gave her and Sally a quick peck on the cheek and rapidly descended the gangway. I had almost made my escape ashore;

'Hey, Doc, hang about!'

The voice was familiar. I put down my cases and turned around. It was Pete, racing after me. 'Where's my walkie-talkie?' he demanded.

'Sorry, Pete. I'm getting you a new one.'

'Never mind a new one, where's the bugger I lent you?'

'Sorry, Pete, it's fallen in the water!'

He shrugged his shoulders in exasperation, turned and strode back up the gangway. 'This is like a sketch from the *Goon Show*!' he muttered. 'Bloody quacks!'

I was feeling rather guilty as I stepped onto firm ground and headed rapidly for the customs shed. But I still couldn't resist one last glance. I put down my cases and turned to look back at the massive vessel that had made such a change in my life that had given me so many new experiences.

There weren't many people still looking over the ship's rail, but I recognized one of them; her blonde hair gave her away. I waved and she waved back.